MEN
in
UNIFORM

ANNETTE
BROADRICK

THE PRESIDENT'S
DAUGHTER

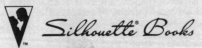

Silhouette® Books

Published by Silhouette Books
America's Publisher of Contemporary Romance

 SILHOUETTE BOOKS

Recycling programs
for this product may
not exist in your area.

ISBN-13: 978-0-373-36284-4

THE PRESIDENT'S DAUGHTER

MEN
in
UNIFORM

Courteous, courageous and commanding—
these heroes lay it all on the line for the
people they love in more than fifty stories about
loyalty, bravery and romance.
Don't miss a single one!

ANNETTE BROADRICK

believes in romance and the magic of life. Since 1984, Annette has shared her view of life and love with readers. In addition to being nominated by *RT Book Reviews* as one of the best new authors of that year, she has also won an *RT Book Reviews* Reviewers' Choice Award for best in series, a W.I.S.H. Award and a Lifetime Achievement Award for Series Romance and Series Romantic Fantasy.

Chapter 1

Washington, D.C.
Monday, December 21

A blast of frigid air swirled around Nick Logan, nipping at him like a hungry animal as he walked the two blocks between the parking lot and his newest assignment. He hunched his shoulders and quickened his steps until he reached the guard's booth at the east gate.

He paused beside the booth, peering inside at the lone occupant. "Hope you have a heater in there."

Ken White, working the uniformed division of the Secret Service, replied, "One of the many fringe benefits of this job, of course." He gave Nick a quick once-over. "What are you doing here, Logan? I thought you were on the VP detail."

Nick shrugged. "I was, until last night."

"Good to see you," Ken said.

Nick walked through the iron-gated fence that surrounded the White House. He adjusted the collar of his heavy overcoat around his ears in an effort to block the raw wind blowing down Pennsylvania Avenue.

The bleakness of the day fit his mood.

By the time he reached the side door located between the White House and the Executive Office building and went inside, he was more than glad to be out of the wind. Nick paused in the entryway long enough to remove his coat, draping it over his arm before he headed for W-16, the large office/lounge that served as the command post for the White House detail of the Secret Service.

Once there, Nick paused in the doorway and looked around. The room contained several folding chairs, a long table with coffee and supplies, and a dozen or more men waiting to be briefed for the next shift. He recognized most of them from other assignments. The Secret Service was a close-knit group.

One of them broke away from a small group and approached him.

"Nicholas Logan?" he asked. "I'm Gregory Chambers, the detail leader. Appreciate your coming on board at such short notice."

"I was sorry to hear about Colin Crenshaw's accident. What happened?" Nick asked as he followed the older man across the room to the coffee area.

"Lost control of his car over in Alexandria," Chambers replied, refilling his cup while Logan poured himself some coffee, allowing the steaming brew to warm his hands. "The investigating officers figure the icy weather was to blame. Ran into a pole. One of those freak accidents nobody can really explain." Chambers motioned Nick to follow him once again. "You'll be covering his four-to-midnight shift," he said over his shoulder. "Colin was a good man. We're going to miss him."

Chambers paused beside a tall African-American who Nick noticed had been watching him since he'd first walked into the room—watching and assessing without betraying his thoughts. "Colin and Ron Stevenson here were partners, so you'll be working together."

Nick held out his hand and Stevenson shook it.

"We working the Man?" Nick asked, referring to the president.

Ron shook his head. "Nope. The daughter."

Not quite the kiddy detail, but close. Keeping an eye on a college-age female was a little better than following the schedule of a couple of active teenage boys.

Before he could ask Ron any more questions, Chambers began the briefing.

"Only one incident to report since your last shift," he said to everyone. "A taxi driver from Baltimore drove up to the front gate. His fare was a woman demanding to speak to the president. The matter was turned over to the police." He continued to read from his notes, making comments and answering questions. Once everything was covered, Chambers nodded toward Nick.

"The last item to be covered is to welcome Nicholas Logan, who's joining this shift. Logan's been working the VP detail for the past three years. Before that, he did his military service in various areas, including the Mideast during the Gulf crisis. Welcome aboard, Nick."

Several pairs of eyes turned his way, Logan noted. He received a few nods and a couple of smiles. This small group of men knew what they were there to do—keep the members of the first family safe—at least from four to midnight. After that, another group came in until they were relieved by the eight-o'clock morning shift. During their off-hours, he'd get an opportunity to get to know some of them better, but now each of them was focused on the business at hand.

In his case, he would be learning more than he ever cared to know about the president's daughter—which, at present, was very little.

Ashley Elizabeth Sullivan, the oldest child and only daughter of James Allen Sullivan and his wife, Juliana Holmes Sullivan, was in her third year at Wellesley, and no doubt currently home for the Christmas holidays. From all that he had read and heard, she maintained an active life-style.

Staying close to the VP had entailed a highly structured, politics-as-usual schedule. Nick had become accustomed to being part of the Washington infrastructure. Keeping a close watch on the activities of someone not in the loop would be a distinct change of pace. Not exactly what he'd visualized as his new assignment when he received the call late last night.

Once Chambers dismissed the group, Nick turned to Ron and said, "So what's the drill?"

"The usual. We do our job, even though Ms. Sullivan has made her opinion of our presence abundantly clear on more than one occasion."

"Let me guess. A twenty-one-year-old single woman doesn't care to be closely monitored by a group of men showing a keen interest in anyone who approaches her."

"You got it. She says it's embarrassing and her friends rib her, especially whenever she goes out on a date. She insists on no motorcades…grudgingly allows a trail car."

"Should we tell her that it isn't our biggest thrill to tag along on those occasions, either?"

Ron smiled. "Not necessary. She's a bright girl, and she's been around politicians and the need for protection most of her life."

"You'd think she'd be used to it, then."

"What she is—from my reading of the situation—is tired of it. Can't really say I blame her, but I don't think our sympathy impresses her much. What she wants is for us to don our invisible cloaks and allow her to get on with her life as inconspicuously as possible."

Nick grinned. "I can see her point, but as you say, we're just doing our job." He glanced around the room. Most of the others were gone. "So where do we find the princess today?"

Ron glanced at his watch. "When she's home from school, Ashley is generally in the gym working out at this hour. Since we weren't notified of any changes, we'll go there," Ron said, leading the way through the labyrinth that made up the interior of the White House.

Before today, Nick had only been in the more public parts of the building, so the area they were covering now was new to him. He made note of the twists and turns. It wouldn't do for him to get lost in the damned place.

"You weren't given much notice on this reassignment," Ron said after a few minutes of silence. "How do you feel about it?"

Nick shrugged. "It doesn't really matter to me where I'm assigned. But the timing didn't make me want to leap for joy. I was due for a much-needed vacation later this week. Nothing less than a national emergency was going to keep me from taking it, or so I thought."

A corner of Ron's mouth lifted briefly. "Sorry to hear about that. I can't remember the last time I had more than a couple of days off." He was quiet for a moment. "Was your family upset?"

"Well, since I was supposed to get together for Christmas with my folks, my two brothers and their families, none of them were too thrilled with this morning's phone call. You'd think by this time they'd be used to my erratic schedule."

"I take it you're not married," Ron said.

Nick shook his head. "You?"

"Not anymore. After months on the campaign trail last year, I got home to find that Janine had moved out, taking our two little girls with her. She said this wasn't the kind of life she wanted."

"This business is tough on marriages," Nick said.

Ron shrugged, as though to release the tension in his shoulders. "I manage to see Corinne and Sasha a few times a month. Not exactly what I had in mind when we talked about having a family."

"Those long road trips can really mess up a relationship," Nick said quietly.

"I do my best to talk to the girls on the phone every

morning," Ron said. "Once they start school, it'll be tougher for me to reach them as long as I work this shift."

"Maybe Ms. Ashley should understand that we all have our crosses to bear," Nick drawled. "Do you think we should be the ones to enlighten her?"

Ron made a sweeping bow. "You first, oh brave leader," he said in a reverent voice. They both laughed.

After another, more companionable silence, Ron spoke up again.

"I hear you were one of the men who parachuted into Baghdad before all the fireworks started a few years ago."

Nick glanced at Ron before looking away. "You heard that, did you?"

"And that you were still there when the attack began."

Nick didn't respond right away. When he did, all he said was, "Somebody forgot to synchronize the watches."

"That's a story I'd like to hear more about sometime."

Nick glanced at Ron from the corner of his eye. "Only if you have some of your own tales to share."

Ron nodded. "Good enough. I like to know the man I work with."

Nick was thinking the same thing about his new partner. Although Stevenson was polite enough, even cordial, there was a quiet air of reserve surrounding him. "Not much hidden about me," Nick replied lightly. "What you see is what you get."

"Uh-huh," Ron replied with a hint of skepticism. "Here's the gym. Come meet our Ms. Ashley." Ron spoke to the two men positioned just outside the door whom they were replacing, and briefly introduced them to Nick before he and Nick entered the gym.

Ashley was working out on the Nautilus equipment specifically designed for the upper torso. From the damp look of her thin jersey top and latex shorts, the woman had been putting some energy into her efforts.

The first thought that crossed Nick's mind was that her photos didn't do her justice. Despite her casual attire and perspiring condition, there was no hiding the fact that Ashley was a very attractive woman.

Her dark brown hair was pulled high onto the crown of her head in some kind of knot, although several strands had worked their way loose, clinging to her forehead, cheeks and the nape of her neck.

The creamy texture of her fair skin—skin now glowing with a faint sheen of moisture—was a stark contrast to her delicately arched dark brows and thick lashes, but it was her eyes that pulled at him. Whiskey-colored eyes seemed to dominate her heart-shaped face.

As soon as they walked into the room, she stopped her workout and moved away from the machine, picking up a towel nearby and blotting her face.

He guessed her height to be about five foot five. She had a slender build, her body well toned with muscles that were subtly defined. The body of an athlete, he thought to himself.

Now that he was face-to-face with the person he'd been assigned to protect, Nick was even less certain how he felt about his new duties. All things being equal, he would still prefer getting his vacation to following this woman around. Even so, the idea of spending time in this attractive young woman's presence intrigued him more than he wanted to admit.

Nick realized he was feeling a little off balance. Somebody should have warned him years ago that choosing to play the role of hero could be damned disturbing at times.

Ashley watched the two men approach her and realized that the man with Ron Stevenson must be Colin's replacement. She'd heard about Colin's accident first thing that morning. She'd liked Colin, and been sorry to hear about his accident.

Now she studied his replacement and was startled to see he was intent on an inspection of his own. His attitude annoyed her. She knew what he saw and knew he wouldn't be impressed with her slight build and her lack of obvious assets.

Not that she cared what he thought about her. What difference did it make to her? She was glad she wasn't the type of woman to attract a man like the one coming toward her. She would bet he had no trouble gaining all kinds of attention from most women.

But not her.

Although he wore the dark suit and tie that was the uniform of the men in the protective service, she did not consider him average. Exactly what it was that disturbed her about him still eluded her. His eyes seemed to probe for secrets she might wish to keep. She shivered, made uneasy by the predatory way he moved.

"Ashley, I'd like you to meet Nicholas Logan," Ron said once they reached her side.

Ashley dropped the towel on the bench beside her and held out her hand.

"How do you do?"

Her instincts were telling her that she wanted to leave a safe distance between herself and this man. Those instincts were right on target, she discovered when he took her hand and shook it.

Ashley felt a strong current of electricity shoot through her that made her want to leap away from him. Instead, she nodded, then casually released his hand, taking care not to rub her palm against her leg to ease the tingling she felt.

Ron cleared his throat before speaking. "I understand you have plans for the evening."

"Yes. Todd and I have tickets for The Nutcracker Suite."

Neither man changed expression, which was a dead giveaway to Ashley, who had been around similar men for most of her life.

"Have either of you seen it?"

When Ron said nothing, Logan cleared his throat. "No, ma'am. I haven't."

"Have you ever been to the ballet?"

Both men shook their heads slowly, their expressions carefully blank.

Briskly she turned away, saying over her shoulder, "Well, you're in for a treat. We'll be leaving at seven."

By the time she finished her workout, Ashley decided she had overreacted to the new agent. She was being silly. He was no different from the other special agents—there to do his job.

As soon as she left the gym, the men followed her at a discreet distance back to the living quarters of the presidential family.

Both her brothers enjoyed having the agents at their beck and call, and spent hours talking sports with them. Jamie, at fourteen, and Matt, at eleven, were still young enough to enjoy the attention, especially since their dad had such a busy schedule.

It was like having male nannies whose attention was always focused on them. All of which was fine and dandy. For now. Just wait until Jamie started to date. She had a hunch he wasn't going to appreciate the security measures quite so much then.

She was thankful that Todd was comfortable escorting her to various functions. They had been friends for years. Todd's family had moved to Washington when her father was first elected to the presidency because Todd's father was a member of the Cabinet.

Their non-romantic friendship was very important to her. Todd's even disposition helped her keep her sanity. He had suggested they go to The Nutcracker because he knew how stifled she was feeling.

She needed to get out for a few hours. She'd been home from school for two days and already missed her life there.

If her dad approved of her plans for a winter vacation she'd be gone in a few days. This year she wanted to have the holiday vacation all her friends took for granted—one away from supervision by older adults.

Somehow she had to convince her father that she could travel without a gaggle of Secret-Service men proclaiming to the world who she was. Just once she wanted to be treated like a normal college student, without a care in the world.

Nick and Ron took their supper break early. Nick waited until they finished before saying, "Not very friendly, is she?"

Ron didn't need to ask for clarification of the "she" in question. "Actually she surprised me this afternoon. Usually she's more talkative. She may be upset about Colin. The accident was a shock to everyone."

"I'm surprised there was no mention of Colin's death during the meeting."

"Chambers spoke to us individually before you got there. We're all having to deal with it."

"How long were you partners?"

"Two years."

Nick noticed that Ron wasn't comfortable with his questions, so he changed the subject.

"Are you looking forward to the evening's entertainment?" Nick asked.

"Are you kidding? The last thing I consider entertainment is watching a bunch of people running around on their tiptoes."

Nick laughed. "I'm with you there." He looked at his watch and pushed his chair back. "Guess it's time to get back to work. I can see this detail is going to be a barrel of laughs."

Chapter 2

Nick sat directly behind Ashley Sullivan at the theater. Her date for the evening was Todd Jessup, son of William J. Jessup, the Secretary of Labor. The two of them seemed engrossed in all the activity taking place on stage. Nick made no effort to watch the stage. He wasn't there to be entertained. Ron sat in the row in front of Ashley, while two men were in the lobby and two more in a car outside, all connected by radio.

Out of habit Nick continued to scan the area, watching the audience and their reaction to the onstage festivities. He wasn't the only one less than enamored by the whole thing. He noticed several bored expressions, and one man nearby had dropped off to sleep.

Intermission finally came. Ron and Nick made certain that one of them was in front of Ashley and Todd, while the other one followed directly behind. Once they reached the lobby

Todd turned to Ashley and offered to get her something to drink.

She glanced around the crowded area and smiled. "That sounds great. While you're waiting in line, I'll go to the ladies' room. I'll meet you back here."

She ignored Nick and Ron, as though they weren't there. Heck, maybe they *were* invisible, Nick decided. That would certainly make their job a good deal easier.

He quietly followed her through the mass of milling people, keeping a general eye out for anything that might be deemed unusual. Ashley stopped a couple of times and spoke briefly to acquaintances. She had just disappeared around the corner of the hallway leading to the ladies' room when Nick saw a flurry of movement out of the corner of his eye.

A woman was making a beeline for the same area, her expression intent, her attitude bordering on rudeness in her rush to follow Ashley through the hallway leading to the ladies' lounge. Nick waited near the entrance to the lounge, keeping an eye on the middle-aged woman. He didn't want to jump to conclusions. There was no reason to think that Ashley might be in danger. However, he didn't intend to take any chances.

As soon as the door opened into the lounge, the woman reached inside her handbag. Nick was right behind her, reaching for the weapon in his shoulder holster.

By the time he realized the woman was pulling out a package of cigarettes and eagerly lighting one, Nick found himself inside the ladies' room, creating a stir among the occupants. Hoping to be as inconspicuous as possible, he backed out the doorway, but not before Ashley spotted him in the mirror, where she had paused to freshen her lipstick.

She spun around and glared at him. Grabbing her purse, she marched after him, following him into the hallway.

"My God, can't I even go to the restroom without being followed?"

Keeping his voice down, he replied, "I'm sorry. I saw a woman who seemed to be in a big hurry to follow you in there."

Ashley folded her arms across her chest and leaned back so she could meet his gaze. Her eyes blazed.

"Well, aren't you the observant one? No wonder they've entrusted you with such a sacred detail—following me around." She straightened, dropping her arms to her side. "I don't suppose it occurred to you, Special Agent Logan, but most people, after having been in the theater for this length of time, tend to rush to the facilities at intermission. Perhaps that idea never occurred to you. Probably not. The sterling guardians who surround us don't have such normal ordinary needs, do they?"

All right, so he'd made a fool of himself. It wasn't the first time and probably wouldn't be the last. In this business he preferred to err on the side of safety. Obviously she wasn't going to take any of that into consideration.

However, she sure as hell didn't need to be so sarcastic.

Nick cleared his throat and fingered his tie. In a carefully modulated tone he murmured, "Look, I said I was sorry, okay? I'm still adjusting to this job. I'll work at being more circumspect in the future, all right?"

Ashley's gaze never faltered. It was obvious to Nick that she was struggling to control several choice remarks that she would, without doubt, love to make.

He had to give her credit for the fact that she didn't make them.

Instead, she shook her head in frustration and, turning on her heel, returned to the lobby. Nick followed.

Todd and Ashley found each other in the large lobby and joined a group of people discussing tonight's performance. Nick and Ron waited a few feet away.

Ron glanced at Nick from the corner of his eye and muttered, "What the hell did you do to our Ms. Ashley, Nick? She came charging out of the lounge area with fire in her eyes. I made the mistake of asking her how she was enjoying the performance so far and she almost took my head off."

Nick glanced at his partner with an innocent expression.

"What makes you think I had anything to do with her reaction? She may be hating the show tonight."

"Because she kept looking over her shoulder as though all the hounds of hell were after her, and when she spotted you, she muttered something about you spoiling the entire evening for her."

"Surely the lady exaggerates—I did not ruin the *entire* evening. I'd have to call that an overreaction on her part. After all, the night is young."

"Overreaction or not, I bet her father will hear her views on the subject before the night is over."

Nick stuck his hands in his pockets and continued to scan the milling group of people. "Fine with me. Maybe they'll fire me and I'll get my vacation time, after all."

"You wish. Come on, those blinking lights must mean the thing is starting up again."

His resigned tone almost made Nick smile, *almost* being the operative word. At the moment he was far from being in a smiling mood. By the time everyone was seated and the lights were dimmed, Nick felt certain he detected steam coming from Ashley's ears. What he had done hadn't been all *that* bad. So maybe he'd been a little overzealous, but it had been an honest mistake.

He sat there and watched her as she slowly relaxed and became caught up in the music and the story unfolding on stage.

Todd reached over and took her hand, and she turned so that Nick had a view of her profile. She'd worn her hair up tonight, with little tendrils falling around her ears and on her neck. Her cheeks were flushed, no doubt from temper. She had the longest eyelashes he'd ever seen on a person…the longest and the thickest. Funny he should notice such a silly thing.

Almost a week later Nick arrived for work at the White House. Upon signing in, he was told to report immediately to the Oval Office. The summons came as something of a relief. The tension whenever he was around Ashley was obvious to any observer. His mere presence appeared to irritate her. He did his best to stay out of her line of vision. When she was forced to interact with him, her icy politeness made her opinion of him abundantly clear.

He'd already admitted to his supervisor that he'd bungled the diplomatic part of his job with his charge. He'd spoken to Chambers a few days after the theater outing about the possibility of switching his assignment. He'd been turned down. Nick had attempted to explain Ashley's animosity toward him but was cut off in midsentence. He was informed that he could make amends or not. It was his choice. It wasn't necessary for the person he protected to like him.

With this summons, however, Nick knew that Ashley's feelings were very important to her father. Since she'd let several days go by, he had begun to think she had kept the theater incident to herself. Obviously he'd been wrong.

As soon as he walked into the anteroom of the Oval Office, one of the aides announced his presence to President Sullivan. Nick was invited to enter. He fought the impulse to straighten his tie and smooth down his hair before he nodded and walked into the Oval Office for the first time in his life.

His first surprise was to find Ron there, casually visiting with the president.

His second surprise was the warm smile of welcome on President Sullivan's face. Before Nick could think of anything to say, James Sullivan walked over to him and held out his hand.

President Sullivan was an imposing, charismatic figure. Tall and lean, he looked as though he would be at home riding the range on the back of a horse. Since he'd been born in, and served two terms as governor of, the state of Colorado, James Sullivan could easily be descended from pioneer stock who had settled the West generations ago.

He was a young president, barely in his fifties into his second term of office. Not only was he known as a tough negotiator and a fierce warrior when it came time to fight for legislation he backed, Sullivan was also widely recognized as a staunch family man.

Nick had assumed that anyone his daughter didn't like would get an automatic veto from the president. Therefore, his friendly demeanor caught Nick by surprise.

"I'm very pleased to meet you, Logan. I've been hearing good things about you. I also want you to know how much we appreciate your willingness to cancel your vacation plans in order to fill the unexpected gap in ranks here."

The man certainly didn't miss much.

"I'm pleased to be here, Mr. President," Nick said, surprising himself that he actually meant it. Other than Ashley's obvious negative reaction to him, Nick had found working the White House detail pleasant enough. He'd quickly adjusted to the new surroundings and considered himself fortunate to be working with Ron.

He glanced at Ron, who now stood behind the president, and was startled to see his partner flash him an almost imperceptible wink.

What is going on here?

President Sullivan continued to speak. "I understand your plans were to head out West for a couple of weeks of skiing in the Colorado Rockies."

Since his vacation plans hadn't been a state secret, Nick wasn't as surprised that the president knew about them as he was surprised that Sullivan mentioned them.

"Plans have a way of changing in this business, sir," Nick replied.

"Why don't you and Stevenson have a seat and let's talk

about the possibility of getting some skiing into your schedule, after all."

Sullivan returned to his desk while Nick and Ron sat down in the chairs arranged in front of it.

With a rueful smile Ron said, "I've already explained to President Sullivan that I've never seen a pair of snow skis in my life, much less been on any. I grew up in Florida."

Nick didn't know of any agency requirement that called for an ability to ski. Since he'd spent his early years in Wyoming, learning to ski had been a natural part of growing up for him. He waited for more information.

Sullivan sighed and shook his head. "You know, gentlemen, children can be the greatest joy and the biggest headache a person can experience."

Uh-oh. Now he was leading up to the subject of his daughter.

"So I understand, sir."

"Ashley has made it quite clear that she does not wish to participate in the family's idea of a winter vacation this year. Ray Clarke has invited our family to spend a few days with him on his yacht doing some deep-sea fishing in the Gulf of Mexico."

Nick knew that Raymond Clarke and James Sullivan had been college roommates who had remained close friends in the intervening years. Clarke had made a name for himself in New York real estate. Nick wasn't surprised to hear that the Sullivans had been invited to spend their vacation time with him.

The president continued, "Jamie and Matt are counting the days until time to leave. Ashley, on the other hand, swears she becomes nauseated watching the waves rush the beach. All she's been able to talk about since she returned home from college is going skiing with a group of her friends."

Nick gave Ron a quick glance, but Ron's full attention was on the president.

Sullivan shook his head ruefully and said, "I'm not certain how she did it, but somehow Ashley managed to get me to agree to her going to Colorado over the holidays. Not only that, she also got me to agree not to have a round-the-clock surveillance team accompany her."

He put up his hand as though to silence any remark that either man might make. "I know all the arguments against such an idea, believe me. I know and I fully understand. However, I also understand the limits that can be safely set for a young woman her age. I've already discovered that there are times when there is no reasoning with Ashley...and I'm afraid this particular instance was one of those times. My dilemma is attempting to find some sort of balance between her need for privacy and the need for her to receive adequate protection."

Sullivan swiveled his chair and looked out the window in a contemplative pause, allowing his chair to sway absently from side to side. Finally he turned back to face the two men.

"I managed, eventually, to get her to agree to a compromise—to be accompanied on this trip by two agents who would blend in with the group by taking part in their activities in order to maintain their anonymity."

Nick leaned forward in his chair. "She agreed to that?" he asked, struggling to hide the surprise he felt.

Sullivan smiled. "Let's just say that she conceded that much, since she knew better than to expect I would let her go without some kind of protection."

"I take it you want Ron and me to accompany her."

Sullivan nodded. "After discussing the matter with the detail leader and going over the present roster with him, your name came to the front, Logan. Not only have you spent time in that area, your recreational skills are more than adequate. Ron can spell you once they're through skiing for the day so that you won't have to spend twenty-four hours on duty."

"Who will cover the night shift?"

"That was another concession Ashley agreed to make. Both of you will be staying in the chalet the group rented. There will be six of them, plus the two of you. Since there are three bedrooms, as well as sleeping sofas in the den area, you shouldn't be too crowded."

"Does Ashley know that you've asked Ron and me to go?"

Sullivan shook his head. "Not yet, but I'm certain it won't matter to her at this point who's going as long as she gets to go." He grinned and added, "I've got to tell you that I had no idea my daughter was growing up to be as tough a negotiator as she's turned out to be. We've had several sessions that lasted past midnight thrashing out all of this. This is the plan we finally agreed upon."

Nick gave a brief thought to mentioning Ashley's obvious antipathy toward him to her father, then thought better of it. Whatever was eating her would have to be worked out between them. In the meantime he was going to accept this unexpected gift as a belated Christmas present.

He was going skiing, after all. For that, he could put up with any amount of cold politeness or being ignored.

"When do we leave?" he asked, unable to hide his pleasure at the prospect.

"I understand transportation arrangements have been made by the detail leader. The official word, of course, is that Ashley is with us. She'll be disguised as usual while traveling in public. The reservations are for an early-morning commercial flight tomorrow. The group will be traveling together, which should help her to blend in with the other students."

President Sullivan stood and offered his hand to each man. "I hope you both enjoy the visit to my home state. I rather miss the skiing myself."

The men shook hands and silently left the room. They were in the hallway before Ron glanced around them, then in a low voice said, "You think she's going to be friendlier to you on this trip?"

Nick grinned. "Let's put it this way. Anything would be an improvement."

Ron chuckled before they went in search of their charge.

* * *

"No! Absolutely not, Dad. You have to find someone else!" Ashley faced her father across the expanse of her bedroom late that night. She had been packing when he dropped by her room to mention the arrangements he'd made for her trip.

Her father shrugged. "Your choice, of course, honey. I just thought you wanted to go on this ski trip. Ray will be pleased to have you with us—you know how much he enjoys your company. Or if you prefer staying on shore, your mother and I will enjoy having you nearby. You'll probably get a nice tan, anyway."

She sank onto the side of her bed, clutching one of the sweaters she intended to take to Colorado. "Why didn't you tell me before now you intended to send Nicholas Logan with us?"

He looked puzzled. "What's wrong with Logan?"

She jumped up and walked to her dresser, carefully studying the contents of an opened drawer as though debating what to take. "I don't like him," she muttered crossly.

James followed her, leaning his elbow on the tall piece of furniture. She refused to meet his gaze.

"Do you have a particular reason for not wanting him to go?" he asked. "Has he done or said anything out of line? Because if he has, I will report him immediately."

He was giving her a legitimate way out of this if she would use it. Ashley was tempted. Oh, how she was tempted. But reporting him because he annoyed her beyond belief would be putting her credibility on the line. What exactly had he done to cause him to be reported? Been his arrogant, loathsome self?

She sighed. "He hasn't done anything out of line, Dad. I mean, nothing specific. He's just a bumbling irritant who annoys me." She forced herself to meet her father's steady gaze. Somehow she had to convince her father that he must find someone else for this trip. But how? He was a very fair person. She couldn't lie. She wouldn't lie. But how could she begin to explain…

"I don't like the way he looks at me," she grumbled, returning to her opened suitcase and meticulously folding the clothes she intended to take on her trip. She concentrated on placing them inside with precision.

"The way he looks at you?" he repeated. "You mean, in a sexual manner?"

"No!" She paused, her frustration mounting as she searched for words to describe how that horrible man made her feel. "It's as though he looks right through me," she began, then stopped. "As though I don't even exist as a person to him!" she blurted out.

"You mean he treats you differently than the other agents do?"

"Yes! No! I mean, no, of course not. He's very efficient, I'm sure. I don't happen to like his attitude toward me, that's all. He's arrogant and smug and…" At the moment she couldn't think of all the many ways she found him offensive. But there were dozens, she was quite certain of that.

"So you don't like him."

What a relief. Her father was finally beginning to understand. She threw her arms around his waist and hugged him with relief.

"Exactly!" she agreed with a big smile, pleased to have finally made her point.

He sighed, patting her comfortingly. "Unfortunately, my dear, he's the best agent we have available for this particular job. He'll be able to stay with you while you're on the slopes…" He ignored her snort of disgust. "He knows the area, which is a plus, and he's agreed to dress like the rest of you so he won't look conspicuous."

He watched her for a moment before asking, "Do you have a problem with Stevenson, as well?"

"Ron? Oh, no. Not at all. Why do you ask?"

"I'm trying to figure out what set off this tirade of yours. I thought you would be pleased that we were able to arrange this trip for you. However, if you don't want Logan with you, then we'll be forced to call off your part of the trip."

She stiffened and pulled away from him. "Let me see if I understand you," she said through clenched jaws. "I either go on the ski trip accompanied by Special Agent Logan or I go to the beach with you, Mom and the boys, is that it?"

He smiled. "That's an excellent summation of this conversation, my dear."

She spun away from him and began pacing. "This is just great. I can't believe I'm going to have to spend the next five days with that man."

"You know, baby, I don't believe I've ever seen you this riled over any man before. Particularly not an agent. You've been around them most of your life. You seem to ignore them most of the time."

"I try. Oh, boy, do I try. But Nick Logan is impossible to ignore."

James smiled. "Ah. I think I'm beginning to get a better understanding of the situation."

Ashley narrowed her eyes and stared at him suspiciously. "And just what is that supposed to mean?"

"Logan is an attractive man. I'm not surprised that you noticed him. What surprises me is your very strong reaction to him. You generally treat your male friends quite casually."

"Really, Dad. It isn't the same thing at all! Agent Logan is certainly not a friend of mine! He works for us, that's all. I don't even think of him as a man, for that matter."

Her father made a noise that sounded suspiciously like a chuckle, but when she looked at him, his face was suitably solemn. She wanted him to take her seriously. This was not a joke. Nick Logan could very well destroy all her pleasure in the upcoming trip. She wanted her father to understand her very real concerns. She just couldn't think of anything else to say to convince him.

"I don't see that there's much that can be done about the situation at this late date, my dear. Ignore the man, pretend he isn't there or that he's just there to enjoy some skiing—which will be true, by the way."

"Except he'll be hovering over me all the time."

"Stevenson will be there, as well." She sighed. "It's only for five days, remember," he added.

She rolled her eyes, then hugged his neck and said, "Thanks, Daddy, for understanding how important this trip is to me."

"We'll stay in touch, you know. We'll only be a phone call away, no matter what happens."

She supposed she would have to be content with knowing that to be true.

Ron and Nick arrived at the Washington National Airport early enough the next morning to contact the security people regarding their presence on the flight. After showing their identification and checking their weapons, the two of them stopped in one of the coffee shops in the secured area for coffee until time to expect Ashley to appear.

They were dressed for a trip to the mountains in sweaters, jeans, boots and parkas. Ron joked about being an impostor, decked out in all his Western finery. Nick reassured him that most people in the area where they were going dressed similarly, whether they skied or not.

They were waiting just inside the security area watching for Ashley when she arrived, accompanied by an agent. He made no effort to pass through the metal detector. Instead, he waited until Ashley passed through with her backpack, then nodded to Nick and Ron and left.

"I almost didn't recognize you two," she said with a chuckle. "You look like you're ready for the slopes, Ron."

He laughed. "Forget that! I only have to look the part."

Nick could have said the same thing about her. She wore a stocking cap pulled down to frame her face, completely covering her hair. Large sunglasses concealed the top half of her face. The rest of her attire seemed to be a uniform for everyone headed west this morning.

She deliberately turned to Nick and looked him up and down, making no comment on what he wore. Instead, she said, "I understand you're an experienced skier."

"I'm not up to Olympic standards, but I enjoy it."

"It was your experience that caused you to be chosen for this trip, you know."

He grinned. "So I was told. I certainly didn't assume that you'd requested my company."

"Just so we understand each other." She turned away, then gave a little bounce. "Oh, here come the rest of them. They must have ridden together to the airport." She gave a quick skip and darted closer so she could greet them as soon as they came through security. She hugged each one, exclaiming how glad she was to be going with them. Ashley appeared to be delighted with everyone and everything this morning.

Except him.

So what else was new?

In the flurry of introductions, Nick studied the other members of the group, watching their interactions for clues to their personalities.

There were three men and two women:

Joe, who looked to be in his mid-twenties, the obvious leader of the group, tall, dark-haired, athletic and ruggedly handsome;

Derek, a couple of years younger than Joe, light brown hair, medium height, with a puckish sense of humor;

Craig, probably close to Derek's age, with a shock of red hair, medium height, and a sunny disposition;

Erin, early twenties, a willowy brunette with a sultry look and a shy demeanor; and

Trish, probably Ashley's age, a diminutive blonde with a flirtatious manner, who seemed to enjoy the glances that came her way in her snug-fitting jeans and figure-hugging sweater.

All of them had been briefed on why Ron and Nick were along. They were obviously enjoying the secrecy and security surrounding the outing and the parts assigned to the agents. Each member of the group assured Ron and Nick that he and she would be watchful and attentive at all times and would report anything that drew their attention as suspicious.

By the time they lined up to board the plane, Ron was shaking his head. "Do we have any idea what we're getting into with these kids?" he asked as they followed the group through the jetway to the plane.

Nick grinned. "I'm beginning to have a hunch that this may not be the vacation of a lifetime."

"Did you see how that Trish gal was eyeing you?" Ron asked in a low voice.

"Afraid not," Nick replied, amused by Ron's expression.

"She looked like she wanted to take a bite out of you and was just trying to decide where she wanted to start!"

Nick could feel himself flushing. "C'mon, Ron. Give me a break, okay?"

They paused as they entered the plane and greeted the flight attendant.

Their seats were grouped together. Trish and Ashley took the aisle and window seats on one side of row eighteen, while Joe and Derek took the seats across from them. Brian and Erin were in row nineteen, behind Joe and Derek, while Ron and Nick sat across the aisle from them, behind Trish and Ashley.

Joe looked behind him at Brian and said, "Want to change places?" Brian glanced at Erin. She smiled and shrugged her shoulders, her cheeks reddening.

"Sure," Brian said, stepping out into the aisle.

Ron leaned over to Nick and whispered, "You want me to trade with anyone?"

"Give it up, Stevenson!"

Ron straightened and laughed. "Well, I offered." He reached into the pocket in front of him and pulled out the airline magazine.

Nick reached into his coat pocket and pulled out the information he'd been given on the resort where they'd be staying, as well as the travel arrangements.

According to his notes, they would be flying nonstop to Denver. Upon arrival at the airport they were to pick up a van, which would get them to the resort where the chalet they'd rented was located.

He knew the area, but hadn't been there in several years. In fact, he hadn't been on skis in at least that long. He hoped Ms. Ashley didn't intend to hotdog it down the slopes to show him up.

He certainly wouldn't put it past her.

Chapter 3

A wave of noise hit Nick when he stepped out of the jetway in the Denver terminal. Loudspeakers were blaring, carts carrying luggage beeped loudly to clear a path, and a mob of people milled around looking for gates, getting off planes, searching for people, and talking at the top of their voices.

It was enough to give anyone a raging headache.

The holiday spirit was alive and well and going full blast, from all indications.

His group immediately fit in—all laughing and talking at once, asking questions, reading the signs, arguing about where they would find their luggage.

Craig took his role as one of Ashley's bodyguards seriously by draping his arm around her shoulders, keeping her snug against his side. Although he was only a few inches taller than Ashley, Craig was twice as wide. She looked smothered in his embrace. From what Nick could see, she wasn't complaining.

Nick glanced around for Ron, who was trying to get through a family group noisily greeting passengers following him off the plane. As soon as he was free of them, Ron gave Nick a thumbs-up motion accompanied by a grin. Nick just shook his head.

Their group finally agreed on the direction they needed to go and were now dodging people and moving toward the exit signs.

The agents hurried after them. Nick realized that trying to keep this group corralled would take all the energy he had and then some.

Ron caught up with Craig and Ashley and stayed with them as well as he could, considering the oncoming foot traffic. Nick followed along behind. Trish showed up beside him, chattering away, giving an occasional skip to keep up with his longer stride. He did his best to ignore her.

Nick felt out of place in the holiday hustle and bustle. Would anyone believe that he and Ron were here to play in the snow and bask in the sun? Nick knew his expression wasn't particularly relaxed. Maybe he could work on that part of it. The problem was that he couldn't relax and do his job. Somehow being around so much exuberance made him more conscious of the wide gulf between vacation mind-sets and attitudes versus his type of work.

When they reached the baggage-claim area, Nick was surprised to see Sam Masters standing near the sliding doors that led to the street, his thick blond hair gleaming in the light. He and Sam had worked together overseas during his stint with Intelligence. They'd both gone to work for the Treasury Department at the same time, but somehow had lost touch over the years.

Nick walked over to where Sam waited and said, "What in the world are you doing in Denver, Sam? The last I heard, you were in L.A. working on a counterfeit ring."

The two men shook hands, grinning at each other like old friends at a class reunion.

"I could ask you the same thing, Logan. I thought you were working the Naval Observatory, keeping Jason Freeman safe for democracy. What happened? Our VP boot you out?"

"Nope. Just a shift in my assignment, that's all."

Sam looked over at Ron, who stood near Ashley while the group watched for the luggage to appear. "So, what are you doing on the kiddy detail?"

Nick cleared his throat. "For your information, the prez and *all* his family left today for a fishing vacation in the Gulf. These are just a group of college kids getting in a little skiing before returning to school."

Sam adjusted his mirrored sunshades and grinned. "My mistake. I brought you one of our vans. Thought it would be more simple than attempting to rent one. Rentals are at a premium this time of year, if you can even find one available."

They turned and watched as Joe, Derek and Craig claimed various pieces of luggage as it was pointed out to them.

"Good grief, how many bags are there?" Sam asked. "Hope the van will hold everyone and the luggage, too!"

Nick was wondering the same thing. "There's my bag. Guess I'd better grab it. We'll meet you outside in a few minutes." He hurried back to the carousel and scooped up his bag, then joined the line to show their baggage claim at the gate.

After they cleared the claims-check area, Nick said, "Okay, everyone. We have a van waiting for us outside." They scrambled into their parkas before following Nick through the wide doorway. Ron brought up the rear. Once outside, he looked across the street and spotted a dark green Dodge van by the curb. Sam leaned against the front fender, tossing the keys, then catching them.

Once they were able to cross to the other side, Sam handed the keys to Nick. "Here you go. By the way, if you have any free time while you're here, give me a call. I'd enjoy catching up on everything with you." He handed him a card. "Here's my number." He glanced at the laughing, boisterous group piling into the van, affably arguing over the seating arrangements. Nick could feel their impatience as they waited for him to join them. Sam chuckled. "Some tough assignment you've got there, buddy."

Nick grinned. "Must be living right, huh?"

"No sampling the merchandise, now."

"Wash your mouth out, man. I'm here to protect and serve, nothing else."

They both laughed, then Sam waved to the group and walked a few feet in front of the van where an unmarked government car waited with a driver inside. Once they drove away, Nick circled the van for a quick visual check before he opened the driver's door and got in.

Ron had taken the front passenger seat, silently designating Nick as the driver. Nick didn't blame him, not if he wasn't used to driving in this kind of climate.

"Everybody present and accounted for?" he asked, adjusting the mirrors. He reached into his pocket and pulled out his sunglasses.

"Oh, wow!" The irrepressible Trish sighed. "Now you really look like a man of mystery."

Nick happened to catch Ashley's expression in the rearview mirror as she rolled her eyes in disgust.

"That's me, all right," he agreed with a grin and pulled away from the curb. Ron laughed.

Trish continued, "Why didn't you introduce us to your friend, Nicky? He was cute!"

Ron had suggested to the group when they first met that they call the agents by their first names. Trish was taking the suggestion an additional step.

"What are we, Trish?" Derek retorted. "Chopped liver?"

Nick glanced into the rearview mirror and saw Trish pat Derek's cheek. "You're cute, too, honey. Don't fret." She gave an exaggerated sigh. "I just happen to go for those tall, dark, mysterious males like Ron and Nicky...and their friends."

"Well, I guess I fit the tall and dark, Trish," Ron replied wryly. "But I don't get the mysterious stuff you're talking about."

Joe spoke up. "Oh, she's referring to all the secret hand-shakes, the code words, the radio signals, all that junk you guys do."

Ron looked over at Nick and mouthed, "Secret hand-shakes?" and Nick just shook his head. An imaginative bunch.

"At least the weather is cooperating," Nick said. There was a chorus of agreement behind him.

The weather *was* beautiful, with crisp, cold air, a sky so blue it looked artificial, and the nearby peaks covered in glistening white. It felt good to be back in the western part of the country. He'd missed it and had really looked forward to visiting and seeing his family again.

Well, at least he was here. The visit with the family would have to wait for another time.

The drive to the ski resort was filled with songs, outrageous stories and laughter. All of them—with the exception of Ashley—were intensely curious about what it was like to be a Secret-Service agent. They were full of questions. Nick kept his mouth shut and let Ron field the questions. The man was good at sidestepping questions that would involve revealing more than was necessary about their security measures.

The more Nick was around Ron, the more he appreciated the way the man handled himself. He'd lucked out, being paired with someone he liked and respected. That wasn't always the case in this business.

He gave Ron the resort map so that when they pulled into the gated area to the resort, Ron directed him to their chalet. The driveway had been cleared of snow. When he pulled in, there was a rush to get out and explore.

The place was a modified A-frame, quite large, with a great many windows from which to view the mountains all around them. The inside was filled with pleasant surprises. There was a large living area and an equally large den off the main room.

A fire was going in the den, making the place seem cozy. Their hosts had been there to prepare a warm welcome.

Everyone explored. They found three bedrooms upstairs, as well as a full-size basement. Nick was relieved to discover that whoever owned it was security conscious, as evidenced by the state-of-the-art security system installed. It made their job a good deal easier.

The kitchen was fully equipped, and someone had provided coffee, cream and sugar, fruit and snacks.

He and Ron returned to the living room and waited while the party of six sorted themselves out and decided who was going to room with whom. It wasn't long until they returned to the foyer where they'd left the luggage. When the group saw the agents relaxed in the living room, they followed them in there.

Derek was the first to say, "Hey, I'll do my patriotic duty and sleep in Ashley's room." His unstinting selflessness garnered a fair share of catcalls and giggles.

Nick watched Ashley's reaction. She blushed before laughing and shaking her head. "No way!" she said. "You probably snore."

"Or walks in his sleep," Craig said with a grin. All the rooms were equipped with twin beds. "So how are we going to do this, anyway? We've got an odd number here."

Joe spoke up. "All right, you clowns. Erin and I are taking one of the bedrooms, so Trish and Ashley can have one, Craig and Derek the other."

Now it was Erin doing the blushing, but Nick noted she wasn't protesting.

Since none of this was his business, Nick chose to keep quiet and watch.

Joe settled the matter by picking up his and Erin's bags and going upstairs. Trish turned to Nick and asked, "But where will you and Ron sleep?"

Ashley spoke up. "Didn't you know? They don't need sleep. Actually they're androids programmed to do their job. I doubt they ever eat, either."

Ron laughed. "You got that wrong, Ashley. As a matter of fact, my poor ol' stomach thinks my throat's been cut. So what do we do about meals around here?"

Since Ron already knew the answer to his question, Nick knew he was attempting to deflect some of Ashley's sarcasm. It also directed everyone to thinking about how long it had been since they'd been served breakfast on the plane. They began to clamor with suggestions, each volunteering the others to do the KP duties.

Nick finally held up his hand in the "T" that signaled time-out in sports. "We eat at the lodge. The kitchen never closes. I suggest we head out now if you intend to get any skiing done this afternoon."

Once the thought was planted, everyone grabbed his or her bag and rushed upstairs, eager to get unpacked and change into ski clothes. While they were upstairs, he and Ron checked out the den. The two sleeper sofas were arranged at right angles to the fireplace, opposite each other. Nick knew they wouldn't be the most comfortable beds, but he could survive. Since the sofas were long, he decided to leave his closed and treat it as a single bed.

Ron peered out one of the windows. "I'm glad I don't have to get out in this stuff," Ron said with a shiver. "Sitting by the fire at the lodge and waiting for you guys to come back inside suits me just fine. Guess you have to be born around this kind of weather to enjoy it."

"I suppose. I know I prefer the cold dry air of the mountains to the heat and humidity at the beaches."

"Good thing, since there's plenty of us who prefer hot sand and cool seawater."

The clatter on the stairs warned them that the troops were on the move again. Nick grabbed his down-filled parka and said, "Guess it's time to head 'em up and move 'em out."

"You know, this is going to be tough, doing round-the-clock protection. Does Ashley have any idea what she's asking of us?"

Nick glanced over his shoulder and lifted an eyebrow.

"Do you really think she cares? I have a hunch she hopes I break a leg first thing and you injure yourself falling off a bar stool."

Ron shook his head. "I don't think she's quite that adamant about having her privacy."

"Don't bet on it!"

Hours later Ashley finished a run down the side of the mountain and paused to catch her breath. This was just what she'd needed—a chance to get away from routine for a few days, a chance to be with friends.

She'd chosen an easy trail her first time, not wanting to come to grief her first day back on the slopes. She looked around, watching as Craig, then right after him, Trish, came down, both of them whooping with glee, exhilarated by the fresh air, the fresh powder and the physical release after having been cooped up for so many hours.

She'd missed winter in Colorado more than she'd remembered. The mountains were home to her and always would be. This was the first time she'd been allowed to join her friends, some of whom came every winter holiday. Thank God her dad had finally agreed to let her go on this ski trip.

She was glad Ron was along. He was fun…and funny. They'd all indulged themselves at the buffet in the restaurant at the lodge. When it came time to see about renting equipment, he'd waved them off with a shiver that may not have been totally faked, promising to be right there by the fire when they decided they'd had all the fun they wanted with that foreign white stuff.

She was sorry that it wasn't Ron who was out there with them.

"Going up again?" Craig hollered, motioning to the nearby lifts.

"You bet!" she replied, and started to the lifts to join them.

She wouldn't have minded Ron being out there with her,

but everything Nick the Noble did grated on her nerves. He'd taken charge of seeing that everyone was properly fitted for their skis, obviously enjoying the teasing and flirting he received from the other two women in the group.

He'd missed his calling. As a professional ski instructor he could have spent his days impressing all the giggly females. He certainly seemed to thrive on all the attention. He wore a black ski suit that emphasized his broad shoulders and slim waist. She noticed that Erin did a quick visual of him when Joe wasn't watching. Oh, yeah. He looked good.

She also had to admit that he was something to watch on a pair of skis. All that controlled energy came to the fore as he swooped down the side of the mountain. Trish was already lamenting the fact that he stayed so close to Ashley, leaving her to ride the lifts with Derek or Craig, while Joe and Erin continued the twosome they'd formed.

Ashley would gladly change places with Trish, but she knew better than to suggest it. At least while winging down the slopes she could pretend to be alone. She wasn't going to do anything foolish that would be reported to her father.

"Let's find us a blue run this time," Craig suggested as he grabbed for the lift. "Green's too easy."

Ashley and Nick grabbed the next bar, sliding onto the seats and holding on. She looked over at him. He was cleaning his goggles and not looking her way. His profile caught at her and she forced herself to look away.

By the time they got off the lift, the others were waiting for them. A large map of the area was posted, naming each trail, color coding them to show their degree of difficulty. They stood there debating various ones. Ashley agreed with Craig. She was ready for a little more challenge.

She followed him to Duke's Run, gave him some time to push off and build up some speed, then shoved forward with a sense of excitement. There was nothing better than experiencing the silence of the mountain, with only the sound of the wind as it whistled past your ears.

Ashley gave herself up to enjoying the moment.

Nick kept her in sight but wasn't worried about her. She handled herself well, didn't take too many chances and was quite good. This assignment wasn't going to be bad, after all. He was actually getting paid for doing something he would have offered to do for free.

Too bad Ashley had taken such an active dislike to him. If she would unbend a little where he was concerned, they could have a great week here. Somehow he didn't see that happening.

By the time the sun settled behind the peaks, the group was more than ready to call it a day. They headed for the lodge, hoping to have some hot beverages and a chance to warm themselves in front of the oversize fireplace that dominated the cavernous lobby at the lodge.

Ron met them at the door, waving them inside, and listened to their tales of spills and near misses. They settled around the fireplace as soon as they had hot drinks in their hands. Nick sat down next to Ron and listened to their stories with a contented smile. He'd enjoyed the afternoon. He'd had no problems with Ashley other than the fact she treated him as though he were invisible. He could already feel some of his muscles protesting and wondered if he was the only one.

"I don't know about the rest of you," Derek announced, "but I, for one, vote for an early night. This has been a long day. Don't forget we're on eastern time. That's a two-hour difference and my body's already letting me know it!"

"You're just out of shape," Craig said. "I'm ready to party tonight."

"Sure you are," Trish said. "Who was complaining about already getting stiff before we even left the slopes?"

Everybody laughed. He shrugged good-naturedly. "Okay, so I lied."

Erin spoke up. "Why don't we have an early supper and go back to the chalet? A hot bath sounds like just the thing to me."

During dinner Nick was amused at how quiet everyone had become. There was very little conversation while they ate.

He drove them back to the chalet, listening to them discuss who would use which tub first. Luckily there was a bathroom with each bedroom. He and Ron had the use of another one downstairs.

Now if only the hot water holds out, he thought as he watched them go inside.

He turned on the television in the den and stretched out on the sofa he'd chosen to watch the national news. It was the usual stuff—tension in the Mideast, increased drug problems along the southern borders, a terrorist group protesting the jail sentence of one of their leaders, increased drive-by shootings in L.A.

The weather looked a little more interesting. A storm in the Pacific Northwest would be heading into the Rockies by late tomorrow. That might curtail some of their ski activities. The lifts closed whenever the weather turned bad. Perhaps the group would have to find another way to keep themselves entertained tomorrow.

He waited until it was quiet upstairs, then went in to take a shower. When he came back, Ron had made up the other sofa and was watching a sitcom.

"Now this is the life," Ron said. "A nice fire—thanks for rebuilding it, by the way—a beautiful view and a comfortable bed. This is one assignment you won't hear me complaining about."

"Glad to know you're enjoying it. I was afraid you'd be bored sitting around inside all day."

"Not so far, but I'll let you know. Although I have to admit I'm feeling the altitude a little. It takes some getting used to." He clicked off the television. Now the only light came from the fireplace.

Nick found the extra bedding and made up his bed, glad to stretch out. He was tired, but it was a good tired.

He found it amusing, or maybe ironic, the way things had worked out. Here he was back in the mountains of Colorado, only a few miles away from the family cabin where he'd spent many an enjoyable visit with his family. Coming to this area was almost as good as coming home. He just wouldn't see his parents this trip—or his brothers and their families.

Maybe he'd call his folks tomorrow and let them know he was at least here in Colorado, even if he'd missed having Christmas with them. He wished he could figure out a way to get up to Casper to see them. Both brothers and their families would be going home the first of January, the same day this group was scheduled to return to Washington.

There were times when he envied his brothers their normal lives. Times like tonight, when he had too much time to think about the roads not taken. Ron was a good example of how the opposing pull of work and family could tear a man apart. Most of the time Nick refused to allow himself to think about what he could have had.

It was a waste of energy. He had a hunch it was his strong attraction to Ashley Sullivan that had him fantasizing about a wife and family. He smiled to himself. He certainly didn't have to worry about that fantasy coming true.

The woman disliked him too much to ever consider a relationship with him. Therefore, she was one temptation that would be easy to resist.

Chapter 4

Rocky Mountains, Colorado
Tuesday, December 29

"They sound like a bunch of birds up there, don't they?" Ron said, seated across the table from Nick. It was early morning. The two men had already finished their first pot of coffee and were working on a second one.

Nick glanced up from his serious study of the steam slowly rising from his coffee. He'd never been one for early-morning conversations. Thank God Ron seemed to share his aversion. This was the first time either of them had spoken in the hour they had been sitting there.

"Birds?" He turned his head slightly, trying to focus his mind on the present. After a moment he smiled. "Sounds like a herd of elephants trampling around, if you ask me."

Ron grinned, his teeth flashing in his dark face. "No, I mean in how it was quiet for so long and then…" He shrugged his shoulders, settling back into the comfortably padded banquette that formed a U around the large table. "I guess I was reminded of the times as a kid when my dad used to take us camping." His gaze softened as his thoughts turned inward. "We'd wake up before dawn. I can remember being amazed at how still everything was. I'd lie there listening and watching as the sky gradually lightened. Then I'd hear sounds of rustling in the bushes. Finally there would be the sound of a lone bird—just one—and it was as though his call was the signal for everything out there. The whole area would suddenly be alive with all kinds of bird noises and songs."

Ron glanced out the kitchen window. Nick followed his gaze and noticed that the sun was, indeed, peeking between the mountains.

Ron went on. "The house was quiet this morning, neither of us talking, and then I heard a voice speak softly upstairs. As though that was a signal, all of them began talking at once, just like birds in the wild."

They were sitting in companionable silence when Trish bounced into the room.

"Mornin'." The jeans she had on today were even tighter than those she'd worn on the plane yesterday. "I don't know about you guys, but I'm starving. Is there anything to eat in this place?"

"There's some fruit and a few snacks, but nothing substantial," Nick replied. "I suppose I could do a run for groceries, or we can all just go over to the lodge for their buffet."

"Oh, that sounds even better. No cooking, no cleaning. I'm all for that." She reached for a cup. "Thank God there's coffee."

Ron chuckled. "Nick had made a pot by the time I woke up this morning."

She turned from filling her cup and gave Nick a very sultry smile. "You are definitely my kind of guy," she said in a throaty voice.

Ashley appeared in the doorway. "Yours and a dozen other women's, I'm sure," she said sweetly. "I bet they all line up for a chance to be with our noble protector, don't they, Nick?"

She was dressed for the slopes, her red jacket unzipped

to reveal a snug-fitting black turtleneck sweater. He had to admit that the color was very flattering with her hair and skin coloring.

"Not so I've ever noticed," Nick replied dryly.

Trish spoke up. "We're going for the breakfast buffet. Sounds yummy, doesn't it?"

Ashley shrugged. "I don't care. I just want to get outside for some serious skiing."

Nick stood, pulling his jacket off the back of his chair. "I'm ready whenever you are."

She rolled her eyes. "Look, you don't have to be so diligent in your duties, you know. Nothing's going to happen to me between here and the ski area."

"You're right about that." He slid his arms into his jacket, pulled his cap down around his ears and removed his sun shades from his pocket. "Let's go."

"Hey, wait for me," Trish said, hurriedly finishing her coffee. "I'll come back to change clothes after breakfast."

Ron stood and shrugged into his coat. "Breakfast sounds good to me, too. Guess I'll join you."

"Oh, great," Ashley said. "Am I going to walk in with each of you holding one of my hands?"

Nick looked at Ron. "Now there's a thought. Maybe we should—"

"Don't even think about it!" she retorted, and stormed out the front door. Trish went to get her coat.

Ron followed Nick down the front steps of the chalet. "I think you enjoy setting her off, don't you?"

Nick shook his head. "Not particularly. I'm just not going to play her little games. She's acting like a spoiled brat. If she wants to get her nose out of joint every time I do my job, then she's going to have a really silly-looking face. In the meantime, I *will* do my job, with or without her cooperation."

Ashley strode along the paved road that led to the lodge several feet ahead of them. Trish was content to walk along beside them, chattering about all kinds of things. Nick tuned her out.

Ron finally interrupted by asking, "Did you tell the others where we're going?"

Trish tossed her head. "They're all grown-ups. If they get hungry enough, they'll figure out where the food is."

Uh-oh, Nick thought. A little dissension in the ranks already. What a fun day this was shaping up to be.

As soon as they walked into the lodge, the savory scents of ham, bacon and hot syrup wafted toward them.

Once Ashley filled a plate, she headed for a table for two located in one of the corners, hoping that Trish was right behind her. She glanced over her shoulder and saw that Nick was already moving toward a table nearby. She gave a silent sigh of relief.

She was going to have to get a grip on her emotions, that was all there was to it. She knew she was acting like an adolescent and there was no excuse for her behavior. What *was* it about the man that set her nerves to screaming whenever she was anywhere around him?

Her behavior wasn't due to the fact that there were Secret-Service men with them. She actually enjoyed Ron and his quiet sense of humor. Somehow she had to get over her irrational dislike of Nick Logan. She just wished she knew how.

"What do you have against Nick?" Trish suddenly asked, sitting down across from her. "You've been on his case ever since we got here."

Ashley rubbed her forehead with her fingers, feeling the hint of a headache looming. "I don't know, Trish. I honestly don't. He just rubs me the wrong way, that's all."

Trish grinned. After taking a big bite of her food and chewing it, she carefully swallowed before saying, "I really don't think I'd care which way he rubbed me, as long as he was interested in trying."

"Yeah, right. We both know you're all talk and no action... so why the siren routine?"

Trish didn't answer right away. Ashley continued to eat and

was taken aback when Trish finally responded by saying, "I didn't know Joe was coming on this trip to be with Erin."

After a moment Ashley responded, "I think we all came to ski, Trish. That's what this trip is about, isn't it?"

Trish sighed. "I came because I thought if I was in a small enough group with him, Joe would finally notice me."

Ashley studied her friend's woebegone face. "Oh, Trish, I'm sorry," she said in a quiet voice. "I had no idea you felt that way."

Trish sighed and continued eating. In a moment she said, "As long as Joe doesn't know, I guess I'll survive. You could have thrown me into a crocodile pit and I probably wouldn't have noticed yesterday when Joe said he and Erin would share a room. I was totally freaked."

"But would you have shared a room with him?"

"Are you crazy? Of course not! I'm not going to bed with some guy just because—" She stopped her tirade and shrugged her shoulders. "I just didn't think this was going to be a trip about sex."

"It isn't. It's about skiing."

"For you, maybe."

"For me, definitely. Do you think my dad would have agreed to let me come if he'd thought I'd be sharing a room with some guy?" She made a face, hoping to lighten Trish's mood a little.

Trish chuckled. "He doesn't have to worry about you, not with two chaperones following you everywhere you go." She nibbled on a piece of toast before adding, "Wow. I just realized. That could really cramp your social life if you were seriously involved with someone."

"Tell me about it. I'll probably end up single for the rest of my life."

Trish gave her a devilish grin. "Either that, or have an affair with one of your guardians." She glanced over at the other table where Ron and Nick were eating. "If I were in your place, I would definitely be tempted."

Ashley replied, "Ron's just getting over a painful divorce.

I don't think he's ready for another relationship anytime soon."

"Not Ron, you idiot! Nick. I bet he could teach you all kinds of things."

"The thing is, Trish, I think you're supposed to like the guy before you decide to have an affair with him. At least that's always been my take on the matter."

"What's not to like? Don't you just adore his eyes? And the way he looks at you, as though he can read your very soul? Not to mention that body? Sometimes I have this urge to walk up and just stroke his backside in unabashed admiration, you know what I mean?"

Unfortunately Ashley had just taken a sip of coffee when Trish nonchalantly threw that suggestion at her. She almost choked when the liquid went down the wrong way at her gasp.

"Trish!" she finally was able to hiss, wiping the tears from her eyes.

"Well, it's the truth. I'm not really into bodybuilding and stuff like that, but I have to admit that I've wondered what that man would look like in the buff. I have a hunch he would be all burnished muscle and sinewy strength." The expression she got on her face was embarrassingly dreamy.

"Could we change the subject now?" she asked, with more than a hint of annoyance.

"Sure." Trish waved to someone and Ashley glanced around. Joe, Derek and Craig had just walked into the room. Trish jumped up. "I'll go see what happened to Erin. See you later."

Ashley took the opportunity to make her escape. She gave a brief wave to the others before she hurried toward the door. She would return to the chalet long enough to gather her skis and poles before she headed up the mountain.

Just as she reached out to push on the door, a masculine arm reached past her shoulder, swinging it open for her. She didn't have to look around to know that Nick Logan had joined her.

This was just great. She wouldn't be able to look at him without thinking of Trish's ridiculous comments. She glanced over her shoulder at him and forced herself to smile.

"Thank you."

His expression didn't change. Since he'd placed his sunglasses over his eyes, she couldn't visually gauge his reaction to her politeness, but his answer came readily enough. "Don't waste your breath, Ms. Sullivan. No one else is around to hear it."

It was that very trait that she found so offensive. She was trying to be nice, for heaven's sake. His response was to be sarcastic.

She decided to retreat into silence.

Even that wasn't good enough.

"Yeah, that's much better," he drawled, matching his steps to hers. "I'm familiar with your silent sulks."

She would not dignify his sniping with a reply. Not even one.

They gathered their equipment and returned to the ski area.

There were eager skiers everywhere this morning. Clouds were beginning to form just above the mountains to the northwest of them. From the looks of things, it could be snowing by noon. If there was a storm coming, she wanted to be off the slopes before it hit.

"Hey, guys, wait up."

Derek and Craig hurried toward them, carrying their equipment. "What's the hurry, Ashley?" Craig asked. "Couldn't you have waited another few minutes for the rest of us? I thought this was a group experience."

She could feel her face heating up. "I'm sorry, Craig. I guess I wasn't thinking." She glanced toward the darkening sky. "I didn't want to miss out on skiing today, and those clouds are certainly beginning to look threatening."

Nick nudged her. "Here comes our ride," he said, suddenly lifting her onto the seat and swinging around to sit on the other side of the bar. Ashley was so startled that she almost lost her poles. She looked back and saw Derek and Craig putting on their skis.

"That was rude," she muttered. "We could have waited for them."

"Yes, we could have. However, if you're serious about getting some ski time in today, we needed to get moving. This may be our only chance before the storm hits."

She frowned. "Not necessarily. I've skied when it was snowing. There's no reason to—"

"Do you enjoy arguing, or is it just with me? You find fault with everything I say."

"I just find you unnecessarily rude, that's all. This is supposed to be a fun trip, but you've certainly managed to take all the fun out of it…for all of us!"

A burst of swirling snow blew past them, and she ducked her head to get away from the stinging spray.

"I had no idea I had enough power to ruin six people's vacation time. Damn, but I'm good."

When she looked at him he was staring ahead of them, watching their progress up the mountain. "Is that supposed to be funny?"

He still didn't look at her. "I should hope not. I'm the guy with no sense of humor."

Ashley had never felt so much animosity toward another person in all her life. If she'd thought she could do it, she would have shoved him off the lift right then and there.

They reached the top of the lift. She got herself ready and eased off, moving through the snow. Only then did she realize that the gusts of snow-laden air blowing around her were not recirculating snow that had already fallen. This was new stuff coming down, growing thicker by the moment.

"Let's go," Nick said brusquely.

"I'm waiting for Derek and Craig. They'll be here shortly."

"Ashley—"

She looked away from him. "If you're nervous about the weather, go ahead. I'll meet you at the lodge." When he didn't say anything, she casually turned her head and looked at him. She was a little alarmed by how fast the snow was falling. He was covered by snow and she was already having a little trouble seeing him. His expression was blurred. She adjusted her goggles and looked around.

There they were! Craig and Derek joined them. "Joe had the right idea. He said he was going to wait to see what this weather was going to do. I don't like this at all," Derek said with more than a hint of uneasiness.

Craig shoved forward. "Last one down the hill pays for lunch," he hollered over his shoulder.

Derek was quick to follow.

"Ready anytime you are, Ms. Sullivan," Nick said quietly.

She pushed away, determined to leave him. The problem with that was the fact that he was darned near a pro on skis. She took the most direct route down, swerving suddenly to miss a slower skier, and inadvertently left the trail she'd been following. With a groan of frustration, she forced herself to slow down while she tried to figure out a way to get back on their chosen run.

She finally came to a complete halt and looked around. None of the men were in sight.

Not even her shadow.

"Nick?" she called, looking around.

She could see others skiing, but no one that looked like the three she had been with. She decided to continue down, hoping to cross another path soon.

Nick would probably think she'd done this just to annoy him. She was now in a wooded area where she moved very carefully. She didn't like being lost. The ski trail had been clearly marked; here there was nothing she could use as a guide down the mountain.

Ashley shivered.

The snow continued to come down in thick flurries.

This was close to a whiteout, she thought a few minutes later. She couldn't see anything in front of her. It was much too dangerous to continue to move with any speed in this kind of weather.

She didn't know how far she'd gone when she finally spotted one of the large midmountain restaurants that were scattered throughout the area for weary skiers. She managed to reach the side of the building, sighing with relief to be out of the heavily falling snow.

It was scarcely ten o'clock in the morning. There was no reason to panic. She'd just wait here for a brief time to get her breath back, maybe get something hot to drink and warm up a little before she continued downhill.

Chapter 5

By the time Nick reached the end of the run, he was ready to wring Ashley's neck. He was really tired of her attitude and her silly games. Did she think she was going to win some points by disappearing on him? He looked around, the thick flakes obscuring his vision, hoping to see Ashley's red parka somewhere nearby. Once he found her, he intended to give her a lecture she wouldn't forget.

Perhaps she wasn't aware of it, but he—and Ron—had the authority to end this little vacation of hers if, in their opinion, they were unable to adequately protect her.

He spotted Derek removing his skis, but there was no sign of Ashley.

He made his way over to him. "Where's Ashley?"

Derek stopped unfastening his skis and looked up at Nick in surprise. "I haven't seen her. I thought she was with you."

Nick scanned the area. There were several red parkas, but none of them belonged to Ashley. He began to feel uneasy. At the rate the snow was falling, it was hard to tell the color of anything.

He muttered an unprintable word and turned away.

"Where are you going?" Derek called.

"To find Ashley."

"Don't worry about her. She was born on a pair of skis. She probably got off course a little. It's coming down like a son of a—"

"I don't need a weather report," Nick growled to himself, moving toward the lifts again.

What really alarmed him was how she had managed to get away from him. One minute she was there just ahead of him, the next minute there'd been no sign of her. Was it intentional? Was she in danger? He didn't know why he bothered to question her disappearance. Of course it was intentional.

He turned and watched as more skiers came down the mountain. One of them looked familiar. He moved toward the snow-covered figure who was moving very slowly in his direction. As he drew closer, he recognized Craig.

"Have you seen Ashley?" Nick asked him.

Craig shook his head. "No. I took a spill up there. By the time I could get started again, I'd lost track of everybody." He looked around. "You mean she isn't down here?"

"Derek hasn't seen her. She was ahead of me, but I lost sight of her about halfway down."

Craig shrugged. "Yeah, well, I was ahead of all of you, for what that's worth. If I hadn't been showing off, I would have been the first one down." He rubbed his shoulder. "You don't suppose she fell, do you?"

"I have no way of knowing. I'm going back to look for her."

"You want me to come with you?"

Nick shook his head. "Thanks, but that won't be necessary."

Craig looked relieved. "I don't envy you going up there in all of this. What a mess."

Nicked waved as he shoved off for the lift. If she was hurt somewhere up there, he needed every minute he had to try to find her. All the while he rode up the mountainside he watched for her red parka. There were so many things that could happen, even to an experienced skier. He didn't want to think about some of the possible problems she may have encountered.

By the time he reached the top, the wind and snow had caused the visibility to be measured in inches rather than feet. Nick was aware of the adrenaline pumping through his bloodstream.

His first full day in charge of her and he'd managed to misplace his charge. How could he have allowed this to happen?

He started down the same run they'd chosen earlier, watching for tracks leaving the marked area, but of course that was a waste of time with the amount of snow that had already fallen. There was no sign of her anywhere.

By the time he reached the bottom of the run, he was ready to call in reinforcements.

"Hey, Nick, she's okay!"

Craig waved at him from one of the wind-protected areas. Nick skied over to him. "Have you seen her?"

"No. But I've been asking people coming down if they had spotted her. One of the guys I just talked with said a young woman matching her description had been at one of the restaurants having coffee. He said he'd chatted with her while they were in line. She told him she'd gotten separated from her party. He said she would probably be down soon."

Nick hadn't taken his eyes off the trails during their conversation, wondering which way she would be coming down. It was then that he saw a bright red dot swooping down in an almost vertical drop on one of the more difficult runs.

Craig pointed. "Look! I bet that's her! Didn't I tell you she'd be down soon? Just look at her go."

Oh, he was looking, all right. Of all the dangerously foolhardy stunts he'd ever seen, she was definitely pulling one now. Did she have any idea how fast she was going? And if anyone got in her way… He didn't want to think about it.

Luckily for Ashley there was no one else on that particular run. Nick stood and watched as she finally slowed her heart-stopping drop downward. She moved into a leisurely curving S down the side of the mountain, looking for all the world as though she was enjoying herself, instead of battling a heavy snowfall that could cause all kinds of damage if she hit something covered by the new snow.

The fact that she made it without a problem did not endear her to him at all. However, at the moment, he was just damned glad to see her safe.

He stood and waited, knowing that she would have to pass by his location on her way to the lodge. It was only when she got closer that he saw her white face. He knew exactly when she spotted him. She called out to him. "Oh, Nick, am I ever glad to see you!" she said, and skied over to one of the benches, where she dropped, exhausted. She removed her goggles with fumbling fingers and began to tug at the straps of her skis.

Nick sat down beside her and took off his skis, then he knelt in front of her and gently brushed her hands away from hers. With an economy of movement he removed hers, as well.

"I didn't know what to do," she said, sounding breathless. "I missed one of the turns on the trail, then I couldn't see anything, it was snowing so hard." She brushed tendrils of hair away from her eyes. "After a while I came across one of the restaurants up there, so I stopped for a few minutes to get warm." She was still out of breath and trying to cover the fact that she was shaking. "Then it seemed as though a break came because the snow lessened and the visibility cleared. I knew I had to go right then, fast as I could, before I lost my nerve and the visibility went back to zero."

Nick stood, then pulled her up and handed her skis to her. He turned and gathered up his, then dropped his arm around her shoulders. Neither one of them spoke during the walk to the chalet. Once there, Nick placed their equipment in the storage area.

Only then did he speak to her. "I think we need to get you

warm," he said brusquely. "The lodge has a big fire going and plenty of hot drinks. I think that's where everyone else is."

She shivered, than laughed with more than a hint of shakiness.

"I don't think it's the cold as much as nerves." She looked back toward the run she had recently come off, which was now veiled in a heavy white curtain of snow. "I can't believe I got down that mountain in one piece."

"Neither can I," he said in a low voice. Once again he placed his arm around her shoulders and headed toward the lodge.

Only then did Ashley seem to realize that she was allowing him to touch her. She stiffened, and Nick figured she would pull away from him. Instead, she relaxed against him. She shook her head as though to clear it, then lifted her gaze to meet his.

"I bet you're furious with me," she said, sounding weary.

"Oh, yeah. Big-time furious." He kept his voice low, almost gentle. "You scared the hell out of me, I don't mind admitting to you. I went back up looking for you. I don't know which is worse, really. I sure as hell didn't want to find you lying somewhere hurt, but not spotting you anywhere didn't mean you hadn't been injured…or worse."

She sighed. "I know. I certainly didn't do this on purpose."

"I'm glad to hear it."

The double doors into the recreation area of the lodge swung open in front of them and several skiers came out chatting with each other and heading for their vehicles. Nick stepped back and motioned her through the doors, then followed her inside.

He nodded toward the conversation pit, which was built around one of the massive fireplaces radiating an enormous amount of heat.

"Wait over there while I get you some coffee. Or would you prefer hot chocolate?"

"Coffee's fine," she replied. He watched her sink wearily

into the comfort of a padded chair. She held out her hands toward the boisterous fire.

Nick turned away, grateful that she would soon be able to shrug off this morning's scare.

Ron met him at the bar. "I hear you misplaced our gal this morning." He glanced over to where Ashley sat. "She looks okay now. How are you doing?"

Nick leaned his elbow on the bar and rubbed his forehead. "It was definitely not one of my finer moments. I'm just glad she wasn't hurt."

"What happened?"

"Damned if I know. She was skiing down the mountain in front of me, then I lost sight of her during a flurry of snow, and when I looked back to where she'd been, she was nowhere in sight."

"Did you think someone had grabbed her?"

"That thought never entered my mind. Which I guess is a good thing. No, I figured she was enjoying one of her stupid games, playing hide-and-seek or something."

"Was she?"

"If so, she had the fear of God instilled in her by the time she showed up. If she wasn't so good on skis, this could have turned ugly."

"So why don't you let me take over for a while? I think you need a break."

Nick rubbed his hand down over his face. "Good idea. Thanks."

The bartender set a cup of coffee on the bar and Nick paid for it, then nodded to the cup, saying, "She's all yours, Ron. I'd just as soon not have to deal with her for the next few hours."

Ron nodded. "Fair enough. Looks as though I won't have to convince her to stay off the slopes for the rest of the day."

They both turned and saw the snow blowing almost horizontally past the wide windows overlooking the ski runs.

A babble of voices caused them to look back at the conversation pit, where Ashley now was surrounded by her friends, all trying to talk at once. Nick watched Craig pull her into his arms and hold her. Then he kissed her.

Nick idly noted she wasn't pushing him away. He shook his head and walked away. He definitely could use a break.

Ashley glanced up when Nick returned with the coffee only to discover that it wasn't Nick at all. "Hi, Ron. I thought you were Nick." She took the cup and eagerly wrapped her fingers around its warm surface.

Craig continued to sit on the side of her chair, his arm around her. "Then we need to have your eyes checked, honey. Your guardians have their own distinctive appearance and are not easily confused for the other."

The other four chuckled nervously. Erin spoke up. "That was really scary, Ashley. Everyone was very worried about you."

Nothing like adding to her guilt, Ashley thought. She needed to apologize to Nick, but she couldn't see him anywhere. She glanced over at Ron, who had found a seat nearby. "What happened to Nick?"

"He had some things he needed to do. How are you feeling?"

She rolled her eyes. "Fine, now. But I sure don't want that to happen again anytime soon." She glanced around at her friends. "So. What are we going to do with the rest of the day? It's almost time for lunch. Any ideas how we should spend the afternoon?"

There was an immediate discussion of all the possibilities. Ashley didn't really care. She sat back and watched the others. Right now she didn't have the energy to move out of the chair she was sitting in. But maybe after a good lunch, she would feel better.

She kept remembering how relieved she'd been when she recognized Nick waiting for her. He'd looked safe and solid, standing there waiting for her. She hadn't cared what sort of lecture he delivered. Even though she hadn't deliberately set out to get lost, she probably deserved anything he had to say.

She kept remembering how she'd felt when he'd held her close against his side for that walk between the chalet and the lodge. She'd felt his heart beating at a rapid pace, almost racing. He hadn't immediately started lecturing her, although he had made his thoughts quite clear on the subject of her disappearance. However, he'd continued to hold her. And he hadn't raised his voice.

Nick's concern had been very real. Of course, it was his job to look after her. There was no reason to read anything into his behavior. What surprised her was how safe and protected she'd felt. All of her animosity toward him was gone.

"What about you, Ashley?" Joe asked. "What do you want to do?"

She grinned and jumped up from her chair. "That's easy. I want to eat. I'm starved!"

They all laughed at her and made a general exodus into the dining area, where once again an appetizing array of food had been spread to tempt the guests and visitors at the lodge.

By the time lunch was over, Ron had volunteered to drive them to town, where the women intended to look at all the shops, and the men planned to find a movie theater.

They headed back to the chalet to change clothes. Ashley felt better once she'd gotten some food inside of her. She wondered if Nick had eaten, then couldn't believe she was actually worrying about him.

Once they reached the chalet, everyone was in a hurry to get ready for an afternoon adventure in town. Ashley decided she might go to a movie, instead of shopping. She was fairly certain that Ron would appreciate her choice!

Nick headed for the chalet as soon as he left the lodge. Thank God Ron had decided to take over. He didn't want to dwell on all that could have happened to Ashley. The fact was that she was safe and had received a good scare. Perhaps it had been inevitable, but he wished that he hadn't lost track of her on the slopes.

As soon as he reached the chalet, he decided to warm up with a shower. Later he dressed, stretched out on the sofa and closed his eyes.

He was still there when Ron walked in an hour later.

"You okay?" Ron asked.

"Oh, I'm all right," he replied, sitting up and stretching. "What's the plan now?"

"I'm taking them into town. They may see a movie or something. I'll stay with her this afternoon. No need for you to tag along." Ron sat down on the sofa across from Nick. "You missed out on a great lunch. Why don't you go on over and get something before the buffet closes?"

Nick stood, arching his back in another stretching motion. He'd changed into jeans and one of his heavy sweaters. Since he didn't intend to stay out in the weather any longer than it took to walk over to the lodge, he figured he was adequately dressed. "Sounds good. I may do that."

While he was at the lodge, he might give Sam a call to see if he'd like to get together this afternoon. They could stay here at the chalet and visit. It would be more private than the bar at the lodge, not to mention having the place to themselves for a few hours. The idea was more than a little appealing.

Nick was at the door a couple of hours later when Sam pulled up in his midsize sedan. He stood in the open doorway and watched Sam walk up the snowy path to the door.

"This is really a mess today, isn't it?" Sam commented, brushing snow off his coat as he stepped inside. "I guess the storm canceled the skiing plans."

"I don't think it matters to these guys. They're off doing something else. Ah, for the resilience of youth." He motioned Sam to follow him into the kitchen, where fresh coffee was waiting.

Sam Masters was thirty-eight years old, but looked several

years younger. His white-blond hair and clear blue eyes reflected his north-European ancestry.

"How do you like working here in Colorado?" Nick asked, placing a steaming cup in front of Sam and sitting down across from him.

"I've had worse assignments. Remember that winter we were in Amsterdam?" Sam shivered at the word.

Nick grinned. "Oh, I don't know. I have some rather fond memories of the place myself."

"But then, you could always find a warm port in any cold area, as I recall. Do you ever hear anything from Brigit these days?"

"Not since a letter a couple of years ago informing me she was marrying into a wealthy banking family and hoped I wouldn't do or say anything to embarrass her regarding her past."

Sam threw his head back and laughed. "Not too tactful, but she got her point across."

The phone rang, the first time Nick had heard the instrument since they'd arrived. Not many people knew they were here.

"Excuse me a moment," he said, walking across to the wall phone. "Hello," he said cautiously.

"May I speak to Ashley, please?" came a pleasant voice that Nick instantly recognized.

"I'm sorry, Mrs. Sullivan, but Ashley and her friends have gone to town. We're having some heavy snow at the moment, and they had to forsake the slopes." He paused, then added, "This is Special Agent Logan. May I give her a message?"

"Oh. Well, yes, please. Ask her to call me when she gets back. We've been missing her and I just wanted to make certain she's happy with her decision. I want her to know that she can still join us on the coast if she wants."

Nick smiled, but made certain his voice was suitably neutral. "I'll certainly have her call you, Mrs. Sullivan."

"No matter how late she comes in, all right?"

"Of course."

Nick hung up the phone and returned to his seat at the table.

"A worrying mother, I take it?"

"Aren't they all? My mother still frets about me for one thing or another."

Sam chuckled. "If she only knew some of the scrapes you've been in, she'd have real cause to fret."

Nick leaned back in the comfortable seat and sighed. "I'm glad you were able to get away today, Sam. It feels good to be off duty, even if it's only for a few hours."

"It was good to hear from you. As I told you on the phone, it's my day off and I'd already decided there wasn't much to do with weather like this. Besides, I'm eager to hear the real scoop on this latest transfer of yours."

Nick gave him a puzzled look. "Scoop? I don't know what you're talking about."

"Don't give me that, Logan. This is me you're talking to. With your background and experience, it makes sense they'd use you to chase down the rumors."

Nick shook his head in bewilderment. "Sam, I'm afraid you've lost me. What the hell are you talking about?"

Sam threw up his hands. "Okay, sorry to have brought it up. If you can't talk about it, I understand. I hope to hell you can get to the bottom of this thing before somebody gets hurt. There's already talk that Colin's death was no accident."

Nick studied the man across from him with narrowed eyes. "Why would there be speculation about that?"

Sam shrugged. "Several theories are being tossed around. Maybe he learned too much and couldn't be trusted to keep it to himself. I happen to know that some big bills have been flashed around lately. I made the mistake of asking about a co-worker's recent windfall a few weeks ago. The next day I was exiled out here. So somebody with clout is behind this."

"You're talking about men in our ranks?"

"Yep."

Nick leaned back in his chair and shook his head. "I find

that hard to believe. Do you have any idea where the money's coming from?"

"Nope, but I figure once we know that, we'll know why. It's got to be something really big or they wouldn't have worked to infiltrate our group."

"Have you reported your suspicions, Sam?"

"And get myself killed by choosing the wrong one to tell? Hell, as far as I'm concerned, I'm reporting it to you. You were my commanding officer at one time, the only person I have no trouble trusting."

"Let me get this straight. You're saying that it's possible that some of our agents are working for someone else, as well? Who's the target?"

"When I saw you at the airport yesterday, I assumed it was the first daughter. Why else would you be assigned to watch over her?"

"The president specifically requested me to be here since I'm familiar with the area. I don't think it had anything to do with a sinister plot."

Sam shrugged. "Maybe my paranoia is getting the best of me, then."

"I'd like to think so, but I'll admit you've got me worried. I believe in your hunches. So let's look at this. If something is planned, why would it be directed toward Ashley?"

"Because the best way to control the president is to have control of a member of his family."

Nick didn't like the sound of this, not at all. Because it made a certain amount of sense, and yet…

"You're talking about traitors within the White House detail? The very men who are sworn to protect the president and his family with their lives?"

"I think someone has been bribed enough to forget his allegiance. The real kicker is to find out who is behind it. I can't get a whisper on that one."

The sounds of slamming doors and voices reached them through the window, and Nick realized the crew had returned. He also noticed for the first time that it had stopped snowing.

"Looks like you've got to get back to work, huh?" Sam said, standing and stretching.

"I appreciate your coming by, especially on your day off. I'm glad you trusted me enough to warn me about all of this, although what I can do about it is anybody's guess."

"Look at it this way, Nick. If you aren't part of their plan, then you may very well be the monkey wrench in the works."

"What are you talking about?"

"I happen to know that nobody expected the daughter to be away from her family at this particular time. In fact, most people still think she's on that yacht with the rest of them. Having you with her is the best thing that could have happened for her safety."

"If what you say is true, then it's more likely that whoever is behind this is planning something where the family is concerned. Do you know who on the detail will be with them on the yacht?"

"Nope. Like I said, I was sent out here a few weeks ago. Not much filters to this part of the country." He met Nick's gaze. "All I'm saying to you is to watch your back and to trust no one."

Nick studied Sam for a long silent moment before asking, softly, "You included?"

Sam shrugged. "That's up to you, of course. I figure I owe you this much. I wouldn't be here today if you hadn't bailed me out of a couple of tight places. I don't forget things like that."

"Come on, Sam. We were all just doing our jobs."

"Some people were, that's true. Then there were those who chose to go the extra mile. I've learned to value those people because they're so rare."

The kitchen was suddenly filled with people, all laughing and talking at the same time.

"Well, hello," Trish said to Sam. Her smile sparkled. "I

hope you're not leaving now, are you, not when we just got here!"

Sam smiled at her and said, "'Fraid so."

"Do you ski?" she asked hopefully.

"Very poorly, I'm afraid." Sam looked over at Nick. "It was great seeing you again. Keep in touch now, you hear?"

Nick nodded. "I'll do that. You do the same." He watched as Sam walked down the pathway, waved at Ron who was locking up the van, before he got into his sedan and drove away.

"You missed a great time," Erin said to Nick. "We had fun."

"Did you see a movie?"

She shook her head. "Nobody could make up their mind which one to see. Besides, we can see a movie anytime. We're in Colorado. I've never been this far west before. I bought a bunch of souvenirs to take home."

Nick happened to turn and catch Ashley's eye. She smiled at him, a truly engaging grin without artifice, the first he had ever received from her. She was inviting him to share in the humor of the moment. It hit him that, personality conflict aside, Ashley Sullivan was a truly nice person. She didn't deserve to be caught up in whatever was going on back in D.C.

It was up to him to protect her. Not only was it his job, it was becoming a personal issue with him.

That thought scared the hell out of him, every bit as much as Sam's news today. He had no business getting emotionally involved with her.

He could remind himself of that fact from now until old age set in, but it didn't change any of the facts.

He was falling for the president's daughter.

Chapter 6

Tuesday, December 29

"There's going to be a live band at the lodge tonight," Joe said, joining the group in the kitchen.

"How did you hear about that?" Derek asked.

"I have ESP, didn't you know?"

The girls laughed at the look on Derek's face. Erin patted his shoulder in a consoling gesture. "There was a sign on the guard's hut at the gate. Didn't you see it when we came back from town?"

Ashley and Trish answered together, "He was too busy talking," and everybody laughed—including Derek.

Craig looked over at Joe, slightly raising a brow. "ESP?"

Joe shrugged and grinned disarmingly. "It was worth a shot. Anyway, I think we should plan to stay for some dancing after dinner. Anybody up for that?"

Nick looked at Ron, who rolled his eyes and shrugged. Where *did* they get their energy?

"I think it's time I relieved *you* for a few hours," Nick said, pulling Ron aside.

"I hope you got a nap. These guys don't ever stop."

"No, but I had a nice visit with Sam. I hadn't seen him in a few years."

"Glad you had the opportunity."

The group, as he tended to think of them, had already charged upstairs by this time, the guys loudly discussing shower order while the gals discussed what to wear for the evening. He and Ron returned to the room they were sharing.

Ron walked over to his bag and began to pull out clean clothes.

Nick watched him for a moment, cleared his throat and said, "Sam mentioned something this afternoon that has me concerned."

Ron glanced around at him. "What's that?"

"He said there's talk that Colin's death was not an accident. I'm curious to know what you think."

Ron met his gaze squarely, but didn't answer right away. "Maybe," he finally admitted. Then he added, "I wish I knew."

"So you've had some doubts?"

Ron looked down at the floor, obviously trying to decide how to answer. Nick could understand his hesitation. This was serious stuff they were dealing with here. If what Sam had told him was true, there was no telling how many agents were involved.

Was Ron one of them? If he was, would Nick be able to discern that? He had to trust that he'd be able to figure out Ron's position. For that matter, Ron was in the same situation where he was concerned.

Who could they trust?

"Colin and I were in the habit of having coffee together after we got off work every night," Ron finally said quietly. "Neither one of us had anyone waiting at home. It gave us a chance to visit. In the course of our conversations, we shared a lot about ourselves that had nothing to do with our job assignments."

"You were friends," Nick murmured.

Ron sighed. "Yeah. We were friends." He rubbed his hand over his head. "That last night we met at an all-night diner as usual. Colin was excited. Nervous. Tense. He started telling me things he'd never discussed with me before. Not much detail, you understand. Just that he thought he was close to gathering proof."

"About what?"

"Some kind of conspiracy."

"A conspiracy? Against who or what?"

Ron sighed. "Hell, I don't know. We're all paranoid to some degree. To listen to Colin, you'd think there was a group trying to overthrow the government. In the past he'd made comments about not knowing who could be trusted anymore. That night he suggested that it went all the way to the top."

Nick could feel a knot forming in his stomach. "That sounds pretty paranoid to me, all right. He thought it might touch the Man?"

"From what he was saying, I got that impression, yeah."

"Who knew Colin felt this way?" Nick asked.

"I don't know. I told him that kind of talk could get him killed."

"So now you're wondering if, in fact, it did."

"Sometimes," Ron admitted. "That and the fact that there was no way he was on his way home when he was killed. He didn't live anywhere near that area, and when I left him, he said he was headed home to bed."

"He could have lied to you…for the best of reasons. Maybe it was a way to protect you."

"Maybe. We'll never know now." Ron leaned forward, his gaze intent. "I have to admit I was more than a little suspicious when you were first assigned in his place."

"Me? Why?"

"Let's say it gave you a valid reason to be in the White House. I figured you might have been placed there to investigate what happened, in case Colin's sudden death had raised anyone's suspicions."

"And have you changed your mind about me?"

Ron's answer was slow in coming. "Maybe. I haven't seen any sign of you investigating anything. Until now, anyway." They were both silent, thinking their own thoughts, until finally Ron asked, "So what do you think all this means?"

"I'm not sure. I just know I don't like it. I can't help but wonder if we were shuttled off to get us out of town."

"Somebody had to do it."

"Yeah."

He could hear amusement in Ron's voice. "The things we're forced to do for our country, right?"

Nick stood and walked over to the window. "Go to sleep. I may need you to spell me before this night is through."

He heard Ron's chuckle, then the soft sounds of a blanket being arranged over him.

Nick's mind was racing. Big money around. Agents with sudden windfalls. Was someone out there buying their loyalty?

Who and why were questions that needed to be answered immediately. The president and his family were at risk until this matter was resolved.

Ron was astute enough to recognize that Nick could have been pulled into this assignment for more than one reason.

There was nothing to be gained by confirming the fact, or by admitting that he was reporting to someone in addition to the detail leader. He glanced at his watch. He had to get this information back to Washington immediately, but not through regular channels.

Before he made his call he went upstairs to tell Ashley to call her mother.

Hours later Nick saw Ron come into the lounge where the band had drawn a large crowd. He was glad to see him. Nick was feeling a little beleaguered at the moment. The three couples were enjoying themselves, no doubt about that. They were making him feel older by the minute.

He was also fighting his very strong attraction to Ashley. She'd chosen to wear an ensemble, the skirt of which was guaranteed to promote pneumonia. It revealed a pair of long legs that unexpectedly made him want to gnaw on his knuckles. Not a good sign.

Erin and Trish were equally decked out in similar outfits that had no effect on him whatsoever. That was when he knew he was in big trouble.

The men in their group kept them all busy on the dance floor, so that Nick had plenty of time to sit and watch the room, the band, the other dancers and the way Ashley moved to the music as though it flowed through her body.

He didn't want to think about bodies. Especially not hers. He'd been fighting his own very natural response to her attractiveness all evening. There was nothing professional about that particular response, but there wasn't a damned thing he could do about it.

So he was pleased to see Ron show up, looking alert and refreshed by his time off. Nick needed the distraction.

Ron slid into the booth across from Nick. "Pretty good music, huh?" Ron asked.

"Loud, anyway."

Ron laughed. "The best kind." He watched the crowded dance floor for a while, then said, "You been out there yet?"

"Me? Are you kidding? No way."

"It's not against the rules, you know. We're allowed to dance."

"On duty?"

"Well, you have to admit this duty is a little unusual. After all, we're supposed to blend in."

"I suppose."

Ron grinned. "Well, here I go, blending in," he said, and headed for a table where three women sat watching the dancers.

Nick smiled to himself. Good for Ron. Unfortunately Nick hadn't seen anyone he was particularly eager to dance with. His eyes strayed back to the dance floor.

Craig and Ashley looked good together. It was obvious they had danced together many times. She had danced with Derek and Joe several times, as well, but Craig was the one with whom she seemed to best communicate. It bothered him that the thought of her with Craig made him knot up inside.

He spotted Ron out there after a few minutes. He wasn't bad. Not bad at all.

When the band finally took a break, everyone arrived back at the booth. Trish said, "We're lucky you're saving this place for us, Nick. But why aren't you out there dancing?" She pointed over her shoulder. "Did you see Ron? Wow! He's good."

Erin spoke up. "I want to dance with him sometime tonight."

"Me, too," Trish added before focusing on Nick. "And I insist that you dance at least one dance with me, too, Nick."

"Your toes will never be the same," he replied.

"I'll take care of my toes. Is it a deal?"

He noticed that Ashley was watching him. Oh, what the hell. "Sure," he said. "Whenever you want."

The conversation became general. When Ron returned to the table, each of the women insisted on having their turn with him, so that by the time the band returned, it had been decided that Ron was booked for at least the first three dances.

He was a good sport about it.

Erin held out her hand to Nick. "Come on. It's your turn."

He looked around as though for reinforcements, but Joe and Derek were already asking other women to dance. Craig led Ashley out on the floor.

They'd been dancing for several minutes when Erin leaned toward him and said, "You're being a good sport about all this."

Maybe so, but he felt like a fool. He hadn't danced since

college. However, it seemed to be a night of freestyle and no one was paying any attention to him, thank God.

When the song was finally over, he was out of breath. They had almost reached the table when Trish touched his arm and said, "It's my turn."

He grinned at her. "Okay, but don't say you haven't been warned." They stayed out on the floor through two songs, and Nick had to admit that he was having fun. Trish was an excellent dancer. When the second song ended he begged to be allowed a chance to catch his breath.

Trish threw her arms around him and kissed his cheek. "You're great, Nick. Thanks so much." Her cheeks were rosy and her eyes sparkling. He escorted her back to the table and ordered drinks for everyone.

By the time another round appeared and he paid for them, the table was almost deserted. Only Ashley continued to sit there, watching him.

He smiled tentatively at her. "Are you enjoying yourself?"

She nodded, then reached over and, with a napkin, wiped a smudge of lipstick off his cheek. "You seem to be enjoying yourself, as well."

"Ashley—"

She stopped him with a finger over his mouth. "I didn't mean anything by that. Not really. I guess I've never seen you quite so relaxed." She held his gaze. "It's very appealing."

His pulse picked up and it had nothing to do with his recent bout of dancing. "I...uh, thank you."

"You really don't have to be serious all the time, do you?"

"Not really. I'm not much on socializing, though."

"That surprises me. Surely you're aware of the way you draw feminine gazes wherever you go."

He could feel his ears reddening. "Uh, actually, no, I'm not."

She grinned. "Look at you. You're blushing!" She laughed. "Now there's a sight I never expected to see."

Nick looked up and was relieved to see Ron returning to the table. He was going to be rescued from this very embarrassing conversation. He thought. Then Ron said, "So why aren't you two out there dancing?"

Ashley replied, "I've been waiting to be asked. He's danced with Erin and Trish, but so far I haven't heard an invitation."

Now he was in for it. "Would you like to dance?" he asked, trying not to clench his jaw.

She gave him a brilliant smile. "Thank you, kind sir. I'd be delighted."

They had no sooner arrived than the band suddenly segued into a slow tune. The already dim lights lowered slightly, causing a stir in the crowd. Nick wondered if fate was actively working against him. This woman stirred his pulse more than any he'd ever known. Why did she have to be someone so totally inappropriate?

Taking a deep breath, he placed his hand tentatively at Ashley's waist, grasping her hand with his other one.

She looked up at him for a moment, then silently followed his lead. He made certain that he didn't brush up against her. There was no way he wanted her aware of his reaction to her. He tried to ignore the fact that every other couple on the dance floor was pressed snugly against each other.

He tried to ignore the scent of Ashley's floral cologne, the way she moved so lightly in response to his guidance. Most of all, he fought to hang on to some kind of control over his body, which was clamoring to pull her against him and kiss the living daylights out of her.

"I never thanked you for what you did today," she said softly, looking up at him. Her soft mouth beckoned. He forcibly pulled his gaze from her moist lips to her eyes and felt as though he were drowning in their amber depths.

"What did I do?" he managed to ask.

"Went back to look for me. Didn't go into a tirade, listing all the things I did wrong."

He smiled and unintentionally pulled her closer. He didn't

really need to be reminded of how he'd felt while looking for her. Now here she was in his arms. He wondered if she could hear his heart pounding. He swallowed. "You're welcome. You really had me worried for a while there."

"You were tempted to tell me off, though, weren't you?"

He nodded very slowly and smiled. "Very."

She laughed and stepped closer to him. He slipped his arm around her waist and pulled her closer, reveling in the way she fit his body so perfectly. They continued to dance until he felt her lips brush softly against his ear. He shivered and realized that this was not going to work.

Suddenly he stopped dancing and stepped away from her, afraid she would notice the effect she was having on him.

"What's wrong?"

His heart was hammering. "This isn't a very good idea," he managed to say, thankful the lighting was low. He was already as hard as a rock. What would she think if she discovered that the man assigned to protect her was attracted to her? He didn't want to think about the possible explosion that could occur.

"What?" She looked around, then back up at him. "You mean dancing together?"

He nodded.

"Are you saying that you don't wish to dance with me?" she asked stiffly.

He tried to find an acceptable answer to that without either insulting her or telling her the truth, but he hesitated too long. She spun around and left him standing there. "Wait. I didn't mean to—" He followed her off the dance floor.

She waved her hand. "Please don't explain. I'm sorry I compromised you in any way, Agent Logan." She grabbed her purse off the table. "I'm going to the restroom now." She gave him a level stare. "Alone. Think you can handle that?"

She spun on her heel and charged across the room.

Nick shook his head at his awkward handling of the situation. He needed to explain to her that... He sat down at the table. *Yeah, Logan, explain to her how strongly she affects you at such close quarters? Explain how you feel about her? That's all you need.*

He watched the door to the women's room and saw Erin follow Ashley inside. He was absolutely certain he did not want to hear any part of their conversation.

"Pompous jerk! Puffed-up, arrogant toad! I really detest him. I can't believe he just…he…" Ashley sputtered out of words. She couldn't remember ever having felt so crushed by someone's behavior toward her. She'd been dreamily following his lead, loving every moment of being in Nick's arms, fantasizing about their becoming friends now, and maybe something more. While all the time he…he was hating every minute of it! She angrily brushed away the betraying moisture in her eyes. He wasn't worth it!

Erin patted Ashley's shoulder. "What in the world did he say to you out there to get you so upset?"

"Nothing. He said nothing, but it was obvious that he was uncomfortable with me. Did you see how he and Trish danced together earlier? She was all over him, rubbing up against him, doing all sorts of things, which he didn't seem to mind in the least. But when I danced with him, he was stiff and acted like he was dancing with his great-aunt Edith or something."

"I was watching the two of you. You looked great together. Then *you* stopped dancing and walked away from him. You're the one who left him standing on the dance floor, so why are you so angry?"

Ashley sank into one of the chairs provided. "Because he said that our dancing together wasn't a good idea. I don't know why he feels that way! I thought we were finally becoming friends. He was so nice to me this morning, when he could have really given me hell. I was hoping…" Her voice trailed off. Her lips firmed and her jaw tightened. "Well, it doesn't really matter what I was hoping, does it?" She opened her purse and found her compact. She took her time powdering her nose and refreshing her lipstick, then turned to Erin and said, "Let's go dance. I refuse to let him ruin this evening for me."

Erin smiled. "Honey, you've got it bad, don't you?"

"No, of course not, I just—"

"I recognize all the signs, believe me."

Ashley slumped in her chair. "He doesn't see me as a woman at all, Erin. I'm just a part of his job."

"I wouldn't be so sure of that."

Ashley glanced at her, caught by something in her voice. "What do you mean?"

"Has it ever occurred to you that because of his job, he may consider you off-limits to him?"

She looked at Erin in surprise. "But that's ridiculous. I—"

"No, it isn't. Just think about it, Ashley. He has to stay detached in order to do his job. Maybe he finds it a little tough to stay detached when you're in his arms like you were earlier."

"Do you think?" she asked, her hopes rising.

"It's a possibility. He seems relaxed enough with the rest of us, but I've noticed he gets all tense and businesslike with you."

"Which irritates me no end."

"Maybe that's the only way he can hide his feelings for you."

"Hah! The way he acts, he has no feelings. He's just a robot who..." Ashley paused. "I'm really being childish. And it's got to stop." She smiled and said, "Enough soul-searching for the evening. Let's go knock 'em dead on the dance floor!"

Nick saw them come out of the restroom laughing. He had a hunch the joke was at his expense. The fact that Ashley ignored him for the rest of the evening didn't make him feel any better.

He'd handled the whole situation poorly. Positive interpersonal relationships with members of the opposite sex were definitely not in his line of experience.

He hadn't meant to offend Ashley. In fact, he'd enjoyed her friendliness toward him this afternoon. He spent the rest of the evening trying to think of something that he could say to help ease the situation, but nothing came to mind.

By the time they returned to the chalet, it was after midnight—officially the day before New Year's Eve. The group was already making plans to attend the big party being thrown by the resort to celebrate the end of the old year and to welcome the new.

The other topic of discussion was the weather forecast. They were promised a day of sunshine and clear skies tomorrow, actually later that day. Nick listened to them on their way upstairs, discussing when to set their alarms. Everyone was in agreement they wanted to get an early start. No one wanted to miss a minute on the slopes while they were here.

Nick seriously began to wonder if he'd be able to keep up the pace they'd set for the next three days.

"What happened between you and Ashley tonight?" Ron asked once they were in their respective beds and the lights turned off. "The temperature suddenly dropped about thirty degrees at our table. I could have sworn Ashley walked off and left you standing on the dance floor."

"Just a result of my natural charm, I guess."

"I thought she was beginning to tolerate you earlier today."

"So did I. Obviously I managed to exceed her toleration limit with very little effort."

"Do you know what set her off?"

"Not exactly, no."

"Something you said, maybe?"

"I don't recall that we were doing much talking."

Ron's laugh wafted toward him in the dark. "Well, I have to admit I enjoyed the evening. I haven't danced in years."

"Same here. That may have been one of the problems."

"You seemed to be enjoying yourself with the other two."

Nick sighed. He'd been relaxed with Erin and Trish. He didn't react to them the way he did to Ashley. He had never reacted to any woman the way he reacted to Ashley Sullivan.

That was the thought that kept him sleepless for several hours that night.

Chapter 7

Wednesday, December 30

A steady beeping finally drew Nick out of an exhausted sleep. He recognized the sound of his cellular phone. He fumbled for the lamp so he could see. As soon as the light was on, he looked at his watch.

It was three o'clock in the morning. He'd had maybe an hour of sleep. What in the hell could be so blasted important that someone needed him at this time of night!

"Logan," he muttered into the receiver, shoving his hand through his hair.

"This is Chambers, Logan. We've got a problem."

As soon as he heard his superior's voice, he knew he wasn't going to like what he was about to hear. "Okay. Let's have it."

Ron sat up and watched him. Nick mouthed the word "Chambers" to him. Ron nodded grimly.

The news was as bad as it could get.

"The president's yacht is missing. We lost contact with her

a couple of hours ago. The Coast Guard is on the way to the area. We had a security ship nearby. We can't raise either of them."

"Dear God," Nick said in a low voice. His phone call late yesterday hadn't been much help, it seemed. If this was part of the plot he'd been investigating, then whoever was behind it was still several jumps ahead of him.

"It's too soon to draw any conclusions, of course," Chambers continued. "There may be some electromagnetic disturbance out there. It's possible it's only a communications snafu."

"Or they could have cruised into the Bermuda Triangle," Nick suggested as a joke.

"You're the third person this morning to suggest that possibility. No one is amused."

This morning. That's right, it was five o'clock in Washington.

"We should know something as soon as the Coast Guard reaches their last position," Chambers continued. "They're watching for flares or for possible debris. It's not a good situation."

"No, sir, it isn't," Nick replied. If Chambers believed it was a communications problem, he would not have called at this time of night. "What do you want us to do, sir?"

"We don't want to set off any public alarms just yet, but the situation is being treated as a national security emergency."

"Understood, sir."

"Vice President Freeman is here at the White House. He was notified immediately as soon as we realized we'd lost contact. He has taken command under the circumstances. Mr. Freeman has suggested that we bring Ashley back here to await news of her family."

Jason Freeman was now in charge. The irony didn't escape Nick. He'd been a member of the VP detail for a few years. Scarcely two weeks had passed since his sudden transfer. And now the vice president was the man in charge of the nation. For only the moment...hopefully.

"Is there any reason to believe the family is in danger?"

Nick asked in a carefully controlled voice. "We have so many safeguards around the president. I don't really see how this could have happened."

"Neither do I!" Chambers replied tersely. "I don't like any of this. We were monitoring them, had both of them on radar when first the yacht, then the other ship suddenly disappeared off the screen. We're afraid there may have been some kind of explosion."

"The Coast Guard will be able to tell, won't they?"

"You'd certainly think so, wouldn't you? But at this point we're all scratching our heads, including the Coast Guard."

"What do you want us to tell Ashley?"

His question was met with a long silence before Nick discerned a sigh on the other end of the line. "There's no need to alarm her."

"I agree. So what should we say? We were scheduled to stay here for two more days."

"Yeah, I know. I'd hate to have you lie to her. Hell, I don't know. Just use your judgment."

"Yes, sir."

"Rather than fly her back commercially, we're having a private plane meet you at one of the smaller airports closer to the ski area. It's already on its way and should be there in another hour." He gave Nick directions to the airport. "There's always the possibility that this thing will turn out more positive than it looks at the moment, you know. Perhaps by the time you get back here, we'll discover it was just a mechanical glitch somewhere."

Neither one of them believed that for a second, but it sounded reassuring. It also gave him a line to take when discussing the matter with Ashley. The truth was, they had no idea at this time what had happened to her family, nor could they guess at a possible outcome. In their business they had to prepare for the worst and pray for the best.

"We'll have her at the airport, waiting."

"If you should run into any problems, contact me immediately."

"Will do."

He disconnected the line and looked at Ron, who was already dressed and waiting. Nick recognized the attitude of alertness. Adrenaline was already pumping in his own veins.

"Good news rarely arrives at this time of night," Ron said quietly.

Nick sank down on his bed, ignoring the fact he wore nothing more than his boxer shorts. "That's for sure."

"The president is missing?"

"They lost contact with the yacht and the security ship a couple of hours ago. There was no sign of an explosion, no flares, no SOS, nothing. They just suddenly disappeared from the radar screen. There was no response to any of the messages sent."

"Damn." Ron looked like he'd been punched in the gut.

Nick knew exactly how he felt. "Yeah, at the very least. They've sent the Coast Guard looking, but so far, no sign of anything."

"In a way that's good news, Nick. If there had been an explosion, they would have seen the blast, maybe, or found debris. Something would have shown up somewhere."

"Who knows how close they are to the yacht's last position. It's my guess it's too soon for them to have found anything."

"The whole family was on board?"

Nick nodded. "Except for Ashley," he said thoughtfully. He was quiet for several minutes. "We have to tell her…something, anyway, because the vice president has sent word that he wants her returned to Washington immediately. There's a private plane on its way to pick us up. They're landing at a nearby field to save us the drive back to Denver."

Ron folded the bedding he'd used. "What are we going to tell the others?"

"Good question…and I don't have an answer at the moment." Nick reached for his clothes. "Why don't we just let Joe know that Ashley's family called and needs her back early? He seems to be the leader of the group. They're due to leave here in a couple of days, anyway. Hopefully they'll understand." He finished dressing, made certain all of his gear was in his bag and placed his bedding on the sofa to be picked up by the cleaning crew.

He thought of how excited all of them were about skiing later today…and attending the New Year's Eve party tomorrow night. What a mess.

"Do you want me to wake Ashley?" Ron asked, standing at the window with his hands in his pockets.

Nick sighed. "This is going to be very difficult, no matter how we handle it. We don't want her falling apart on us." He shook his head wearily. "And, yes. I think you'd better be the one to talk to her. She'll take any news better from you than she would from me."

"We could tell her the same thing we intend to tell Joe and wait until we're airborne to explain the situation more fully."

Nick nodded. "Good idea. In the meantime, I'm going to make some coffee. We have to be on the road in thirty minutes so she needs to pack as quickly as she can. It would help if we could avoid waking Trish, but I'm not certain that's going to be possible."

Ron turned away from the window. "At least the weather is holding, although there's the possibility of a storm in the forecast."

"I thought it was supposed to be clear tomorrow."

"So they said. The storm was just a possibility. Probably nothing to be concerned about."

"I hope not. All we need is to get socked in here due to weather conditions. That will really make the VP happy with us."

"Hey, he can't hold us responsible for the weather, you know. We do what we can. That's got to be good enough."

"Yeah, you'd think so, wouldn't you?" He waited until he reached the kitchen and shut the swinging door to the hallway before turning on the lights and making coffee.

The president and his family was missing. He wondered what Sam might have to say when he heard about this.

Nick tried to recall which agents were with the president. A chill went through him. He needed to talk to Chambers, but this wasn't the time. As soon as they got back to Washington he would discuss his suspicions with him.

Then he remembered Sam's warning—trust no one.

He rubbed the furrows in his brow, trying to think all this through. The main thing was to stay calm. Once the three of them were on that plane, his duties would be virtually relieved.

What was Ashley going to do if something *had* happened to her entire family? She was too young to have to face such a possibility. But he knew better. Whole families were wiped out all the time—through fire, floods, tornadoes. But not like this. Not a family as closely guarded as the first family.

Nick fought the urge that made him want to wrap her in his arms and promise her that he would always be there for her.

He could just imagine her reaction to such a declaration.

Regardless of any possible response from Ashley, falling for the daughter of the President of the United States had to be right at the top of the list of suicidal ways to destroy a career. He had braced himself to get through the remaining days. Now those days had shrunk to a matter of hours of close contact before they were back in Washington.

The brutal facts were that there was a strong possibility none of her family was alive, which meant the life she had known up until now would be changing radically in the next few hours. He wanted to be there for her in any way she would allow.

The door swung open. Ashley stepped into the kitchen, wearing a robe over thermal pajamas. She hadn't bothered to comb her hair and it tumbled around her shoulders. She looked vulnerable and bewildered.

"Nick? What's going on? Why are we supposed to leave now?"

"Didn't Ron say?"

"No. He came in and woke me, then pantomimed that I wasn't to say anything to wake Trish. He just pointed me down the stairs, then went into Joe's room."

Nick filled a cup with coffee and silently handed it to her, then poured two more, setting them on the table.

Ron slipped in behind her without making any noise. He was the one who said, "Sit down, Ashley. We don't have much time, but we'll try to explain."

His voice coming from close behind her startled her, and Ashley flinched, almost dropping her cup. "Oh. I didn't hear you." She sat down at the table and looked up at them impatiently.

Ron sat down across from her. With a muttered thanks to Nick, Ron sipped on the coffee and waited for Nick to join them.

Ashley watched them both, her gaze darting from one to the other.

"Something's happened, hasn't it? What's wrong?"

Nick picked his words carefully. "Something has come up. Your father wants you back earlier than was originally planned. There's a plane arriving shortly to take us back to D.C."

Still looking at Ron, she asked, "My father? He's still fishing, isn't he? They aren't due home until the weekend." When Ron didn't answer, she went on, "This doesn't make any sense. We're going home day after tomorrow, anyway. Why can't I wait and go back with the rest of them?"

This time Ron answered her. "Ashley, in this business we don't ask a lot of questions, you know what I mean? We got the call that they want you back in Washington and that the plane is on its way. It's our job to get you to the plane."

She frowned. "But what about the rest of the group?"

"I've already told Joe that you have to leave early and he will explain to the others in the morning. All he needs to do is to arrange a ride back to the airport for everyone on the first. He'll be able to do that with no problem through the resort.

I imagine they have a shuttle that runs between here and the airport." Ron patted her hand. "Sorry you can't finish your stay with them, but at least you've had some time out here with your friends and have lots of stories to share when you get home."

Nick looked away, concentrating on what needed to be done, not wanting to dwell on the news that might be awaiting her in a few hours. "Do you think you can get dressed and packed without waking Trish?" he asked brusquely.

The look she gave him was filled with disdain. "Of course. Trish is a heavy sleeper, anyway. I won't need much light to find everything."

He looked at his watch. "You have twenty minutes. It's cold outside, so bundle up. I'll go warm up the van." He finished his coffee and walked out of the kitchen without looking back.

Ashley looked at the door, and said, "I better go get packed. If I'm not ready in twenty minutes, he'll probably leave without me."

Ron smiled broadly. "Somehow I doubt that very much. Ashley, just try to remember that Nick is doing his job the best way—the only way—he knows how. I'm sorry he upsets you. I'll admit the guy doesn't know much about relaxing. This may have been a vacation for you, but it's his job and he takes his job seriously."

"Oh, I don't have a problem with that. The problem I have with Nick Logan is that he takes *himself* entirely too seriously."

"Well, you won't have to put up with either one of us for much longer. Once we're back home, there will be others who, perhaps, will make you feel more comfortable."

She reached over and touched Ron's hand with hers. "I'm sorry, Ron. Please don't think this is about you. You've been so much fun, willing to join in even when you don't ski. Your attitude actually proves my point. There was no reason why Nick couldn't have relaxed and enjoyed himself, as well, instead of being so officious all the time."

"Well, like it or not, our time here in the Rockies is pretty much done. You'd better go get ready, okay?"

She nodded and slid out of the banquette. Ron was right. She would have to take all of this up with her father when she got back. He'd better have a darned good reason for causing her to miss another two days of skiing, plus the New Year's Eve party.

Ashley silently went upstairs and slipped into the bedroom. Luckily Trish slept near the windows while Ashley's bed was close to the door and the bathroom. She quickly dressed, then went into the bathroom and gathered her things, placing them in her bag. She removed the clothing she'd placed in drawers and the closet, then slipped out once again.

Trish never stirred.

Ron was waiting for her when she got downstairs. He took her bag and backpack from her, helped her with her parka, then ushered her out the door, silently closing it behind them.

When they reached the van, Ron opened the sliding door and helped her into the backseat, stowing her luggage with theirs, then closed the door and got into the passenger side of the front seat. Nick was already behind the wheel.

He looked up at the clouds in disgust and wished the weather people would get it right. They'd practically promised clear skies for a good skiing day. Instead, their possibility of more snow was showing a very strong probability.

Nick had written down the directions, then had reviewed them while he was waiting for Ashley. He took his time; he didn't want to do anything to alarm Ashley.

The headlights of the van eventually illuminated the sign that announced they were approaching the regional airport. The road into the area had been freshly graded. No lights were visible in any of the ground buildings.

He spotted a small tower up ahead. He drove toward a dark building located near the runway. No one was stirring, which wasn't surprising. They were early.

"The place looks deserted," Ron said quietly. "Shouldn't there be some landing lights or something?"

"They wait until the approaching plane radios for instructions for landing before turning them on."

"Oh."

Nick allowed the van to roll forward along the narrow road that ran parallel to the landing strip. They would leave the van parked by the hangar for now. He'd call Sam once they were on their way and let him know where to pick up their transportation.

He never knew, consciously, what triggered a warning signal, but suddenly the hair on the back of his neck rose. Ron leaned forward in the seat, peering through the windshield, staring ahead. "I don't know about this, Nick. It doesn't look—"

That was when Nick saw the tiny red light of a scope being trained into the van. He yelled, "Get down!" at the same time that he stepped on the accelerator. He heard the ominous sound of glass shattering and the distinctive thud of a bullet entering flesh.

Ashley screamed.

"Ashley!"

"I'm okay, I'm okay! It's Ron! I think he was hit!"

Icy wind blew in through the shattered window, sucking out the warmth of the van as it barreled along the road, gaining speed. They had to get back to the highway, but Nick sure as hell didn't want to take a chance of returning by the hangar.

Nick spotted a side road and turned the wheel sharply, heading back to the highway. In the rearview mirror he saw lights flash on at the same time a powerful engine came on. Whoever was shooting at them was not giving up.

Nick threw a brief glance toward Ron. He couldn't see much in the dim lights from the dash. Ron was slumped toward him.

"Ron? Talk to me, man. Where are you hit?"

Thank God there was no traffic on the highway. Nick didn't slow down any more than was absolutely necessary when he turned onto the highway. The van rocked, not being made for this kind of driving—nor high-speed chases.

He glanced into the rearview mirror once again and saw the car pull smoothly onto the highway behind them.

How far out of town were they? he wondered. He wished he'd gone to town with the group yesterday. He needed some idea of the layout of the place. He knew there was a medical facility there—a necessity in a ski area.

How badly was Ron hurt?

"Ron?" he said again. "Can you hear me?" He wanted to touch him but didn't dare take his hands off the wheel at the moment. "Where did those bas— Where did they hit you, man?"

The car behind them was steadily gaining on them.

Ashley answered him. "He's unconscious." She was reaching across the seat toward Ron when Nick caught a brief glimpse of her in the mirror. "I think—"

"Get the hell down in the floor and stay there!" Nick ordered. He heard Ashley move and could only hope she would follow orders.

At least the van was equipped with a powerful engine. He planted his foot to the floor and followed the winding road back to the town they had just passed through.

Watching the lights behind him, he saw that they were staying with him. "Damn," he muttered.

At least they weren't gaining. At this point, he would take any advantage he could get. The road was straightening out some. He took a chance that it would stay that way. He needed to find some backup. And fast.

Nick fumbled for the cellular phone in his pocket and punched the speed-dial number that would connect him to the local agency. There was someone there twenty-four hours a day.

Now there was no answer.

He didn't have Sam's number handy and wouldn't be able to see to use it at the moment.

What in the hell was going on?

Somebody had been waiting for them back there. They had walked into a trap. Only blind luck had gotten them away. He had no idea if Ron was dead or alive. Nor did he have any certainty for their chances in the near future.

Somebody had set them up. The question was who—and why. They may not live long enough to find out, but he was going to do what he could. Risking yet another maneuver that took his hand from the wheel, he reached over and touched the slumped figure beside him. His fingers came away wet.

With his eyes on the road he checked for a pulse and was relieved to find one, but from the look of things, Ron was losing a lot of blood. Something would have to be done fast, despite the fact that his first priority was to protect Ashley.

The lights of the town shone up ahead and Nick took a moment to take a deep breath. They weren't out of the woods yet, not so long as those yo-yos were behind him, but he was feeling a little better with every mile gained toward help.

Chapter 8

Ron moaned and moved his head slightly.

"Hang on," Nick said quietly. "We're almost there."

They had reached the outskirts of town. Nick looked for a sign that would direct them to a hospital. When he saw the distinctive marker with an arrow pointing to the right, he took the corner in a controlled skid, praying there was some alert law-enforcement officer around who might be interested in discussing his driving habits.

He wanted all the attention he could get from a uniformed cop.

As though his mind had conjured it up, a patrol car came wheeling out of a side street with lights flashing. The car that had followed them to town suddenly lost interest and immediately turned the other way.

He tried to identify the make and model, but all Nick saw was rapidly diminishing taillights. The car appeared to be a large, dark town car.

Ignoring the flashing lights coming up behind him, Nick drove toward the emergency entrance of the hospital without slowing down until he reached the well-lit entrance, where he came to a skidding stop.

He threw open his door and sprinted to the car behind him. The officer was already out of the car, but paused in the opening of his door with his hand resting on the revolver strapped to his waist.

"I've got a man wounded in my car," Nick said. "It was some kind of drive-by shooting." Then he flipped open his federal ID. "Or it may be something more. He's my partner. We have the president's daughter with us and we're trying to get her back to D.C."

The patrolman looked to be in his late forties and wore his gray hair in a crew cut. Nick watched him study the ID. *Please let this officer have some field experience,* Nick prayed. He was reassured by the cool, assessing gaze of the older man.

"Let's get him inside," was all the officer said.

While the patrolman went into the hospital to get help, Nick hurried back to the passenger side of the van. He opened the sliding door for Ashley, then the passenger door to check on Ron.

"Is he going to be all right?" she asked in a shaky voice as she slowly exited the van. "I don't understand. Why was someone shooting at us?"

There was blood seeping through a hole in the back of Ron's parka where the bullet had gone into the right side of his body. There was also blood on his chest, which told Nick the bullet had passed through him, ripping a much larger hole in his chest.

Every minute was going to count if they were going to stop Ron from bleeding to death.

He stepped back when the ER personnel arrived with a gurney. He offered his hand to Ashley. When she clasped it, her fingers were icy and her hand was trembling. Ashley was trembling so she could scarcely stand. From the light being cast around the emergency entrance, he could see there was no color in her face at all.

"Are you going to be able to walk inside on your own, or do you want me to carry you?" he asked quietly.

She stiffened. "I'm not hurt. Of course I can walk."

The small burst of temper helped to put a touch of color in her cheeks.

They went into the hospital and were met by one of the nurses. "Can you give us any information on this man?" she asked, scribbling on a clipboard.

"All I know about him is that he's been shot and needs help," he replied tersely. He gripped Ashley's arm just above the elbow. "Where's your waiting room?" He held up his ID to the nurse and her eyes widened.

"Right through those doors," she replied, pointing.

He propelled Ashley through the doors.

"Wait. We've got to see about Ron. We've got to…"

He continued to guide her into a waiting area that luckily was empty at this hour. "Look, Ashley, Ron is now in the hands of trained medics. If anyone can help him, they will, okay? Right now, we've got a more serious problem."

She stared at him as though convinced he'd lost his mind. "What could be more serious than Ron's getting shot?"

"Finding out who was shooting is just as important. And why. What were they doing at the airport? And who were they aiming at?" He kept his gaze on hers, willing her to listen to him and understand the gravity of what happened tonight. "Now, I want you to sit down and wait right here for me, okay? I've got to make some phone calls and try to get some answers." He paused and looked around the dreary room with impatience. "And somehow I've got to get you back to Washington."

Ashley sank into one of the chairs. "This doesn't have anything to do with me, does it? *Or does it?* Is there something you aren't telling me?" She jumped to her feet. "I want to talk to my dad. He's got to know that—"

"Not now, Ashley. There's no reason to disturb him at this time of night."

"But none of this makes sense! Why does he want me back

in Washington when he isn't even there? They're all on the Gulf somewhere. What are you trying to do, anyway? Are you kidnapping me?"

"Ashley, you're getting hysterical and I'd hate like hell to slap you, but I'm certainly willing to if you keep this up."

She took several gulping breaths and put her hands up as though to ward him off. In a calmer voice she said, "All I'm saying is that none of this makes sense—flying back to D.C. early, Ron being shot. I want to talk to my family," she added in a firm voice. "There is nothing hysterical about that."

He sat down on the sagging sofa beside the chair where she'd first sat, nodding to the chair and waiting until she seated herself before saying anything. "All right, Ashley. I'll give it to you straight. We were going to wait until we were on board the plane, but all those plans have gone out the window for now, so—"

"Something has happened to my family!" she said in a rush. "Oh, my gosh, that's it, isn't it?"

"We aren't sure, but yes, that's the way things are shaping up. We lost communication with their ship. It may be nothing—nothing at all. But the vice president felt it wiser to have you back in Washington. So that's what we're trying to do."

He watched her as she tried to deal with the information he'd been forced to convey to her. He had to admit that she handled herself well. Tears rolled down her cheeks, but she quickly brushed them away. He could see the struggle she made to gain control of her emotions.

After a few minutes she said, "So what do we do now?" with only a slight hitch to her voice.

"I want you to wait here while I find out what I can about Ron. I've got to make some phone calls and figure out how to get you back home as quickly and as safely as possible." He stood and looked down at her. "I believe you're safe enough right here, but if for any reason you feel threatened, go to the ER and ask for me. I'll check back as soon as I know something."

"I don't want Ron to die," she whispered.

"Neither do I."

"My family's safe. I know they are. It's probably some silly fuse or something that went out on the radio. I bet if I called, I could get through to Dad right now."

"You can try if it will make you feel any better." Nick would dearly love to have someone answer a phone call from that yacht.

Ashley dug into her purse and got her phone card, then determinedly went over to the pay phone across the room from them.

Nick took that opportunity to slip into the hall and check his phone numbers. He would call Sam and see if he could get some help.

Unfortunately he got Sam's answering device. Not a good sign. All agents knew they could be called at any time. Nick didn't have another number for Sam, besides the office, which still didn't answer.

Before calling Chambers, the detail leader in Washington, he wanted to find out how Ron was doing, so he headed back to the ER to find out what he could. He spotted the patrolman waiting in the lobby.

"I didn't get a chance to introduce myself earlier," the man said. "The name's Harvey Cameron."

Nick held out his hand. "Nick Logan. Thanks for your help. Have you heard anything about my partner?"

Harvey nodded. "He's in surgery, and if all goes well, he should recover. He lost a lot of blood, but they were able to stop the bleeding. The bullet passed through his chest."

"Yes, that's what I figured happened."

"They want to do some repair work on him. They were already pumping new blood into him when they wheeled him by."

"Was he conscious?"

"Naw. They might have already given him something, I don't know. Why? Do you think he has some information for us?"

"Not really. He'd leaned forward in the seat, which means they probably were aiming for me and he blocked the shot."

"Why you?"

Nick shrugged. "I was driving."

Harvey had a notebook in his hand and was making notes. "Do you think whoever was shooting knew Miss Sullivan was in the van with you?"

"I've got to believe they did. Why else were they at that particular airport, where we were told to take her to meet a private plane? For all I know, she may have been the target. Until we know who did it, we won't know who they were after or why."

"Looks to me like you're going to need some backup here."

"You're telling me. Somehow I don't think I'm going to get it from my group. There seems to be a communication breakdown between me and the local headquarters."

"What do you need?"

Nick looked out the front door and saw the van with its broken window. "Whoever's out there expects us to be in that van. So my first thought is to take Miss Sullivan somewhere safe in a car that won't be recognized."

"Any ideas where to take her?"

Nick was quiet for a few minutes, then nodded. "Actually, yes. My family has a cabin not too far from here. Not too many people know about it. Although I doubt the road into that area has been cleared lately. The road used to be a logging road and there aren't many houses out that way." He thought for a moment. "I guess the best thing would be to get some cross-country skis and go in that way."

"Tell you what. I'll drive you in as close to the place as possible. We should be able to find you the necessary equipment to go in. Later today I'll see about getting the road cleared, if that will help."

"That will help a lot. I've got to report to Washington what's happened. The sooner I get her situated, the better."

Harvey started toward the door. "I'm going to go check in

and go off duty. I'll be back in my own car. Less conspicuous. We'll get that little gal all the protection she needs."

"Thanks."

Nick found a quiet corner and called Washington. The phone was answered on the first ring.

"Chambers."

"This is Logan."

"Logan? Something wrong?"

"You could say that. We were ambushed at the airport before the plane arrived. Ron was shot. He's in surgery at the moment."

"My God! Has the whole world gone insane?"

"I'm beginning to think so. I can't get anyone from the local office to answer. I tried Sam Masters's home number and there was no answer there, either."

Chambers was silent. Finally he said, "I need to report this to the VP. He isn't going to want to hear it."

"I know. Any word on the first family?"

"Nothing so far."

"Have you heard anything from the plane that was sent to pick us up?"

"As a matter of fact, I haven't. Someone should have notified us immediately when you weren't there when they arrived."

"I think you're right. The whole world has gone mad," Nick muttered.

"Where are you now?"

"At the hospital."

"I'll get to work on this from here. In the meantime…" There was a longer silence. "Damn, you don't have a backup plan, do you?"

"Unofficially, yes. I've got a place in mind where I'll take Ashley. She'll be safe and we'll wait to hear from you. As soon as you can figure out some transportation for us, we'll be there."

"Don't go too far."

"Never fear." Nick hung up and returned to the waiting room, where Ashley waited, her expression tense.

"Any luck?"

She shook her head. "You knew I wouldn't reach them, didn't you?"

"Well, I figured if our security forces couldn't do anything, a phone call might have just as much luck."

"So you were humoring me."

"It worked, didn't it?"

"How's Ron?" she asked, changing the subject.

"He's in surgery, but they feel he's going to make it all right. In the meantime you and I are going to have to disappear."

She looked at him suspiciously. "What do you mean?"

"I mean that for the time being the less people who know where you are, the safer you'll be. At present we're working on a way to get you back East. Until then you'll have to stick with me."

She just looked at him, then said, "I wish Ron was here."

"Believe me, so do I. Here's the drill. I'm not going to have time to listen to your arguments and objections to everything I have to say. We're in dangerous territory at the moment in more ways than one. You have got to trust me. Do you understand that?" he asked.

"Or else what?"

"Or else...well, maybe you have friends here in Colorado that you feel you can call on in an emergency. If that's the case, then go ahead."

"I don't want to involve people who might get hurt," she replied.

He smiled. "Good girl. I know this is tough for you and that you prefer Ron to look after you, but we've got to accept that this is where we are and this is what is happening. I need to know that you're with me on this. I'll try to consult you whenever possible, but there will no doubt be times when I have to call the shots, and you'll need to trust what I decide and go with it right then. Think you can do that?"

She studied him for a long moment in silence, then nodded.

"Good. Let's get out of here," he said, turning on his heel and heading for the door.

Ashley followed Nick out of the waiting room. He stopped at the nurses' station and gave them the number of his cellular phone so that he could be notified as soon as Ron regained consciousness. Then he went outside and spotted Harvey leaning against an aging Buick. Nick stopped by the van and removed their bags, then pocketed the keys. He'd give them to Harvey later so he could put the van somewhere else. At the moment he wanted anyone who happened to drive by to see the van still at the emergency entrance of the hospital.

As they approached him, Harvey held out his hand to Ashley. "I know you don't remember me, Miss Sullivan, but I used to work a security detail when your father was first elected governor. I don't think you were old enough for school back then. I'm sorry you're having such a rough time of things now."

She gave Nick a quick glance, and he made a slight negative gesture. She was quick to pick up that Harvey knew nothing about her family's disappearance.

"I'm going to take you two up the road a spell to pick up some skis."

Once again she looked at Nick. This time he just smiled.

Harvey continued, "Until we know who's taking shots at you, I'd just as soon not let anyone know you're here in Colorado. The general public believes you're vacationing with your family, anyway. So we'll just keep it that way."

Nick placed her between them on the wide bench seat of the car. They pulled out of the parking lot with Harvey explaining his plan.

"I've got some friends who have a little store on the edge of town. They live right next door and I explained that we needed to get some cross-country skis for the two of you. Once we've got that taken care of, I'll get you up to the family cabin for some rest. By then, maybe we'll have some leads on what's going on."

If only he knew the full extent of it, Nick thought to himself, he probably wouldn't sound so optimistic. Thank God the man had the security training and knew what he, himself, was up against. Even if he thought the shooting was some isolated incident.

Nick could only hope that was the case, even when he knew differently.

Chapter 9

Ashley sat between the two men and stared out the windshield into the cold darkness, unable to control the shaking of her body. So this was what life had come down to for her—having to obey a man she'd only met a little over a week ago, trusting that he would be able to protect her in the event someone was actually trying to harm her.

She couldn't get the mental image out of her mind of Ron slumped over in the front seat of the van, his life blood draining away. Or seeing him on the gurney as the hospital personnel worked to stop the bleeding. Everything had happened so fast. That could have been her lying there.

Or she could be with her family right now, even though they now seemed to be out of touch. What was happening to her safe little world, anyway? What was the use of all the interfering, officious people constantly infringing on her family's privacy if none of them could protect them from what had happened in the past several hours?

"Looks like they're waiting for us in the store," Harvey

said, sounding relieved. "I'll wait out here while you go inside and get whatever you need."

Ashley glanced at her watch and was surprised to see it was almost six o'clock. The sun would be coming up some time in the next hour or so. This had to be the longest night of her life, but surely with the sun everything would be better. Somehow darkness seemed to make everything more threatening.

Nick helped her out of the car, took her arm and guided her over the icy spots of the driveway until they reached the front of the small general store. A man stood behind the front door and peered through the glass at them. Although he was dressed, his graying hair stood up in spikes around his head, a silent reminder that they had gotten him out of bed.

"You the friends Harvey called about?" the man asked.

When Nick nodded, the store owner opened the door. "He says you've been having some trouble and thought I could help you out."

Nick waved Ashley into the store before him, saying, "We really appreciate this." Then he rattled off a list of supplies they needed to the man, who nodded and headed toward the back of the store. Ashley glanced at Nick in surprise. He seemed to have memorized a rather comprehensive list without faltering. The most surprising thing was his request for two sets of cross-country skis. What in the world was he planning?

He had her try on boots and made certain the skis were the correct length for her.

"I really appreciate your help," Nick said to the storekeeper. "It's not often a shopkeeper will get out of bed just to make a sale."

"Glad to help you out. Any friends of Harvey's deserve whatever I can do," the man replied.

Nick smiled. "He's one of the good guys, that's for sure," he said quietly.

While he paid for everything, she gathered up some of the supplies and returned to Harvey and the car.

Nick followed her, carrying the larger items. It was a good

thing Harvey's car was so big, otherwise they would have had trouble getting the skis inside. As it was, Nick worked with them for several minutes to find the right angle so he could close the back door.

Once Nick was back in the car, Harvey said, "I'm going to need some directions from here," and Nick gave them to him.

So Nick had some particular destination in mind. Too bad he didn't feel it necessary to share that information with her. Nonetheless, at this point all she cared about was getting some rest. Maybe after a few hours' sleep she would feel ready once again to deal with the bizarre circumstances with which she was faced.

It seemed as though they drove forever, turning off main roads and finding secondary roads until finally there was nothing but unbroken snowdrifts all around.

"Looks like this is as far as we go on wheels," Harvey said cheerfully. "Good thing you decided to come prepared."

Nick looked at Ashley as though expecting an argument. "You're going to need to go through your bag and bring only what you can carry in your backpack."

"Oh, darn, and here I thought you'd have a sled to carry our luggage behind us."

He looked away from her for a long moment before returning his gaze to hers. His lips twitched into what she might have thought was the beginning of a smile on anyone but Nick Logan.

"It's a relief to know you're returning to normal. I was beginning to worry." He got out of the car and began to wrestle with getting the skis out while Harvey went to the trunk and retrieved their bags.

Ashley sat in the backseat and sorted through her belongings, quickly pulling out essentials, including her ski pants. Thankful for the darkness, she quickly changed into them, putting her jeans into the backpack along with everything else.

She looked up at the sky. There was very little difference

between the sky overhead and the surrounding mountains. Only, the snow gave off a lighter glow. This was not her idea of a great time to begin a cross-country ski trip.

After fastening her backpack and adjusting it on her back, she returned to the front of the car. "I hope you know where you're going. I'd hate to get lost in all of this." She waved her hand at the wilderness around them.

Harvey spoke up. "I was thinking the same thing."

"I do know where we are, plus I have my compass, a flashlight and, if all else fails, the phone."

"If the battery holds out," she muttered.

"Now there's a happy thought," he retorted.

Harvey chuckled. "If I didn't know better, I'd believe the two of you have been married for years, the way you bicker."

Ashley didn't like the sudden shortness of breath she felt at the thought of being married to Nick Logan. The very idea gave her the shivers.

Nick made no comment. He knelt and helped her with her skis, then put on his.

Harvey checked them over, then nodded. "I'll take the rest of your things back home with me. Let me know if you need anything more."

"We'll manage. We can meet you back here, if that's agreeable to you."

"Sure," Harvey said. "Just let me know when and I'll be here."

Harvey turned around on the narrow road and drove away.

Ashley felt as though she'd been abandoned by her last friend—left in the wilderness with one of the original mountain men.

"Do you know anything about cross-country skiing?" he asked.

"It's a little late for you to be asking that, don't you think?"

"I'll take that as a yes."

"Do you mind telling me where we're going?" she asked.

"My family owns a cabin a few miles farther up."

"Why couldn't we have just gone to a hotel, instead of playing survival of the fittest out here?"

"Because the game of survival, as you like to call it, is a very real one. Until I know what is going on, I want to be in the safest place I can think of in order to protect you. There are too many security hazards in and around a hotel that need to be dealt with and at the moment we don't have enough trained personnel for the job." He gave her one of those penetrating looks that always made her want to squirm. "Now do you intend to come with me, or do you want to continue this time-wasting discussion a while longer?"

She didn't want to be grateful to Nick for any reason, but she had sense enough to know that he was her best hope at the moment of getting back to Washington in one piece.

Ashley just wished she was with any other agent than Nick Logan.

"I just want to go home," she said quietly.

"Yeah, I know, Dorothy. But you and Toto are going to have to put up with me for a while longer."

"Very funny."

"None of this is funny, Ashley. I'm doing my job the best I know how. I don't know what's going on, who shot Ron, who knew we were going to be there at that particular time and were waiting to ambush us. What I do know is that we're in a precarious situation where we aren't certain whom we can trust. When in doubt, I don't trust anyone."

"Except me, of course," she added with a fake smile.

He studied her for a long moment. "I trust you to obey me, yes. I trust your desire to see your family again. I trust you to do your best to get to a place of safety."

He was rude. He was egotistical, but she had to admit he was good at what he did. Not that she would ever admit to him that she admired his skills. There was no reason to feed the man's already overblown ego.

She followed his trail as he started up the long hill ahead of them, resigned to the inevitable.

Instead of dawn bringing the sun, about half an hour into their trek the clouds hanging low overhead began to release thick fat snowflakes all around them.

She had no idea how long they'd been following some invisible trail through the wilderness when Nick stopped and pulled out some packaged food and water, pointing out a wooded area nearby where she could find some privacy if necessary.

Breathless from trying to keep up with him, she asked, "Is all of this rushing really necessary, or do you just enjoy the idea of playing hide-and-seek?"

"Being shot at makes it real enough in my book."

That silenced her. For a while. The snow fell steadily, and as time passed, the wind began to pick up, making it more difficult to see their surroundings.

By the time Nick stopped the next time, Ashley was several yards behind him, mechanically moving her arms and legs, all but the motor functions of her brain turned off. The swirling snow around her had formed a cocoon of sorts, creating a world of icy hell where the only other occupant was the robotic fiend ahead of her, who was impervious to the wind and the snow and anything else but his own mysterious destination.

"Ashley!"

There was something about his tone of voice that sounded irritated. What was his problem? Did he think she should be moving faster? Too bad. She didn't care if—

"Ashley, we're here. Can you see it? In the clearing over there."

Ashley blinked several times, feeling as though she was only now waking up after having been in a trance. She squinted her eyes, trying to see through the blowing snow.

There was something over there, something that could be a building, but she couldn't really make it out. She shook her head and tried to quicken her pace despite the fact that she could scarcely move her legs.

By the time she was out of the direct blast of wind, Nick had already removed his skis and was reaching for her.

"Let's get you inside." He muttered something about hypothermia, but she was having a little trouble concentrating to figure out his meaning.

Blearily she peered at the building that had mercifully blocked the wind from them, causing the snow to eddy around the corners of the building.

She had given their destination little thought, other than frequent prayers that they would reach it soon. Now that they were there, she was surprised to see a large, apparently well-built log-cabin home, with a sweeping porch across the front, one end screened in.

The six steps leading up to the porch were piled high with snow. Drifts decorated the porch; some piled high in front of the heavy-looking storm door.

As soon as she was free of the skis, Ashley took a step toward the stairs.

"Hold on," Nick said. "I need to check out the place first."

She looked back at him and wearily shook her head. "You're really too much, do you know that? If there is something lurking inside ready to grab me, they can have me."

Ashley forced herself to climb the stairs, idly watching the snow fly up in little puffs with each step she took. She wanted to lie down somewhere, that was all. Was that so much to ask?

She scuffed her boots in the snow on the porch until she reached the front door. "It's locked," she said, puzzled.

"Somehow that doesn't surprise me," he replied without inflection. He walked over to the wall beside the door and began to tap lightly along one of the logs, then pressed along its bottom curve. A small part of the log swung open, revealing a minuscule enclosure that held a key.

He reached around her and unlocked the door, then stepped back with a smile.

Ashley pulled the door open only to find an inner door, locked, as well. "Your whole family must be paranoid."

He offered her the key.

Once it was unlocked, Nick came in behind her and closed the door, leaving them in dusky shadows. He stepped past her and headed down the hallway toward the back of the house.

Ashley panicked. "Where are you going?" she asked before she could stop herself.

He paused in a doorway and looked over his shoulder. "I need to turn on the electricity so we can have lights and hot water. The electrical box is in the basement, as well as the pump to the well."

"Oh." She took a few steps down the hall and looked through an archway into a large room. A stone fireplace took up most of one wall. Stacked firewood was arranged neatly beside it. She leaned in and saw that a staircase went up one wall to a long open balcony upstairs. Several doors opened off the balcony.

She shivered, feeling the deep chill in the place. She continued down the hallway to the kitchen where an open door revealed a set of stairs that obviously led to the basement.

She looked around the fully functional kitchen. The place was arranged with a minimum amount of fuss and bother.

A light suddenly flickered in the shadowy room and she spun around in alarm. She realized that the refrigerator door was open and the light came from inside. Only then did she hear the comforting hum of the appliance and realize that Nick must have turned on the electricity. She immediately flipped on a wall switch and was relieved to banish the shadows in the room.

She closed the refrigerator door, then opened what looked to be a pantry door. There were canned goods and sealable canisters sitting on shelves inside. At least they weren't going to starve.

Nick came into the kitchen and looked around. "Everything seems okay in here," he commented. "I'll go start a fire in the other room."

She followed him into the great room and sat down on the long sofa in front of the fireplace. With fumbling fingers she tugged off her mittens to remove her boots. Once they were off she massaged her toes and sighed.

Nick paused and glanced over his shoulder. Seeing her sitting there, he said, "You did really well today. I was impressed."

After dragging her all over the snowy countryside, he was now going to patronize her. "Sure you were," she muttered under her breath. She curled into herself and closed her eyes, resting her head on her knees.

"Look, Ashley," Nick said, jolting her out of her peaceful stupor. She opened her eyes and saw him standing in front of her, his hands on his hips. "I know I'm not one of your favorite people, but we're going to be in each other's company for a while yet. If you've got something to say to me, then say it. I've got a lot on my mind, and I'm getting fed up with being the object of your barbed remarks."

Ashley felt as though he'd hit her with a flame-thrower. Why did he have to choose this moment to confront her?

He really looked angry. What had she said to set him off?

All right. If he wanted to know what she had against him, she would tell him.

Ashley took a deep breath, released it and said, "You may be the best agent the Treasury Department has, but your people skills leave a great deal to be desired, Agent Logan. I find you arrogant and egotistical. It you don't like the way I talk to you, then we definitely have something in common. I'm tired of you either barking orders at me or patronizing me. If my responses offend you, then I suggest you might try a more cordial form of communication—or maybe they don't teach that at your Secret-Service school."

She flopped back down on the sofa and closed her eyes once again.

The silence that filled the room seemed to suck all the air out of the place.

Later Ashley opened her eyes and realized that she was alone in the room. She felt disoriented. How much time had passed? Where had Nick gone? Her mind was so fuzzy that she was having trouble remembering what she'd said to him. Whatever it was had effectively silenced him.

Chapter 10

Nick stood in the master bedroom with his fists clenched, forcing himself to take deep breaths to cool his temper. All right, he'd asked for that, he supposed, and if it helped her to speak her mind, then maybe it had been a good thing. Problem was, he resented the hell out of her attitude, given their present situation. It was obvious to him now that it wasn't going to improve.

So the best thing for him to do was to get them back to D.C. as fast as possible. As safely as possible.

In the meantime they were both past hungry and close to exhaustion. He looked around the bedroom, pleased that whoever had been here last had left the room ready for its next occupant. Sheets, blankets and pillows waited neatly on the foot of the mattress. He quickly made up the bed and found a couple of extra comforters in the closet before returning downstairs.

He paused at the bottom of the stairs and looked over at Ashley, who was curled up beneath the blanket, still wearing her parka.

She was sound asleep. Nick stood for several minutes watching her, feeling his anger fade away. If he had to deal with an attitude from her, he much preferred the one she had adopted to one of whimpering, or hysterics, or even a "I can't go on, this is too much" attitude.

She'd kept up with him today and he'd set a hard pace. He'd never been so thankful for anything as he'd been when he finally spotted the cabin. He'd begun to think he'd missed it.

Nick went into the kitchen and opened several cans of vegetables and dumped them into a big pot for stew. He found some canned beef that would add a little flavor.

He'd always enjoyed coming here as a kid. Nothing ever happened that couldn't be resolved by a long hike in the woods. He'd missed those times in his life, he realized. Unfortunately a hike wouldn't resolve anything he was dealing with at the moment.

While he waited, he called Washington. Chambers answered on the first ring.

"This is Logan. Do you have an update for me?"

There was silence on the line. Nick waited. Quietly Chambers said, "The Coast Guard located the yacht earlier today. There's still no sign of the security ship."

"Were they all right?"

"We don't know. We found Clarke, his captain and two crew members bound and gagged. The captain was on the bridge, the crew members were in the galley and Clarke was in his stateroom. He said he'd just taken a shower and come out of the head. He got a fleeting glimpse of a black-clothed figure wearing a black ski mask before he was hit over the head, leaving a gash. He was airlifted to the nearest hospital. The others said they didn't see anyone before they were knocked unconscious. Each of them appeared to be okay. Just shaken."

"And the Sullivans?"

"No sign of any of them. There was a board game set up in the boys' cabin as though they'd been interrupted playing.

They found an open book lying on the table beside the bed in the Sullivans' stateroom. No sign of a struggle anywhere."

"How about the agents who were on board?"

"Not a sign of them."

"The whole deal sounds like a sci-fi movie—an abduction-by-aliens sort of thing. Was there any sign of debris that might have been from the security ship?"

"Not so far."

"Any subs spotted in the area?"

"Nothing has been reported. We were in constant contact with the security ship. They were returning business-as-usual reports—then all communication suddenly went dead. We have aircraft checking the vicinity, plus Coast Guard units from New Orleans, Pensacola and all points in between searching the Gulf." Chambers changed the subject. "What's happening out there?"

"We're at the safe house, so to speak. Ashley is understandably upset with everything—being ambushed, witnessing Ron's shooting. I told her we'd lost contact with the yacht, but tried to downplay it. Have you discovered anything regarding the ambush?"

"Now there's another peculiar thing. After I spoke to you this morning, I contacted our local office—and got right through. They say they haven't heard from you, nor have they heard any information about the plane we dispatched to pick you up. I told them to get out to the airport and see what they could find."

"Did you mention we had an agent down?"

Chambers didn't answer right away. When he did, his voice dropped. "No. Until we better understand what's taking place, I chose to keep Ron's whereabouts from everyone."

Nick felt a certain amount of relief. He had a hunch that Ron was safer the fewer the people who knew where he was. Given that Chambers had decided not to give the local agents all the details, there was reason to believe he suspected their tight-knit group might have been compromised.

"I appreciate your discretion," Nick replied dryly. He also

realized that by keeping him current on the news regarding the president and his family, Chambers must believe Nick could be trusted. That counted for something.

Chambers continued, "I spoke to Sam Masters. He said he'd visited with you yesterday."

Nick picked up a change in Chambers's tone.

"And?"

There was a pause. "He said you were under a great deal of stress and probably needed that vacation you were knocked out of by this assignment."

Now there was some interesting news. He didn't recall having discussed his vacation plans with Sam at all. So how had he learned of them?

"Oh, I'm stressed, all right. Maybe I just imagined Ron in the hospital with a nasty bullet wound."

Chambers chuckled. "Easy, Logan. No need to take offense. What I find most interesting is the report that came back from the airport. They found the plane sitting in front of one of the hangars, waiting to be boarded."

"What did the pilot have to say?"

"Are you ready for this one? There was no one on board. The agents found no sign of anyone out there—just the empty plane."

"That makes no sense."

"It certainly stops us from bringing you back using that avenue of transportation. If the plan was to stop Ashley from getting back to Washington, they were successful."

"If that's their strategy, then all I have to do is keep her hidden."

"Exactly. I don't want to know where you are. As a matter of fact, Sam was quite insistent that I tell him how to find you. How close did you say you two are?"

Nick reviewed the visit he'd had with Sam, and Sam's report to Chambers. "Not close enough to trust him with more information."

"My suggestion is that you sit tight for the time being. As

long as Ashley is safe and well taken care of, we can concentrate on what's going on at this end."

"What's the VP saying?"

"He's already upset about the family's disappearance. He doesn't want something to happen to Ashley, too. When I told him about the ambush, he agreed to trust your judgment in the matter."

"Would it be all right if I have Ashley speak to him? I think she needs some contact with someone other than me at the moment."

"That's right!" Chambers replied, as though remembering something. "You did mention at one time that Ashley has taken an aversion to you."

"That's putting it mildly. She would have much preferred that I had taken that bullet, instead of Ron. It might even have made her day."

"Surely you're exaggerating. Let me talk to her."

"She's asleep right now and I prefer her that way. However, as soon as she's awake, I'll put in a call so that you can speak with her, and hopefully you can patch her through to the VP to explain everything that has happened. I need the support, believe me."

"If anything breaks on this story, I'll contact you immediately."

"Thank you, sir. I appreciate it."

He ended the call, and before he could put the phone down, it rang.

"Logan," he said tersely.

"Nick!" It was Sam. "Where the hell are you? I hear you had some problems getting away from Colorado. I thought you weren't leaving until tomorrow, anyway. What's the deal? Ashley get homesick or something?"

"Something like that."

"So where are you? We went out to the airport and there was no sign of anyone there. Nor any sign that you had been there."

"Uh-huh. Well, it irritates me when people start shooting at me for no reason. I get downright cranky."

"Don't I know it! I didn't know about a shooting. Was anybody hurt?"

"We're fine. Someone shot the passenger window out of the van, though."

"You were damned lucky that no one was hit. So when do you plan to go back to Washington?"

Thinking fast, Nick replied, "Oh, we'll use our planned itinerary, after all. After the scare she had, Ashley decided she wasn't in as big a hurry to get home as she thought."

"Do you need a ride to the airport?"

"Nah. We've got everything worked out just fine."

"Well, if you need me, just give me a call. You've got my numbers, at home and at work."

"I know."

"I'll give you a call next time I'm in D.C."

"Sounds good, Sam. Thanks for checking on us."

Once again Nick concluded the call and absently stuck the phone in his jacket.

Something wasn't right. Why was Sam looking for him? How much did Sam really know about the shooting? He hadn't been home when Nick tried to reach him. Had Sam set him up? Had everything that Sam told him been a lie?

His main priority right now was to keep Ashley safe. He also wished he could get back to the hospital to see Ron.

He reached for his phone and punched in the numbers for the hospital. After several minutes he finally got through to the supervising nurse on the surgical ward.

"This is Agent Nick Logan. I'm calling to find out about my partner, Ron Stevenson."

"He is out of recovery and has been assigned a private room in ICU in accordance with instructions. He also has private nursing care around the clock."

"That's good news. Has he regained consciousness?"

"Yes, but he's heavily medicated at the moment. It's necessary that he remain quiet until the damaged area has been given an opportunity to heal."

"Could you put me through to his private nurse?"

"Certainly. One moment."

After a few clicks on the line a female voice said, "This is Hazel."

"Hi, Hazel. My name is Nick Logan and I'm—"

"Oh, Agent Logan. I'm so glad you called. Our patient has been asking for you. Would you be able to speak to him?"

Nick grinned. "You bet I would. Thanks."

Ron's voice was faint when he said, "Nick?"

"That's right, partner. How're ya doing?"

"Feeling no pain, as they say. What happened?"

"We still don't know. Someone was waiting for us when we got to the airfield."

"Yeah. I managed to figure that out, since that's the last thing I remember. The next thing I know I'm laid up in a hospital somewhere with no one to answer any of my questions."

"I've spoken to Chambers. You might want to give him a call when you're feeling up to it. He's not telling anyone that you were hit. I wouldn't be surprised to find you've been registered under another name. And who's your nurse?"

"Don't know her, but she says she's with the agency."

"That figures. And not the local one, I bet?"

"She says she's been working in Virginia and was put on an early morning flight out here. All I know is, she was here when I finally figured out where I was."

"You get some rest. They tell me you're doing fine."

"Any news from back East?"

"They found the yacht. Everyone on board was all right. The Sullivans are missing. Sounds like a terrorist attack to me."

"Doesn't sound good for our side. Does Ashley know?"

"Not yet. I told her we'd lost communication with the yacht, but that's all."

"Is she okay?" Ron asked.

"She keeps wishing you were here. So do I, for that matter."

"That's good to hear. I'd like to think I'm indispensable."

"You want me to call your family or anybody?" Nick asked.

"Better not. No sense setting off any alarms."

"What about your girls?"

Ron was quiet for a long moment. "No," he finally said. "I explained I was going out of town and would call when I got home. So they won't be expecting to hear from me."

"You take care now. You've got my number. Call me anytime. I mean that. Day or night," Nick said.

"Thanks."

Hearing Ron's whispery voice was the best news he'd had. Nick wished he didn't feel so damned responsible for Ron's getting hit. He couldn't come up with anything else he could have done. He'd trusted his instructions. He'd done what he was told to do. As a result, he'd almost gotten his partner killed.

Nick didn't like that. Not one bit. He was trying very hard not to take the shooting personally. He couldn't afford to lose his objectivity in all of this.

He walked over to the stove and checked the stew. It was ready and so was he. He couldn't remember the last hot meal he'd had, but it was close to twenty-four hours ago.

"That smells good."

He glanced around and saw Ashley in the doorway of the kitchen, looking rumpled, sleepy and vulnerable. She had removed her parka.

"Sit down and eat."

She needed no further prompting. She hadn't bothered putting her boots back on and wore only socks on her feet. Ashley silently crossed the room and sat down. He placed a large bowl of stew in front of her, together with a package of crackers he'd found in a sealed container. He set down another bowl across from her, poured them coffee and joined her at the table.

They ate without acknowledging the other's presence. Only after they had eaten two helpings apiece did Ashley carefully place her cup back on the table and look at him.

"I want to apologize for my very rude behavior earlier. There was no excuse for what I said to you. You have been doing everything in your power to protect me, and I have done nothing but give you a bad time. It isn't fair. It isn't right, and I hope that you will forgive me."

"There's nothing to forgive, Ashley. You have the right to express your opinions, which I believe you did, quite succinctly."

Her face flushed, but she didn't drop her gaze. "I guess I've behaved so badly because I've never been around anyone like you. I find you very unnerving. And when you snubbed me the other night at the dance—"

"Snubbed you? What are you talking about?"

"When you didn't want to dance with me."

"I did dance with you. You're the one who walked off the dance floor. Not me."

She looked down at her empty bowl for several seconds before she shrugged and said, "I guess it doesn't matter. You were so friendly with everyone else and seemed to enjoy dancing with Erin and Trish. But with me...well, it was obvious to me you didn't want to dance with me, and it hurt my feelings. Somehow I thought that we'd managed to break through the barrier between us. You'd actually been a little friendly toward me earlier in the day. I guess I had some expectations that you didn't meet that night, so I acted like a brat."

"I certainly didn't mean to hurt you, Ashley, and if I did, then I owe *you* an apology."

She tried to smile and her bottom lip trembled slightly. "Have you heard anything about my family?"

"Oh! You're supposed to call Washington. I meant to have you call as soon as you were awake."

"I really needed to eat before I did anything else. Does that mean they've located them?" she asked hopefully.

"I'll let the VP fill you in on the details." He hit the speed-dial number for the detail leader and spoke to Greg Chambers, then handed the phone to Ashley.

In a moment she greeted Jason Freeman and asked if there was any news from her family. She was quiet as she listened to a lengthy response.

Nick got up and began to gather their dishes in order to give her some privacy.

She wasn't saying much, he noticed. Each question must be receiving full answers.

Ashley finished the call and handed the phone back to Nick. She quickly wiped her eyes and left the room. He decided to give her some time to adjust to the latest news she'd been given.

Besides, he needed to adjust to her apology. Damn, he really hadn't meant to hurt her. He'd been trying to protect himself and his own feelings, using his job as a barrier between them. Ron had tried to warn him that he was being rude, and he hadn't listened. So his own behavior was now coming back to haunt him.

She'd had the courage to admit why she'd behaved toward him as she had. He wondered if he had the courage to admit to her that his behavior toward her had been triggered by his own attraction to her.

Chapter 11

Nick paused in the archway to the great room. The room was in shadow. Moonlight filtered through the east window, casting a silhouette of bare tree limbs across the floor. The only other light came from the flickering flames of the fire. The scent of the burning wood wafted to him from across the room, bringing with it a sensory reminder of his past.

Ashley knelt in front of the fireplace, adding small pieces of wood to the increasing flames with the kind of intensity generally reserved for meticulously detailed occupations. Brain surgery came to his mind.

Nick could feel his nerves jumping. The two of them were in an intimate environment together. Despite what she'd said to him earlier, she'd also admitted that she had hoped, once, that they could be friends.

What he felt for her could hardly be described as friendly. The woman had managed to get under his skin like no other woman had. He couldn't understand how one person could throw his emotions into such turmoil so quickly. His emotions bounced around like a yo-yo on a string whenever he was in her vicinity.

What in the world was he going to do about her?

Nick shoved his hands in his pockets and entered the room, suddenly understanding how Daniel must have felt when he entered the lions' den. When she heard him behind her, she quickly wiped her cheeks with her fingers before she turned and attempted a watery smile.

"Your family has a lovely place here. Has it been in the family long?" From the light tone of her voice, they could have been having afternoon tea together and she was attempting to put him at ease by choosing a neutral subject.

She looked back at the fire and she furtively wiped her eyes.

He knew she was hurting and he wished he knew what to say to her for reassurance. She'd been right. They hadn't taught him too many social-communication skills when he'd gotten into this business. So maybe he'd just follow her lead.

He sat down at one end of the sofa and took off his boots before responding.

"Actually it has," he finally said, looking around the room that held so many pleasant memories for him. "My grandfather had it built some time ago," he continued when he saw her shoulders relax slightly. "We've modernized it as much as possible. If it had been up to us, I think we would have picked a place a little more accessible. My grandfather was more of a hermit. After my grandmother died, he just walked away from everything and everyone and spent most of his remaining years up here alone."

Ashley quietly blew her nose before saying, "No doubt without electricity or running water."

He smiled, remembering the fuss over that. "True. My mother absolutely refused to spend any time here until Dad got the electrical company to run lines to the place. That took a great deal of talking on his part, let me tell you. I think he was ready to personally pay each man a bonus if they'd get the lines run so we could spend our summers up here. He also had the septic system installed so we could have indoor plumbing. My grandfather already had the well here, but we had the electric pump put in for running water." He hadn't thought about all that in years.

Ashley curled her legs beneath her and faced him. She looked very much at home there, which he found more than a little unnerving. He had a sudden flash of insight that almost paralyzed him—his family would fall in love with this woman without hesitation.

A fine time to have that thought sneak up on him!

The faint scent of her floral fragrance teased him, and the light from the fire gilded her in a warm rosy glow.

Say something, he thought to himself. The only thought that came to mind was much better left unsaid—such as telling her how beautiful she looked sitting there, her dark hair tumbling around her shoulders, her pale skin making the tips of his fingers tingle with the need to touch her.

Nick gazed into the fire, willing himself to think of anything other than his response to the woman he was supposed to be protecting.

He didn't know how long they sat there in silence before she finally said, "After speaking with Vice President Freeman, I understand that you and I are going to be in each other's company for a while longer."

He'd been fighting these feelings ever since he met her.

"Um, yes." He cleared his throat. "I want you to know how very sorry I am that—"

She stopped him with a small wave of her hand. "Please don't. I'd rather not talk about the reasons we're here. What I was hoping was to use our time together, for whatever length that's going to be, to get better acquainted."

He hoped his reaction to her innocent suggestion didn't show on his face.

She smiled, a conciliatory smile that warmed him despite the warning bells going off inside of him. "We got off to a bad start, I'm afraid," she said. "I'm perfectly willing to accept the blame for that. I can only tell you that I've never been so rude to anyone as I've been to you, and you never did anything to warrant my behavior."

"It doesn't matter," he replied gruffly.

She stared into the fire for several minutes before looking at him again. "I was hoping you would share a little about yourself with me. Don't you think it would make the time we spend together a little more comfortable if I knew you better?"

Whoa. That was the last thing he'd expected her to say. She was trying to find a middle ground somewhere between them where they could function together. He appreciated it more than he could say.

She was being very honest, forthright, and he knew that he could do no less. He shifted so that he faced her, his knee resting on the sofa. He propped his elbow on the back of the sofa and rested his head against his hand.

"If you really want to get to know me, then I need to begin with an explanation."

Her eyes seemed to widen slightly as she watched him intently. "All right."

This was every bit as hard to say as he'd expected it to be. He wished he'd brought something from the kitchen to drink. His throat was so dry he could scarcely swallow. "About the other night…and the way I danced with you," he began.

She immediately stopped him. "Oh, please. You've already apologized, and even that wasn't necessary. *I* was the one acting childish." She sounded amused, only her eyes didn't reflect her tone. He saw a hint of pain in their golden depths.

"I never should have danced with you in the first place," he said baldly. "I should have lied and said something about my job description not including dancing. You mentioned that I danced with the others with more enjoyment. It wasn't that I enjoyed dancing with them more. It's that I could relax a little with them. I couldn't allow myself to relax with you."

She frowned. "I'm not that bad of a dancer, am I?"

He was saying this all wrong. He didn't want her to feel worse.

He shook his head, feeling his frustration level rising. "You're one hell of a dancer, and you know it." He rubbed his jaw, searching for words. "My problem with you, Ashley, is that the only way I can do my job is to stay detached from you. Having my arms around you shoots my objectivity all to hell."

She looked at him in surprise. "I'm sorry, but I'm afraid I'm not following you here."

Well, hell. Maybe his communication skills *were* nonexistent. The thing was, he didn't want to have to explain any more than that. Surely she could understand about being detached and objective.

Now he was definitely feeling cornered. He'd started this explanation. He had to finish it. He sighed. There was no way out for him on this one.

He leaned closer. Watching her intently, he said, "All right. I'll lay it out for you." He paused, took a big breath and said, "I'm attracted to you."

She stared at him blankly, her eyes wide.

"Very attracted," he added. "I've been battling this thing ever since I was assigned to you. I've been fighting it, but I'm afraid I haven't done a very good job of conquering the attraction. I'm supposed to be protecting you. I'm not supposed to allow any personal feelings I may have for you to affect me at all. I knew better than to dance with you. As soon as I put my arms around you, I knew I'd made a really bad decision."

He watched her intently. "Now do you understand?"

Her face softened and she moved closer to him, so that his knee now rested against her thigh. "You're attracted to me?" she repeated wistfully, her voice scarcely above a whisper.

He reached over and brushed his knuckles against her cheek. He smiled and touched a tendril of her hair with his finger. "Oh, yes, ma'am, I am."

She rested her head against his hand, which lay along her cheek. He shifted once again so that he could put his arms around her, something he'd been aching to do again since they'd stopped dancing so abruptly the night before.

With a slight tug he managed to move her so that her head rested on his shoulder. He wrapped his arms loosely around her. She tilted her head back so that she could see his face, her eyes filled with wonder. "I find that more than a little hard to believe, considering everything that has happened between us since we met."

He grinned, unable to resist stroking her hair. "Let's just say we certainly do strike sparks off each other." Once again he touched her cheek, gliding his fingers back and forth over the satiny surface.

"So that when you were being so...so..."

"Arrogant and egotistical?" he offered helpfully.

"I was thinking more along the lines of stiff and formal," she said, blushing.

"I had to keep forcibly reminding myself of all the rules and regulations that I was contemplating breaking. It's a breach of trust and borders unethical behavior for me to feel what I feel. It's probably stepping over that line to be telling you now. However, considering our circumstances, I figure I owe you an explanation for my behavior."

He swallowed and looked into the fire. "I want you to know that I'm sorry you've found me arrogant and egotistical and all those things you called me..."

She reached up and touched his jaw, causing his pulse to leap. "Please don't remind me of the things I said. I didn't mean them. Not really." She turned so that her breasts now brushed his chest. "As long as we're being truthful here, I have to admit that my behavior was probably based on the hope that I could provoke you out of your stern, efficient demeanor. What you should have done was to treat me like the spoiled brat I was being by turning me over your knee."

"There were definitely times when I was tempted."

"Like now?" she whispered, touching her lips to his mouth in a tender caress.

Oh, yes. He was absolutely tempted to do all kinds of things to her and with her, and the temptation she offered to him now was too strong for him to resist. He lost himself in the feel of her delectably soft mouth opening beneath his. He groaned and gathered her closer. This was what he'd been so afraid of, now that they were alone. He couldn't take advantage of the situation. He needed to…hold her for a little longer, taste her and lose himself in the wondrous response she offered him.

When he finally forced himself to lift his head, they were both having trouble breathing. "See what I mean?" he managed to say. "I lose all reason when I'm around you."

She placed a small kiss on his jaw, another one on his cheek. "I can't tell you how happy I am to hear you say that." She melted into him and gave him another soulful kiss.

This was getting out of hand. He lifted his hands and settled them on her shoulders in an effort to create some distance between them. His mouth didn't follow suit. Instead, it clung to hers as though starving for the connection.

She ran her hand across his chest in a sensuous move guaranteed to make him forget everything but loving her. He finally forced himself to break the kiss, fighting to hang on to his sanity. It was hard enough to fight himself. It was next to impossible to fight both of them.

"Ashley," he managed to say. "We can't do this."

She opened her eyes very slowly and looked at him. Her eyes glowed and her mouth looked thoroughly kissed. "What?" she asked innocently. "We're just getting better acquainted. Didn't we agree that would be a good thing?"

"Have you ever heard the saying about too much of a good thing?"

"No, but I'm certainly willing to find out what that would be," she said, and slid her arms around his neck. He didn't fight the kiss. However, when he realized several minutes later that they were now stretched out side by side on the sofa, their bodies pressed together from chest to thigh, he knew that if he didn't call a halt to this *right now,* they were not going to stop.

He pulled away from her and sat up, then stood, forcing

himself to walk over to the window and look outside. He had to get his mind on something else—anything else—other than the woman with whom he was very close to making love.

His body was calling him all kind of names, demanding to return to Ashley and all she offered. He sternly resisted, concentrating on all that very cold snow outside that could cool off his overheated system.

The moon was making its way across the sky, lending its light to the snow that had draped itself over every surface. There were no tracks now leading to the cabin, nor were there any lights that would proclaim anyone was there. Outside of the smoke from the chimney, the place would look deserted to anyone who might be in the area.

Should anyone happen to investigate, he could honestly report that his family owned the place and he was checking to see that everything was all right. Of course there was no reason to believe that anyone would be interested enough to—

He'd been focusing so hard on anything outside of the room that he hadn't been aware Ashley had moved until he felt her brush against his back in a tantalizing move. She leaned into him, the length of her body pressed against him, her arms snug around his waist.

He couldn't have moved if his life depended on it. He could feel the heat of her. His hard-won victory over his body during these past few minutes was lost. He returned to rigid and aching in seconds. If she allowed her hands to drop even a few inches, she'd be in no doubt of his condition.

She rubbed her cheek against the back of his sweater, very much like a kitten seeking attention. He could feel her breasts pressing against him with every breath she took.

"I think I'll go on to bed, Nick," she said softly. "Does it matter which bedroom I choose?"

"Th-that's a good idea. I know how tired you must be." He placed his hands on top of hers and gave them a gentle squeeze. "I put your bag in the first bedroom at the top of the stairs."

She leaned around his shoulder so she could see his face and smiled when he turned his head. "Which bedroom do you intend to use?" she asked innocently.

"No. That can't happen, Ashley. You know that."

She released him and turned away, then paused. "Nick?"

He made himself turn to face her, thankful for the deep shadows where they stood. With the moonlight behind him, he knew she would only see his silhouette. "Yes?"

She stepped back toward him, stopping within arm's reach. "Why are you fighting what's happening between us?"

"You know why."

"But you're more than your job, Nick. This is scary for me, too, you know. I've never been in a serious relationship before, and I—"

"Ashley, we don't have a relationship, serious or otherwise. Please don't let a few kisses cause you to think…"

"That you love me? I know that. Of course I know that. I'm not trying to trap you into some kind of a commitment. But we're both adults. I see no reason why we can't explore what's between us."

"I know of several reasons—at least for now. Once we return to Washington, once we find your family, then we can talk about what may be happening between us."

"You're doing it again, you know."

"Doing what?"

"Patronizing me, patting me on the head and telling me to run along to bed while the professional goes about his work."

"Damn it, Ashley, that's not what I mean."

"What you're saying is that you are the one who decides when and how any relationship we might have will work. Well, I have a news flash for you, Nick. I'm a part of this equation you seem to be working on. So if all this stuff you've been handing me about being attracted to me was said to make me more biddable, then you've been wasting your time. I am my own person and I make my own decisions. Do you understand?"

"Yes, ma'am, I read you loud and clear," he replied sardonically, shoving his hands into his pockets.

"Ooh!" She spun on her heel and marched across the room to the stairs in obvious agitation.

"Ashley?"

She was halfway up the stairs before she finally paused and looked down at him. "What?"

"I would never make the mistake of thinking you could ever be biddable." He grinned and said, "Sweet dreams, Ms. Sullivan."

Ashley closed the bedroom door behind her before her knees gave away. She managed to make it to the bed without falling, sinking onto its side in gratitude. She had never been so aroused in all her life. Dear Lord, she'd practically begged him to make love to her! Even worse, he'd turned her down!

How could she have allowed herself to get into such a situation? Kissing him had been the biggest mistake she could have made because she no longer had to fantasize about it. The reality was much more mind-blowing.

It would have helped if he'd been stirred a little, as well.

She pushed off the bed and knelt beside her backpack. Of course he was right, darn him. Maybe that was the biggest reason she found him so annoying. The man never made a false step, no matter what. Even when he admits he's human, he's heroic about it. It was enough to drive a person insane.

Now that she was alone, everything that she'd been pushing out of her mind came hurtling back to haunt her. She missed them so much—her dad, her mom, Jamie and Matt. Who could have done such a horrible thing to her family and what did they hope to accomplish?

She'd never wanted her father to worry about her safety. She wondered what her father must be going through, knowing that his entire family had been taken.

Tears slipped down her cheeks once again. How could she survive the pain if she never saw her family again?

* * *

Nick added more wood to the fire, his mind still on Ashley. She was something else. More biddable. That'll be the day.

Well, he'd proved something to himself. He couldn't trust himself to stay here alone with her. He needed to call Greg Chambers and tell him that he'd changed his mind about the security of the place. He knew that was the wisest thing to do.

He quickly put in the call.

"Don't you ever sleep?" he asked when Chambers answered.

"Not much. I catnap when I can. What's the problem?"

"I'm having second thoughts about our staying here. We're safe enough for the night, but I think we'll be pushing our luck to be here any longer. I was wondering if you could send a chopper in here in the morning and get us to the Denver airport. We've got tickets for that flight already in our pockets. I doubt it would be a problem to get them moved up a day. If we keep this just between the two of us, I don't think any security will be breached."

"You think there's a leak?"

"I think something is definitely wrong. There should have been no way terrorists could get close to that yacht, much less board it and make off with six people, which presupposes that they didn't kill the two agents who were on board and toss them in the drink."

"We're doing some investigating along those lines, going into deep background checks on the agents on both ships. If one of them turned, we'll find him."

"What about the chopper? Can you get it here in the morning?"

"Yes, but as late as it is, I doubt we could have it there before noon."

"Good enough." He gave him some visual landmarks to pass on to the pilot. "I'll go out in the morning and stamp out a large *X* in the snow to help them locate us, but I don't think they'll have any trouble, particularly if you go through the local authorities who know the area."

"I'm not going to tell them who they're picking up."

"Makes sense. Hopefully we'll see you tomorrow evening."

Nick hung up, feeling relieved. They were doing what was necessary. Plus, he felt he could do more once he was back in Washington. Putting some distance between him and Ashley was an added bonus.

Sometime during his rounds of checking to make certain all the doors and windows were safely locked, Nick decided to sleep downstairs. It wasn't that he didn't trust himself to sleep in the room next to Ashley's. It made more sense to him to stay close enough to the fire to replenish it. Thank God his family had left all the chopped wood that he'd found stored in the basement, seasoned and dry.

He should have told Ashley to leave the bedroom door open to allow the heat from the fireplace to warm her room and the attached bathroom. He went upstairs and listened at her door. After this length of time she was probably asleep.

Nick opened the door and peeked inside. As he'd expected she was in bed with the covers pulled around her ears, her back to the door. The angle of the moon provided a night-light for the room. He didn't want to disturb her, so without saying anything, he left the door open and returned downstairs.

Nick found a pillow and some blankets in the hall closet. Without bothering to undress, he stretched out on the couch and fell asleep within minutes.

A pounding on the front door brought Nick from a restless sleep several hours later. He bolted off the couch, his weapon in his hand before his feet hit the floor. He glanced at his watch. It was a little after four o'clock in the morning.

He moved silently to the door, thankful that his grandfather had installed a camouflaged peephole to the side of the door so that he could see who was outside.

He was not relieved to discover that Sam Masters stood there. There was no way that Sam should have been able to find him. The fact that he was here spelled trouble.

"Logan? I know you're in there watching me. I need to talk to you, buddy. We've got an emergency on our hands."

Nick quietly backed away, then bounded up the stairs and into Ashley's room. She was still asleep. He placed his hand over her mouth before whispering her name.

She jerked awake, her eyes wild, until she saw who stood there. Then she quieted. He leaned over her and said, "Grab your things and get into the bathroom. Get dressed and stay as quiet as you've ever been in your life. Something's going on and until I can find out what it is, I need to convince someone that you aren't here. Do you understand?"

She nodded.

He smiled and whispered, "Good girl."

He waited until she was safely inside the other room. Then he sprinted back down the stairs. He could hear Sam's voice.

"I know you're wondering how I found you. Well, you'd better be glad I did. Just let me in, will you?"

Nick took time to check the perimeter of the area. The moon gave off enough light to show only Sam's ski tracks were leading to the house. That didn't mean there weren't others waiting behind the line of trees in the distance.

He went back to the door.

"C'mon, Nick. Stop fooling around. I know you're there. I can see the smoke coming from the chimney. It's freezing out here. Give me a break, will ya?"

Nick made certain his shirt was out, then placed his pistol in his waistband at the small of his back and unlocked the inner door. Then he unlocked the outer door. Sam immediately pulled it open.

"Don't let the heat out," Nick said grumpily, deliberately turning his back on Sam. "What in the hell are you doing here in the middle of the night?"

"Trying to save your neck. You sure don't sound particularly grateful." He slipped off his gloves and blew on his hands. "Got any coffee? It's miserable out there."

"There are closer places for coffee, you know. What are you doing here?" he repeated, turning and facing Sam in the middle of the great room.

Sam ignored him while he pulled off his cap and jacket, then sat down and unbuckled his boots. Nick continued to watch him without expression.

"How did you find this place?" Nick asked.

Sam just shook his head wearily. "You went to ground, Nick, so I figured you had to be around here somewhere close. This property has been in the Logan family for several generations. It wasn't hard to locate on a plat. And you were smart, coming here. Really smart."

"Look, I don't know what you're doing here, but I finally got a few days off for my belated vacation, and I don't appreciate your uninvited visit. So if it's all the same to you, I'd like to go back to bed and get some sleep."

"Vacation? Don't give me that! I know you and Ron have Ashley here. The news is out and you're in danger. That's what I'm trying to tell you."

"And you're full of it, Sam. Ron and Ashley left Colorado late yesterday. They're probably in D.C. by now."

Sam straightened slowly, studying Nick carefully. "That's bull and you know it."

"Do I?"

"There's a chopper coming to pick you up later today. If the three of you get on it, you'll never be heard from again."

"Really? I don't know anything about any chopper. Why would anyone want me?"

"Not you. They're after Ashley."

"Too bad. They won't find her here."

The tenseness in Sam's body suddenly released and he grinned. "Damn, you're good. But I always knew that. So you aren't working the detail, is that what you're saying?"

"That's what I'm saying."

"Then you're staying one step ahead of them."

"Ahead of who?" Nick asked suspiciously.

Sam looked around. "I really need some coffee. If you'll make some, I'll try to fill you in on what's been happening."

"That would be nice." Nick walked down the hallway to the kitchen and headed for the coffeepot. He said nothing, waiting to hear what Sam had to say.

"Remember what I was telling you earlier? That there was something going on?"

"Yeah, I remember," Nick said without turning around.

"They're making their move."

"By grabbing the president's daughter? How do they know she isn't with the president?"

"Because they're holding him and his family at this very moment."

Nick spun around, spilling some of the coffee grounds.

"I thought that would get your attention."

"How do you know that?"

"Nick, there are some things it's better that you not know."

"How do I know you aren't feeding *them* information? Did you tell them she might be here?"

"Yes."

Nick stared at him with disgust.

"I knew they would be checking here soon enough," Sam said in a rush. "It was a trade for information, and what I needed to know was more valuable than what I passed on."

"You're saying that a chopper plans to come here to the cabin? Who's sending it? Chambers?"

"I'm saying that you don't really know whether Chambers is part of this or not. And until I get more information—which I'm trying to do as fast as I can—I'm telling you not to trust anyone who says they're here for Ashley."

Nick shook his head. "Anyone who shows up here looking for Ashley is in for a surprise. They're going to be disappointed when all they find here is a burned-out agent trying to get a few days of R and R."

"How did Ron manage to get her away?"

"He arranged to have a friend of Ashley's pick them up."

Sam didn't say anything. After a while he said, "I forget that Ashley grew up in this state."

Nick smiled. "Good thing, huh, or she'd be a hostage, too."

"Not if I can help it. That's why I'm here."

"What did you have in mind?"

Nick poured the coffee and sat down across from Sam. The scene was reminiscent of their visit earlier in the week, with one major difference. Nick no longer trusted Sam. He intended, however, to hear what he had to say in hope of better understanding what was going on.

"Well, if she'd still been here, I was going to have you guys come with me. I know of a safe house where no one would think to look for her."

"It's probably better this way, though," Nick replied slowly. "I'm sure she would rather be in Washington where she can hear any news of her family." He took a sip of his coffee, then asked, "What can you tell me about the president? How did they get to him? The yacht was under constant radar surveillance. Didn't anyone pick up that something unusual was going on?"

Sam smiled. "They used a massive surge of electromagnetic energy from a new technological marvel—confused all the machines, including the ones on board the yacht. The confusion gave the invaders the time they needed to get on board and subdue any opposition they ran into."

"So you're working with these people, is that right?"

"That's what they think is happening. I might have shown some interest in what they were doing early on, before they became so radical in their ideas. By that time I decided the safest thing I could do was play along and see what information I could get. Only a handful knew that the plot included abducting the president and his family. By the time I found out about it, there was nothing I could do. That's when I thought of you."

"Me?"

"Yeah. If anyone could help him now, it would be you."

"How?"

Sam leaned back in his chair. "It was a damn good plan, you know. The people needed on board were carefully chosen. They followed all the procedures, so that the reports came back on schedule with no suspicions being raised. They rendezvoused with an oil tanker. The Sullivans' sons were captured first and placed on board the tanker, which made getting mom and dad to cooperate a great deal simpler."

"I can imagine. Where's the tanker now?"

Sam grinned. "That's the beauty of the deal. They plan to dock in New Orleans, following the regular schedule of the tanker. Once they reach New Orleans, the ones behind this will go public, stating their demands and announcing they hold all the cards."

"We can't let this get out to the media."

"Tell me about it."

"So why aren't you in New Orleans to see about his release?"

Sam shook his head. "Because they don't trust me that much. I'm being watched because of my connection with the establishment."

"I see. And whoever is behind this is against the establishment, is that it?"

Sam laughed. "Yeah...so that should narrow down the number of suspects to about half the country's population, right?"

"They recruited you in order to use you."

"That pretty well sums it up, yeah."

"Now you want to turn that around."

"I'm doing my best without getting myself killed. It's getting dicier with every day that passes. Why do you think I came in here at night? I needed to warn you not to get on that chopper and to tell you about the Sullivans."

"What are the contingency plans if their demands aren't met?"

Sam looked down at his coffee. "I don't want to think about it."

"Do you know what their demands are going to be?"

"I would just be guessing, but I have a fair idea."

"Is it something the government would accept?"

"Who knows? Do you want to take the chance? Somebody needs to get down to New Orleans to be there when that tanker arrives. You're the only one I trust with this information. What you do with it is up to you. I'd just be careful giving it to anyone in Washington whose agenda may not coincide with the successful release of our presidential family."

"My God, Sam. Are you accusing everyone in Washington of being in on this thing?"

"No. What I am suggesting is that since it has happened, there are those who would use it to further their own gains without ever being exposed."

Nick shook his head. "I wish I had your confidence in my abilities, but I don't see how I can do anything. I'm way overdue for a leave, and I'm pretty much marooned here. I just hope that Ron and Ashley are all right. Maybe I'll put in a call to him and see if they made their connections with no problems."

"Good idea." Sam looked around the room. "Where's the phone?"

Nick went into overdrive, trying to decide what to do. "I'll get it," he said, and went back to the great room. He gave a casual glance upstairs and saw that Ashley's door was still open. He knew she didn't hear their conversation in the kitchen. She needed to know what was going on. He'd make his call to Ron here, rather than return to the kitchen.

He quickly dialed the direct number into Ron's room, and when the nurse answered, said quietly, "Put Ron on, please."

"He's asleep, and I—"

He heard Sam coming down the hall. "Now!" he demanded.

"Yes, sir!"

Ron's sleepy voice came over the wire.

"Hey, partner, thought I'd better check to see how you and Ashley are doing. I trust the two of you made it back to Washington with no delays."

"Oh, you can count on it, Logan. What's the matter with you?" Ron asked with more than a hint of irritation. "You been drinking?"

"There are some strange things happening all over the place. You be careful. It's hard to know whom you can trust these days. Just ask Colin."

"I take it you're not alone."

"Tell Ashley not to worry about her parents. They're safe for now. I know she'll be pleased to hear that."

"Who's there? Someone I know?"

"Affirmative. Tell Ashley she hasn't missed much since you guys left."

"Sam? Is it Sam?"

"That's right. So how was the flight?"

"Do I need to report this to anyone?"

"What? You're stuck in Denver!" Nick began to laugh. "You'd have been better off staying here than snoozing in an airport all night. Have you talked with Chambers?"

"I'll call him right now. What do I tell him?"

"If not, don't bother. Keep him guessing where you and Ashley are."

"Oh, my God. Is Chambers in on this thing, too?"

"Never can tell how things will turn out, can we? At least you'll be able to catch that morning flight. It's good to know Ashley's in safe hands. You take good care of her, okay?"

Sam tapped him on the shoulder. "Let me talk to him, okay?"

"Oh, Ron. You won't believe who stopped in this morning to help me enjoy my first full day of vacation. Remember Sam? He wants to say hello."

Nick handed the phone over and went to the fire, rebuilding it now that there were only hot coals remaining. He folded the blanket and put it at the end of the couch, together with the pillow. He deliberately showed no interest in Sam's conversation. He hoped he'd given Ron enough information to keep the ruse going. If Sam was one of those looking for Ashley, he might decide he needed to get to Denver right away.

When Sam hung up, he looked over at the couch and said, "Why aren't you sleeping upstairs?"

Nick said, "I was. I had this out last night before I went to bed and never put it away."

"Oh. Ron said everything's under control at his end."

"That's good to know."

"You know, I've been thinking. Since that chopper's coming here, anyway, I could just hitch a ride back with them. No reason to hang around here and push in on your vacation time."

Nick smiled. "It would sure be an improvement to coming in on skis," he replied.

"How about something to eat? I'm starving," Sam said.

"Sure. I'm afraid I don't have much that isn't in a can. The family keeps the power off when no one is here. Of course there's a generator in the basement in case some of us are here during an outage. I hope I won't have to fall back on it." Nick hoped he was making sense, trying to make casual conversation, as though Sam's visit hadn't thrown all his plans into complete confusion.

They were just finishing their meal when they heard the distinctive sounds of a helicopter. The sun had not yet appeared, although the sky had lightened. As Nick recalled, Chambers had said their ride wouldn't be there until noon.

He had a hunch that whoever was out there had not been sent by Chambers.

Sam stood. "Guess I'd better get out there and explain the change in plans. You take it easy now, you hear me?"

"You, too. Thanks for catching me up on the news. Maybe by the time my vacation is up, all of this will be resolved."

"We can always hope," Sam said. "See ya."

A few minutes later Nick and Sam waited on the porch and watched as the chopper landed. Sam ran to the open door and was helped in. Nick waited as it lifted off. He had a hunch they'd be heading for the Denver airport. He'd have to call Ron back in a few minutes and find out what he'd told Sam.

Nick stepped back inside and closed both doors. He returned to the great room. "You can come out now," he said, raising his voice.

Ashley appeared in the bedroom doorway and sprinted downstairs. "Did you really hear something about my parents?"

"Yeah, I did. There's food in the kitchen. Why don't you help yourself? Then we need to get out of here. Too many people have discovered this location for me to feel comfortable."

As soon as Ashley disappeared down the hall, Nick called Chambers.

"This is Logan. Another change of plans, I'm afraid. We've got too many leaks at the moment. I'm going underground."

"You want me to cancel the chopper?"

"Yeah. I'll check in when I can. This is beginning to look ugly."

"Can you tell me what's going on?"

"Not until we pinpoint some of these leaks. I'll be in touch."

As soon as he disconnected that call, he made another. When it was answered, he said, "Harvey. This is Logan. There's something I need you to do for me."

Chapter 12

It was early afternoon when Nick and Ashley came out of the trees and saw Harvey's car waiting at the county road. The snowplow had saved them miles of trekking on the mountain. Ashley was grateful they didn't have to wait for a ride, although the trip down the mountain hadn't been as strenuous as the one they'd made to the cabin.

She was excited to know that, if the agent had been right, her family was still alive. Anything that Nick wanted to do at this point was fine with her. She had been impressed that he wasn't taking any chances with her safety.

If he was wrong, then Nick was going to be in deep trouble with his supervisor. He was taking lots of chances with his career in order to protect her. How could she not love a man like that?

And that was the trouble she was having. After a very restless night filled with some R-rated dreams, she'd had to face the truth about her feelings for this man. She'd tried to convince herself that it was merely a crush. She really wasn't buying that explanation, however.

If anything, his manner toward her had become even more brusque today than it had been before. The difference for her was now she understood why. He was determined to treat her as part of his job without a personal involvement. The more impassive and distant he was toward her, the more she knew how much he was fighting his own reactions.

Once they returned to Washington, she was going to confront him about his attitude. Did he really think if he ignored his feelings, they would just go away?

Not if she could help it.

"You two don't look any worse for the wear," Harvey said, greeting them with a wave of his arm. "Need some help taking off those things?"

Ashley knelt and unfastened her skis. "No, but if I don't see a pair of these things for a while, that will be just fine with me."

"Got all the skiing you wanted, eh?" he said, smiling, as he took the skis and worked to get them into the back of his car.

"I really appreciate your help, Harvey," Nick said, leaning inside the car to help guide the skis. "You've been my ace in the hole during this entire operation. So far, no one knows that you've been helping us."

"Guess that's good until you find out who you can trust and who you can't, right?"

"Have you talked to Ron?"

"Yep. Went in to see him right after your call. Checked with the doctor. They say it's too soon to be moving him. We agreed he was as safe there as he would be anywhere."

"Maybe. I wish I knew if Chambers is a part of this. After all, he's the one who sent us out to that isolated airport in the first place."

"He also sent someone to look after Ron who knows how to protect him," Harvey replied. "Right now, you have one agent's word against another's. Until you have the facts, you'll just have to keep all your cards close to your chest."

The three of them got into the car, Ashley once again

seated between the two men. Nick stretched his arm across the back of the bench seat and she unobtrusively leaned into him, allowing her head to rest against his arm. She could feel his body tense, but he didn't move away.

"Everything else go okay?" Nick asked.

Harvey laughed. "Yep. All your belongings are here in the trunk. We can transfer them into your new wheels."

Ashley looked up at Nick, her cheek brushing against his neck. "What wheels?"

"I had Harvey rent us a car." He looked past her. "Is it in your name?"

"That's right. No way anyone is going to put that name with you."

"Good."

"Keep me posted on how things go, now, you hear?" Harvey said miles later when he pulled into a mall parking lot beside a late model, dark blue sports sedan. He reached into his pocket and gave Nick an envelope. "Here's the paperwork and keys."

Nick got out and unloaded their bags from the trunk while Ashley grabbed their backpacks from the rear seat.

"I keep finding myself in your debt, it seems," Nick said.

"Don't worry about it. Just look after our gal, here." Harvey turned to Ashley. "Hope everything works out for you."

"Thanks, Harvey. Thanks for everything."

Nick helped her into the car before getting in on the driver's side. She waved at Harvey before turning her attention back to Nick. "Are you planning to drive back to D.C.? Not that I care, you understand," she reassured him with a smile. "I think being on the move will keep anyone from locating us."

"We're going to New Orleans."

She stared at him in disbelief. "New Orleans? Why in the world would we go there?"

"If I can believe what Sam told me, we should be able to locate your family there." He glanced in the rearview mirror before turning to head south. "We should be down there in about three days if the roads aren't too bad. Once we're out of these mountains, we should be able to make some time."

"Sam told you my parents are in New Orleans? How does Sam know?"

"Good question. This may well be a wild-goose chase. At least I think I convinced him that you and Ron are headed back to Washington and that I'm on vacation. There's no reason for him or anyone to be looking for us together."

"What about Greg Chambers?"

"My gut feeling tells me he's trustworthy. But there's a leak somewhere, or Sam wouldn't be getting the information as fast as we are after Chambers specifically told me Sam wasn't in the loop. At least Chambers didn't question me when I called and canceled our ride."

"Did you tell him about Sam?"

"No. There's a chance that Sam is doing what he can to help. Time will tell. In the meantime, we're on our own."

"Today is New Year's Eve," she said after they had been driving for a while. "I imagine Trish and the rest of them are getting ready for the big party at the lodge." She looked over at him. "Has the news gotten out about my dad being missing?"

"According to Chambers, Freeman hoped to keep the news from reaching the public for as long as possible."

She sighed. "Good luck on that one. What will he do if reporters start asking about the family?"

"I would imagine they will give periodic reports on how much the family is enjoying the fishing trip."

"I bet Jamie and Matt are so scared. I wish I was there with them. Do you think the family is being held in the same location? I hate to think about them being separated and alone."

"It's anybody's guess at this point. Sam may be having a big laugh right now, if he discovers I've left the cabin. He knows me well enough to know that I wouldn't sit on the kind of information he gave me. I'd act on it."

"So he may be watching for you."

"He may send someone else, but if so, I can think of no reason for me to be watched, unless he wants to take me out before I can act on the information he gave me. At the moment, I can't figure out what Sam's game is and where I fit in."

"You're going to be watching for anyone interested in us, though."

"You bet I am. Hopefully, if Sam is having me watched, whoever is looking for me will think I'm traveling alone, so they may overlook a couple traveling together. Another thing in our favor is that they have no way of knowing that we're driving. After checking plane, train and bus schedules they might check car-rental places. If so, they won't find anything in my name."

"What if they recognize me?"

He gave her a quick sideways glance and said, "You're doing just fine. You haven't looked anything like your photographs all week. It's no wonder no one has recognized you."

She gave him a sunny smile. "That's the best compliment you've ever given me." She paused, then added thoughtfully, "Actually it's the only compliment you've ever given me."

"Chalk one up for me," he said tersely.

"You don't want to be reminded of how you feel about me, do you?"

"I'm not going to get into that kind of discussion with you, all right? Find another topic of conversation."

Ashley peered through the windshield at the snow piled on either side of the highway and noticed that it was already dark, even though it was just after five o'clock.

"Do you intend to drive through the night?"

"No. But I want to hit the New Mexico border before we stop. We'll be traveling as Mr. and Mrs. Harvey Cameron."

"But we don't have any ID to that effect."

"If we find ourselves in need of ID, we'll have more serious problems than using an alias."

Ashley settled into the corner of the car and closed her eyes, content to be on the road with Nick. Her eyes blinked open. "What are we going to use to pay for gas and lodging? You can't use your credit cards, can you?"

"I'm in luck, there. I generally travel with extra cash in case of emergencies."

"If you run low, I have some you can have."

"Fine."

She closed her eyes again and eventually Ashley fell into a deep sleep.

When she opened her eyes, they were parked in front of a small motel. "Where are we?" she asked, sitting up straighter and blinking.

"We crossed the New Mexico border a few miles back. I'm not going to be able to drive any more tonight." He rubbed his eyes and arched his back, then peered through the windshield at the well-lit motel office. "I hope they have a vacancy."

"I can drive, if that would help."

"No. You need your rest, too. If they don't have a vacancy, I'll have them check the area for me for an available room somewhere."

Ashley watched him get out of the car and stretch before he shrugged into his heavy coat and walked across the parking area to the entrance of the motel. She found herself fascinated by the way the man moved. She could sit and watch him all day long without becoming bored. Mmm-mmm. He was really something.

Because of the large plate-glass window, she was able to see him ring the small bell on the desk, then wait. He looked around the small lobby, then glanced back to the desk when a sleepy room clerk came from a back room in answer to his summons.

She watched Nick pull out his wallet and hand the clerk some cash. He waited until he was handed a key and what was probably the receipt, then came back outside. He slid behind the steering wheel and said, "He finally managed to find us something. It's a room they generally set aside for the district manager of the chain. The only drawback is there's only one bed. It's a king-size, but—"

"I promise not to attack you in your sleep, Agent Logan, sir. You may build any barriers between us to make you feel safer from me."

"Very funny."

"Well, you could afford to lighten up just a little, Nick. You've managed to get us this far without incident. I don't see a problem now. We're both adults. I think I can share a bed with you without my lust overpowering us both."

He turned his head slightly so that the light from the motel fell across his previously shadowed face. "I'll remind you of those words later, Ms. Sullivan."

One side of his mouth actually quirked up into a sort of smile.

She found that half smile adorable.

He drove slowly, watching the numbers. "There it is—second floor on the end, near the stairs."

When he parked, Ashley got out and walked around to the back of the car. Nick was already there opening the trunk. "I can carry my things."

"You sure?"

"Positive." She turned away and started across the parking lot.

"I wish you wouldn't do that," he said, coming up fast behind her.

"Do what?"

"Walk off without me. I want you to stick as close to me as glue, do you understand? We're still not out of the woods on this trip, even though I think I've managed to confuse everyone as to our whereabouts."

"I wish you'd make up your mind, Nick," she said in a low voice. "One minute I'm supposed to see you only as a professional, the next you want me sticking to you like glue."

"A mere figure of speech and you know it. Don't try to dodge the issue."

"Me? Dodge an issue? Not on your life. I'm willing to confront all issues. You're the one hiding behind your badge."

He didn't say anything in reply, which was just as well, she thought. She didn't know why she was teasing him. Actually she admired his attitude toward her and toward his work. But she couldn't seem to keep from nipping at him like a playful puppy attacking its shadow. Only in this case her shadow could actually nip back. Hard.

Nick stepped around her when they reached the top of the stairs and unlocked the first door they reached. After he flipped on the light, he motioned for her to step inside, following immediately behind her. She heard the lock slide into place and the chain rattle as it engaged.

No doubt she should feel much safer, but looking around the room didn't reassure her. For one thing it was a very small room, which explained the one bed. Although the carpet and drapes were worn and faded, everything looked clean enough. As for the bed, it really was large enough for two to rest comfortably. Perhaps it was her emotional safety she felt was in jeopardy in such close quarters.

Just to the right of the front door was an alcove with a dressing table and sink. An open door past that revealed a full-size tub and commode. She peered inside. "Plenty of towels," she offered brightly.

He muttered something that sounded like "That's just dandy." When she turned and saw the expression on his face, she decided not to ask him to repeat it. Now that she saw him in the light, she could see how exhausted he was. He'd been driving for hours without a break.

"Go ahead and shower and get ready for bed, okay?" he said, setting his bag on the long table provided.

She turned to him and impulsively took his hand. "I'm really not being argumentative, Nick. Please hear me out. I must have slept for hours on the road and now I'm wide awake. Why don't you go ahead and shower? Once you're in bed, I may take a leisurely soak. I promise not to disturb you."

"Fine," he said gruffly. He opened his bag and pulled out some clothes, then went into the bathroom and firmly closed the door. She heard the shower go on.

She sighed, and sank onto the bed. She rubbed her hand over the surface, pressing slightly. It gave, but wasn't too soft, which was good news. She opened up her bag and looked for her thermal pajamas before remembering they were in her backpack.

Only they weren't. She dumped everything out on the bed. They were not there. She'd worn them last night. Then she'd hurriedly dressed in the bathroom of the cabin this morning while that man, Sam, was there. She could have sworn that she had packed everything, ready to leave at a moment's notice.

But the pajamas weren't there. She must have hung them on the back of the bathroom door and overlooked them.

Well, that was great news. Not. They were her warmest pajamas. For that matter, they were her *only* pajamas. So now what? She upended her bag and sorted through her things. She'd brought extra sweaters, extra ski pants, an extra parka, plenty of underwear, but somehow she'd managed to go off without anything else to sleep in.

She wanted to laugh, but she was afraid she'd become hysterical. Here she was in a motel room with Nick Logan, sharing a bed. In her fantasies, perhaps, she would have pictured herself in a clinging, see-through nightgown, hoping to stir him into a passionate response to her. However, if she actually owned something like that, she would certainly freeze to death wearing it here.

She heard the water being turned off in the other room. Well, she had to do something. She looked down at the clothes she'd worn all day. No way could she wear them to bed. Maybe a sweater, maybe a—

The door opened. Nick stepped out wearing a T-shirt and sweatpants, his hair tousled from being towel-dried. "It's all yours," he said, then stopped and looked at the bed that was now covered with all her belongings. The look of surprised exasperation was too much for her and she started laughing— which only made matters worse. She covered her mouth, but it was no use.

Finally, she fell back on the bed and rolled to her side, pulling her knees up to her chest, laughing.

"Care to share the joke?" he asked testily.

"I don't have anything to sleep in," she finally said, sitting up and wiping her eyes. She grabbed items of apparel and hastily folded them, jamming them into her bags. "I must have left my pajamas at the cabin."

He didn't say anything. He just went to his bag and pulled out another T-shirt and another pair of sweatpants and handed them to her. "Now, would you please move your things so that I might lie down?"

She jumped up, grabbed the last piece of apparel—which happened to be a pair of her hip-hugger panties—and pushed them into the bag. "Sorry," she muttered, biting her bottom lip in an effort to prevent another bout of giggles. She cleared her throat. In a suitably solemn and dignified voice, she said, "Um, thanks for the loan."

Nick ignored her. He walked over to the thermostat and adjusted the heat, returned to the bed and flipped back the covers on one side before he paused and asked, "Do you have a preference as to which side of the bed you sleep on?"

She shook her head, biting her lip to quell yet another bubble of giggles that threatened to escape. What was *wrong* with her, anyway? A person would think she'd never shared a room or slept with a man before. Actually she hadn't.

Once inside the bathroom, she had turned on the water for a bath and stripped off her clothes. Oops. Forgot to put her hair up. After wrapping a towel around herself, she quietly opened the door and tiptoed out. Nick had left a small lamp on next to her side of the bed. She made her way to her backpack and pulled out her hairbrush, comb and bands for her hair.

He didn't move. She'd given him a quick glance when she'd first come out. Now she looked again. He was on his stomach, his head buried beneath the pillow. She couldn't help but notice that his cell phone and pistol were beside the bed.

After pinning her hair, she returned to the bathroom and

closed the door. She turned off the water and slid into its depth with a sigh of pure, sensual satisfaction.

Nick listened to the slight splashes she made. He wished to hell he knew what he'd ever done in his lifetime that he should have to go through such a test. At least the bed was comfortable. He sat up and looked around. There were no extra pillows that he could see, and he wasn't giving up his pillow in order to use it as a barrier between them.

He got up and looked in the small closet. No extra blankets. He shook his head and returned to bed. He was almost too tired to sleep.

He was still awake when she came out of the bathroom. He lay on his side facing her and pretended to be asleep. A sweetly feminine scent surrounded her, which automatically increased his heart rate.

He peeked at her through his lashes. His T-shirt hung almost to her knees. She'd tied her hair on top of her head in some kind of knot, but pieces were already falling in tendrils, reminding him of how she'd looked that night at the theater. Her cheeks were flushed from the warmth of the water. He imagined that her whole body was equally warm. Memories from the night before flooded his mind. He almost groaned out loud. He didn't need to be reminded of how she felt nestled in his arms.

She moved very carefully to her side of the bed and lifted the covers, making an effort to slide into the bed with a minimum of movement. Then she turned off the light.

A soft glow came through the drapes, but not enough to be distracting. Nick preferred the room that way. If anything moved, he'd be able to see it.

He didn't know how long he lay there listening to her breathing before he finally relaxed and fell asleep.

Sometime during the night he was awakened by her leg pressing against his. He forced himself awake and realized that Ms. Sullivan believed in taking her half of the bed in the middle. He shook his head. He should have known. He adjusted as best as he could, turned over and went back to sleep.

Chapter 13

Nick heard a slight noise that brought him out of a sound sleep. He opened his eyes without moving and saw a shadow moving toward the bed. Instinctively he leaped toward the figure, only to realize—just before he made contact—that it was Ashley. By that time, he already had her clutched to him, effectively immobilizing her from striking him.

Given his momentum, there was no way for him to keep his balance, so he twisted, holding on to her as he fell back onto the bed. In addition, he did his best to muffle her scream before someone called the police to report a possible murder in progress.

"Shhh. It's just me," he said irritably.

She moved her head away from his hand. "I *know* that. What in the world is wrong with you?" She was sprawled across him, lying sideways on the bed.

"I didn't know you were up. I saw a moving shadow and

I just reacted." He lifted her off him and moved over to his side of the bed.

"Well, you managed to shorten my life by several years. I almost went into cardiac arrest!" She crawled back to her side of the bed and peered at the window. It was still dark.

"I said I'm sorry."

She jerked the covers over her and settled into her pillow, muttering, "I can't even get up to go to the bathroom in the middle of the night without being attacked on my way back to bed, for Pete's sake."

They lay side by side staring at a ceiling they couldn't see.

Nick knew he should ignore her grumpiness. After all, he *had* startled her. No doubt she'd been more than half-asleep when he tackled her from out of nowhere.

"Would a written apology help?" She didn't reply. "Somehow I didn't think so." He glanced at his watch. "It's almost dawn. We might as well—"

She turned so that she was facing him. "No. It's much too early to get up. We haven't been asleep that long. And as long as we're on the subject of rest, I'd like to point out that you are the worst cover hog I've ever known. I had to fight for every scrap of blanket."

He turned, facing her. "Well, at least I leave you some room on the bed, which is more than you did for me."

With each accusation they moved infinitesimally closer until they were nose to nose.

"I gave you plenty of room. I've been hanging off the bed on this side the entire—"

"Oh, to hell with it!" he muttered, and grabbed her, kissing her with all the pent-up frustration inside him. He thought he'd meant the kiss as punishment, pure and simple, and as a means of shutting her up. The kiss served the last purpose admirably, but somehow in the process he lost sight of the original purpose.

He felt as though he were part of an explosion. As soon

as his mouth touched hers, she threw her arms around him, kissing him with an abandon that took his breath away.

Nick allowed the overwhelming passion that had mushroomed between them to sweep through him. He ran his hands over her, wanting to learn every inch of her delectable body.

Her fingers moved through his hair, kneading and tugging at him while their first kiss became one of many.

Ashley pulled away slightly and brushed her lips against his cheek, his nose, and returned to touch his mouth with hers once again before whispering, "Love me, Nick. Please. Just love me."

She slipped her hand from his head and slid it beneath his shirt, stroking lightly across his chest. He was definitely going down in flames.

"Oh, Nick," she whispered on little more than a sigh, her hand drifting downward and finding that part of his anatomy that was alert and ready for action. He reached for her hand, thinking to brush it away. Instead, he found himself placing his hand over hers and pressing her closer.

There were all kinds of flashing lights and sirens going off in his head, dire warnings of why this was not a good idea. None of that seemed to matter to him.

This was Ashley he was in bed with and making love to. She was no longer his assignment or the president's daughter, but the woman he'd fallen for, had been lusting after, the woman who'd distracted him on a daily basis since the first day he'd met her, the woman who had caused him many a restless night.

He lifted the too-large T-shirt from her, tossing it across the bed. She tugged urgently on his own shirt, and he obligingly pulled it over his head and sent it sailing after the first. She kept kissing him wherever she could reach—his chin, his chest, until he lowered himself over her and caught her mouth with his, indulging himself at last by enacting some of his late-night fantasies.

Eventually he allowed himself the pleasure of caressing the tip of one of her breasts with his mouth, savoring the luscious

sensation. She moved her hands restlessly over his head and
down to his shoulders, making tiny sounds in the back of her
throat that were rapidly pushing him to the brink. He felt like
an explorer who had just discovered a previously unexplored
continent. He wanted to see everything there was to see and
touch everything, claiming possession.

Ashley could not stop quivering as she fiercely held on to
Nick. A silent mantra replayed itself in her head—*Don't stop,
please don't stop, please don't ever stop.* She'd never experienced so many sensations at once, all of them more pleasure
than she could possibly have imagined.

She couldn't seem to touch him enough. She wanted to
read his body with her fingertips, to memorize each and every
contour, every dip and hollow, every muscled plane.

He paused and her eyes flew open, afraid that he was
already bored with her. In the dim lighting she saw him
fumbling with his billfold and suddenly recognized what he
was reaching for.

She hadn't given protection a thought. She was thankful
that he had the presence of mind to remember. He leaned back
on his heels and she watched him in the shadows and learned
what she considered a very erotic lesson. When he knelt over
her once again she instinctively shifted to accommodate him,
her arms snaking around his neck once more. She kissed him
with an urgency she hoped would mask the fact that she wasn't
at all certain what happened next.

She could hear their harsh breathing echoing in the
darkness, an erotic sound that heightened the sensations that
surrounded her.

She tried not to stiffen when he first touched her so in-
timately, not wanting him to know, not until sometime
later—

"Damn it!" he said, suddenly rearing back from her.

No way was he going to stop now. She pulled him toward
her and tightened her legs so that she was able to raise her
body toward him, forcing him into her body. Despite the dis-
comfort, Ashley almost laughed out loud with the sheer joy

of becoming a part of this man. She nestled her head into his shoulder, kissing him over and over.

With a groan that sounded like despair, he lowered them both to the bed. She took no chances that he might change his mind at this stage. Ashley kept herself plastered against him, moving with him, learning his rhythm until she knew nothing else but the pleasure he offered her with his body. She never wanted these marvelous sensations to end. She wanted them to go on and on—and then her world seemed to explode around her, her body seemingly disconnected from her. She felt as though she were free-falling through a sensation of unbelievable satisfaction.

Nick moved faster, his breathing more ragged until he gave one final lunge that seemed to meld them in a cosmic sort of way. Ashley knew at that moment in time that she belonged to this man and always would, regardless of what might happen in the future.

His head drooped to the pillow beside her and he groaned as though in pain. After several deep breaths Nick carefully shifted so that his weight was no longer on her. He still held her close, while she clung to him, never wanting to move. He muttered something beneath his breath.

"What did you say?" she whispered, nibbling on his ear.

He half-laughed, half-groaned. "You really don't want to know."

She lazily stroked his back, feeling the dampness, and smiled. "Probably not," she agreed.

"This is a hell of a time to discover that we can finally agree on something."

"Oh, I'm sure we'll find other things," she replied, smiling to herself.

After several minutes of silence he finally said, "You know I never meant this to happen."

"If you dare to tell me that you're sorry…"

"Ah, Ashley." Words seemed to fail him. "How could I say that with any sincerity? You've driven me crazy." He searched for and found her mouth, giving her a very thorough and leisurely kiss.

She could feel him growing between them. She reached down and gently stroked him.

"Happy New Year, Nick."

There was no more conversation.

Ashley awoke some time later when she felt the bed shift. She reluctantly opened her eyes, then blinked. Nick sat on the side of the bed, fully dressed, watching her.

"I let you sleep as long as I dared, darlin'. We've got a long drive ahead of us and need to get on the road."

She yawned and stretched, looking at him in wonder. "I never heard you get up."

He leaned over and kissed the tip of her nose. "My training shows in some areas more than others."

"Mmm, you smell good." She stroked his jaw. "You've already showered and shaved. Darn. I wanted to shower with you."

He groaned. "I wish you wouldn't say things like that. You completely destroy my concentration. Please remember that I'll be driving all day."

She shoved the covers away before she remembered that she was nude. She started to grab them when he took them out of her hands.

"A little late for modesty, isn't it, Ms. Sullivan?"

She knew she was blushing, but couldn't help it. She'd never seen this warm-eyed, teasing, gentle Nick before. Whatever battles he'd been waging, he was no longer including her in the warfare.

"There's a twenty-four-hour restaurant next door to the motel where we can have breakfast without bothering with the car."

The thought of food made her realize she hadn't had anything to eat since noon yesterday. She stretched down to the floor and picked up her discarded T-shirt, wrapped it around her and made a dash for the bathroom.

She could hear his chuckle before she closed the door.

Nick was a different man this morning. Only now could she appreciate how much of his personality he'd been holding back since she'd met him.

If she hadn't been in love with him before, she certainly was now.

Nick stood with his hands in his pockets looking out the window at the parking lot. He probably should have awakened her earlier because they needed to drive until they reached El Paso before stopping. He hadn't been able to make himself awaken her.

When he slipped out of bed, she had been curled on his shoulder. He'd carefully disengaged himself, amused at her frowning acceptance of the pillow in lieu of his shoulder. Once he'd showered, shaved and dressed, he'd returned to the bedroom and sat nearby, watching her sleep and thinking about what had happened.

The fact was that it *had* happened. There was no going back now. He didn't want to look too far down the road, whether it was the physical distance they needed to cover in the next few days or the emotional distance that stretched out ahead of them.

She was so blessed young, not so much in years, although she was at least ten years younger than he, but in experience. She'd led a very sheltered life, due in part, he was sure, to agents like him who curtailed her social life quite nicely. She looked even younger asleep.

He didn't know what they would find in New Orleans. Sam had mentioned the name of the tanker, which helped, but Nick had no idea how accessible it would be or what he might find if he managed to board her. In addition, he had to make very sure that Ashley remained safe.

Now was when he could use some backup. He knew that

the local police could always be called upon in an emergency,
but the problem here was that no one wanted this to get out,
if it could be prevented. He knew that Harvey would speak
to no one about anything to do with the president.

Outside of Harvey, he knew he needed to do this one
alone—and count on Ashley's basic good sense to stay as
safe as he could make her.

She was singing in the shower. The tension that had been
building up between them had been eased, at least temporarily.
He no longer intended to fight what was happening between
them. Resisting Ashley took more energy and effort than he
was capable of expending at the moment.

She walked out of the bathroom with a towel wrapped
around her head, another one around her torso. "I'm starved,"
she said, reaching into her bag for fresh clothing. "I'm sorry
to keep you waiting."

He turned and smiled. "No problem. I've worked up quite
an appetite, too, and seeing you in that skimpy towel is making
it worse."

She laughed. "Now who's teasing?" She hurriedly dressed
in what had become their uniform of jeans and a sweater.
After combing the tangles out of her hair, she pinned it in a
knot of some kind and covered it with her stocking cap. She
grabbed her jacket, made certain everything was repacked
in her bag and looked at him with a dazzling smile. "I'm
ready."

All he could think about was just how ready he was, too…
and there wasn't a damn thing he could do about it.

He took her bag, as well as his, and placed them in the
trunk of the car. Afterward, he wrapped his arm around her
and guided her toward the restaurant. She slipped her arm
around his waist, matching her step to his.

When they entered the restaurant, Nick asked for a non-
smoking booth. They were led into the interior of the spacious
area. It was still early for New Year's Day. Very few people
were there.

The waitress took their orders and left a carafe of coffee

at the table. Nick poured them each a cup, and they sat there quietly drinking it. Nick knew that his gaze kept returning to her face, but he could no more look away from her than he could tap-dance on top of the table.

"What?" She wrinkled her nose. "Do I have something on my face?"

He grinned and wiped an imaginary smudge from her cheek. "You'll do just fine, darlin'." He loved to see her blush because her eyes sparkled, as well.

The waitress returned with their orders. Ashley's stomach growled at the scent of pancake and eggs, bacon and sausage. They both laughed.

"You folks are up awfully early," the waitress said with a smile. "Or maybe you haven't been to bed yet."

Nick glanced at Ashley and saw her take an inordinate amount of interest in her breakfast. "We're up early."

"Just passing through?"

He nodded. "Visiting my wife's family in Albuquerque."

The waitress nodded. "Let me know if I can bring you anything," she said, returning to the front.

"Albuquerque?"

"Oh, you don't mind being referred to as my wife, just the destination bothers you?"

She shook her head with a smile. "You're very good with the glib lie. I'll need to remember that."

He thought it more politic not to touch that one, so he followed her example and began to eat. Within minutes there was nothing left on either plate. Ashley sat back and sighed before pouring herself another cup of coffee. She held the carafe up in a silent offer and he slid his empty cup toward her. After filling it for him, she returned to her cup and took a sip.

"Are you always this quiet in the morning?" he finally asked.

"Usually. Why?"

"Just wondered."

Nothing more was said until they were ready to leave. The

same waitress took their money. "Was everything all right?" she asked.

"Great," Nick replied, then was startled when Ashley suddenly took his arm and leaned against him. He raised his brow and looked at her, and she gave him another sparkling smile back.

He waited until they were in the parking lot before he asked, "What was that all about?"

"What?"

"You nuzzling my arm back there."

"That woman was flirting with you. I was just staking my claim."

"What are you talking about? She just asked if everything was all right."

In a patient voice Ashley said, "It wasn't what she said, it was how she said it. She was undressing you with her eyes."

He laughed. "Right." He paused beside the passenger door of the car and opened it for her. "I thought I felt a draft."

When they drove out of the lot and headed south, Nick realized that he was still smiling.

Chapter 14

There was no reason to believe that anyone was looking for them in New Mexico, Nick decided, but he planned to take no chances. He followed the highway south, intending to go as far as the Texas border where he would catch Interstate 10 heading east. Eventually it would take them all the way to New Orleans.

He glanced over at Ashley and smiled. There must be something hypnotic about being in a car for Ashley. They'd been on the road about an hour when he noticed she'd fallen asleep. She'd removed her cap once they were in the car and her hair had dried in thick waves around her neck and shoulders. He envied her the ability to sleep so soundly.

Of course, she hadn't gotten much sleep last night. Visions of their lovemaking filled his mind, not a good idea at the moment. Instead, he concentrated on the reason for this trip.

Sam Masters.

He and Sam went back a long way. It would be like Sam to get himself involved in something before he fully understood what was going on. That much of his story Nick believed. He also believed that if the president had been placed in danger, Sam would not betray him if he could help it.

However, Sam was up to his eyeballs in this mess. He knew who had kidnapped the president. And why. Knowing Sam so well, Nick concluded from the way Sam acted that there was a good chance the hostages wouldn't be freed when this was over.

If that was Sam's concern, it was now Nick's greatest fear. He had to do whatever he could to find them before something happened to them.

His next concern was Sam's other warnings—about Greg Chambers and his not-so-veiled allusion that if something were to happen to James Sullivan, Jason Freeman would benefit by automatically becoming his successor.

Damn Sam, anyway. If he had evidence of any of this, why wouldn't he give it to him? Who was Sam's pipeline and where was he or she located? Had he learned from a Colorado source that Chambers had ordered a helicopter to pick up a couple in a remote cabin and decided it had to do with Ashley? A reasonable assumption, Nick had to admit.

Who had sent the earlier chopper that had picked up Sam? It came too early to have been from Chambers, and Sam wasn't surprised when it arrived. If he and Ashley had gotten on either helicopter, would they have been returned to the Denver airport or taken somewhere else?

Would Sam have allowed them to become hostages, as well? He'd actually seemed relieved that Ashley wasn't there, so it was a good bet that he might not have had control over where they would have been taken.

He was thankful Sam bought his story about Ron and Ashley. He'd been able to use Chambers's omission to protect her. Getting Ashley out of the area was the safest thing he could do now that Sam, and possibly others, knew where she was.

If he could reach New Orleans by the time the tanker appeared there, he might get some answers. He hated being cut off from all lines of support, but he didn't dare take a chance of alerting the wrong people that he might know where the presidential family was being held.

Ashley stirred and sat up straighter in her seat. "Where are we?" she asked, yawning. She looked around and frowned. "This doesn't look like planet Earth, that's for sure."

He grinned. "It's part of the White Sands area," he said.

"We're still in New Mexico?" she asked, sounding disappointed.

"'Fraid so. I don't want to take a chance on getting stopped and having to answer a bunch of questions. So I'm staying just below the speed limit."

"This looks so desolate."

"Mmm."

"Have you been here before?" she asked.

"Yep."

"Doing what?"

"If I told you, I'd have to kill you."

"Very funny."

"Do you need to stop for any reason?" he asked.

"Is that your delicate way of suggesting a rest stop?"

He chuckled. "I suppose."

"I could use one."

"I intend to stop for gas the next town. It's about ten more miles."

She was quiet for a few minutes, then said, "I'm hungry, aren't you?"

"A little, I guess. I haven't given it much thought."

"We never stopped for lunch." She sounded disgruntled.

He knew better than to smile. "I know."

She leaned forward so that she could see his face. "Is there some particular reason why?"

He gave her a quick glance. "I didn't want to take the time. I figured we could make do with the snacks we picked up last gas stop."

She sighed. "You aren't into nutrition much, I take it."

He smiled. "Not much."

She shook her head. "Figures." She reached over and turned on the radio.

"…and the latest from the first family is that they are enjoying their vacation at sea. We spoke with one of the White House staff who assured us that everyone is enjoying this break from the heavy duties demanded of the first family," a reporter said.

Another voice said, "At least they aren't bothered by the press. I understand that the area where they are has been closed to other seagoing vessels, or so some reporters are saying."

Ashley looked over at Nick. "What do you suppose that means?"

He shrugged. "The VP is doing whatever it takes to keep all of this quiet. If word leaks out that the family is missing, we'll have massive problems."

She swallowed hard. "Won't whoever is holding them want it known?"

"Not until they've accomplished whatever it is they hope to accomplish. If I can just get to the family in time, we'll be able to deal with this from a new angle."

Ashley continued to look at the scenery for several minutes without speaking. Suddenly she straightened. "What if that news report was right? I mean, we really don't know where they are, or if they were actually taken off the yacht and are now being held on a tanker. Maybe they really are out there fishing and enjoying themselves and all of this has been some gigantic hoax by who knows who. How are we going to know?"

"I've thought of that, too. However, the attack on the van was real enough. Ron can certainly attest to that. Unless we want to consider that ambush a random act, then we have to assume it had something to do with your father's disappearance. How many people knew that we would be at that deserted airfield in the middle of the night?"

"Good point."

"I do intend to speak to the VP as soon as we get to El Paso, which is where we'll be spending the night. If he *is* involved in any of this, I can't let him know that we're on our way to New Orleans. However, I can report that you're safe but I don't intend to bring you in just yet, and see what his response is. He was expecting us back in Washington yesterday."

"What if he is involved? Doesn't that make everything more dangerous for my father?"

"Without a doubt. Jason Freeman has full access to everything that is going on."

"You used to work for him. What do you think?"

"Right now, I'm not willing to stake your family's lives on trusting anyone."

He saw a sign for a service station ahead and began to slow down. Once they were parked by the pumps, he said, "Go on inside. I'm going to stay here and fill the tank."

He waited until she was out of sight, then he reached for his phone. He keyed in a number that would automatically connect him to a private number that only a few people knew existed.

As soon as the phone was answered, Nick said, "Logan here. Change of plans. I won't be flying back today as scheduled. I'm afraid the situation has mushroomed on us. I'll be in touch as soon as possible."

He hung up and walked into the convenience store to pay for the gas. As soon as he stepped inside, Nick spotted Ashley at the counter laughing at something the young man behind the register had said. Nick froze, then forced himself to walk casually over to where she stood. He dropped his arm around her shoulder, pulling her against his side. "Find everything you wanted, honey?"

When she looked up at him in surprise, his gaze did not falter. She grinned impishly, which should have given him fair warning. However, he wasn't quick-witted enough. Before he could step away she went up on her toes and kissed him on the mouth. When she stepped back, her cheeks were glowing. "Oh, I think so," she murmured provocatively.

She'd managed to steam up his sunglasses, not to mention

caused his temperature to climb. He pulled out his billfold and paid for the gas, ignoring the grinning clerk. He looked over his shoulder at Ashley and said, "I'll be out in a moment," which to him was clear enough instruction for her to be in the car when he returned from the restroom.

No such luck. He found her browsing through the books and magazines.

"Are you going to buy one of those?"

"Uh-uh. Just waiting on you."

"I'm touched."

Her grin was still filled with mischief. "Oh, you should be." She turned and walked out ahead of him, her hips swaying slightly.

She knew exactly what she was doing. He opened her door for her, then closed it firmly before walking around to the driver's side.

Once inside, he turned and looked at her. "You know you're playing a dangerous game, don't you?"

She arched her brows. "Am I?"

"You'd better believe it." He started the car with jerky movements and drove out of the filling station.

"I'm scared," she replied, obviously teasing. "Nick the grouch is back. I've already gotten to know that part of your character quite well."

"How do you know that isn't all there is to my character?"

She settled back into her seat and smiled seductively. "Oh, I know."

Why was it that Nick was feeling less in control than ever?

The sun had set but there was still some light in the sky when they drove into the outskirts of El Paso. Ashley had been quiet since they'd gotten gas. He wasn't certain that was a good sign. She seemed to be entertaining herself with some amusing thoughts.

She'd also fiddled with the radio, looking for strong enough signals to be able to keep music going in the car. Nick meanwhile concentrated on what he intended to tell Vice President Freeman when he called.

There had been other times when he'd been on his own, having to make decisions that could get him killed. At those times, he had placed his own life in danger, not another person's. His feelings for Ashley were a jumbled, very chaotic mess. The only clear thought he had where she was concerned was that he didn't want to place her in any danger.

On the other hand, he was taking her to what he hoped to be the center of this whole mess. He didn't like his choices, but he would do what he had to do.

"There's a nice-looking place. I figure you don't want to stay in one of the big hotels?"

"Not if I can help it. I want to make our cash last as long as possible."

The hotel was one of a chain that was known for its economical rates. It looked newer than the one they'd stayed in the night before. The parking lot wasn't completely filled. He hoped that meant they were early enough to get a decent room.

He pulled up in front of the office and went inside. He'd requested an upstairs room. The ground floors had sliding doors that opened onto a pool area, which was one too many doors to watch as far as he was concerned.

When he returned to the car, he glanced at Ashley. "Let's get cleaned up and I'll take you out for a big steak."

"Oh, yes. We're in Texas now. Cattle country."

"Actually we've been in cattle country since we crossed the Mississippi. Texas just makes a lot of noise about the industry."

"Where are you from? I don't think you've ever mentioned it."

"Wyoming."

"I was born in Colorado."

"I know."

"Did your family ranch?"

"Yep. Until my dad retired."

"You never wanted to raise cattle?"

"Absolutely not."

During their conversation Nick had found a parking space near their room and parked the car. She helped him by carrying her bag while he got his, then he followed her up the stairs.

This was getting to feel comfortably familiar, he realized. The thought was dismaying.

He had a sense of déjà vu when he opened the door and waited for Ashley to enter. There was very little difference in the layout of this room to the one the night before. At least this one was large enough to accommodate two queen-size beds, and the bathroom was larger. There was a sink in the bathroom, as well as one at a counter outside the bathroom.

Ashley walked over to the two large windows and looked outside. "People are actually swimming out there. The pool must be heated."

"Better them than me," Nick responded, placing his bag on the luggage rack. "I don't know about you, but I'm starved. Do you want to change before we eat?"

She turned and smiled at him. Her smile did something to him, he wasn't certain what. Somehow the stiffening left his knees and he felt wobbly just looking at her.

"I can wait. We need to get you some food. You've had a long day since breakfast."

They returned to the car and continued along the access road until they spotted a Western-style restaurant that seemed to have attracted a fairly large crowd of cars.

The Western motif had been carried on inside, as well. While they waited to be seated, Ashley studied the Western prints on the walls. By the time they were shown to a booth in a quiet corner of the place, she was telling him about a place she'd visited when she'd lived in Colorado. Her story reminded him of one about growing up in Wyoming.

By the time they reached the coffee-and-dessert stage,

Nick realized they'd been chatting like old friends. Ashley no longer wore her concealing cap and her hair glinted in the soft lighting around them. Her eyes sparkled as she shared various memories with him.

He was taken off guard by how similar they were in many respects. Their life experiences were vastly different, but their view of the world around them coincided to a surprising degree.

On an impulse, Nick picked up his glass and nodded to her. "Happy New Year, Ashley. My toast is for a happy reunion for you and your family very soon."

With a smile she picked up her glass, which, like his, contained iced tea, and said, "Thank you, Nick. I appreciate the thought."

"It's too bad all of this had to happen. Otherwise, you would have flown back to Washington today with your friends."

"If I can help to find my family, I would much prefer to be here than sitting back in Washington wringing my hands."

He looked at the table, then asked, "Would you like anything else?"

She shook her head, smiling. "I'm very content, thank you."

He signaled the waiter, who brought the bill. After paying, he helped Ashley with her coat before stepping outside.

They returned to the motel and their room in silence. Nick glanced at his watch. "I need to call Washington," he said.

She nodded. "While you do that, I think I'll take a shower." She removed some items from her bag and went into the other room.

As soon as Chambers answered, Nick asked, "Any news?"

"The vice president received a call a few hours ago. The caller said members of a well-known terrorist group are holding the president and his family at an undisclosed location. They played a tape of his voice to prove they had him."

"Which means nothing. He's always being taped."

"This one addressed Vice President Freeman, quietly asking him to agree to their demands."

"Does the VP believe the tape is authentic?"

"He's been closeted with presidential advisers since the call came in. It was recorded, of course, and they've been studying it. He's also quietly contacting the cabinet members who are gathering here at the White House. The family is due home tomorrow. I don't think we're going to be able to keep this quiet after that."

"What are the demands?" Nick asked, curious.

"I wasn't told, but it's my guess they have to do with some of their leaders being held at Guantanamo."

"Any guesses where they might be holding them?"

"Someone suggested the islands in the Caribbean would be a good place to look," Chambers replied. "There would be easy access to any number of islands from the water."

"Is that what you think?"

"Hell, it's as good as any. I want to know what happened to the security ship and the agents on board. We had some good men on those two ships," Chambers said.

"It's possible they're all being held together."

"Somehow I doubt it. I'm afraid our men would be considered expendable."

"I was going to ask to speak to the VP, but under the circumstances, there's no need to disturb him," Nick said.

"Everything all right where you are?"

"Couldn't be better," he said cheerfully.

"You sound better. I've been worrying about your state of mind. Ashley still giving you trouble?"

"No. We've managed to come to an understanding."

"Good. Well, bring her home when you feel it's safe to do so."

Nick hung up and looked around the room. He'd heard the shower shut off some time ago.

Ah, now he heard her hair dryer. He piled the two pillows on one of the beds into a stack and stretched out with a sigh, thinking about what he'd just learned.

They needed to get to New Orleans as quickly as possible, which meant driving straight through. Ashley had offered to drive earlier on this trip. Maybe he'd take her up on her offer.

Ashley stepped out of the bathroom wearing the T-shirt he'd loaned her. It certainly never looked that good on him.

"You look comfortable," she said, smiling, "and relaxed."

"Looks can be deceiving."

He sat up on the side of the bed. "Come here…"

She walked over and paused in front of him. He placed his hands on the back of her thighs and slowly moved them upward. She shivered. He could feel her bare buttocks. He smoothed his hands over the rounded shape. "You aren't wearing anything under this, are you?" he said gruffly.

"Uh-uh," she replied, sounding a little breathless. "You, on the other hand, are wearing entirely too many clothes."

He'd taken off his shoes while he'd been on the phone. He immediately pulled off his sweater and undershirt together, unfastened his jeans and pulled them off along with his underpants. With a swift tug his socks were off, as well.

"You were saying?"

"Wow. You're fast. Did you learn that at school, too?"

"Let's face it, darlin', we're trained to be men of action." Her eyes widened when she saw that he had a full erection. "See what you do to me? I've been in this condition most of the day."

"Is that what you meant when you said I was playing a dangerous game?"

He slipped the T-shirt over her head, then cupped her breasts with his hands. "Mmm-hmm," he murmured, his tongue outlining the darker flesh at the tip of one of her breasts.

She placed her hands on his shoulders and with steady force pushed him onto his back, his feet still on the floor. She straddled him and leaned over him so that once again her breasts were enticingly close to his mouth.

"How dangerous?" she whispered.

He lazily flicked his tongue over her offering, enjoying

watching her skin ripple in reaction. "Speaking of moves, where did you learn that one?"

She chuckled. "In a movie. I've always wondered how it would feel to take control like this."

"Darlin', you've been in control all along if you'd just known."

"You mean I could have done this to you at the chalet?"

"I, uh, believe we might have attracted an audience if you had."

She stared down at him. "Oh, Nick, I want you so much."

"The feeling's mutual…so why don't you have your wicked way with me?"

"This is the only move I learned," she admitted. "The scene ended and the next scene they were, uh, in another position and—"

"You seem to be doing just fine without more instruction." He lifted her slightly and eased her down on him.

She felt so good and he wanted her so badly he was about to burst. She teased him with a slow, rocking rhythm that had him clutching the bedclothes beneath him.

She looked radiantly happy, her gaze fastened to his in silent communion. He began to meet her thrusts with his own, increasing the pace until she suddenly froze in place for a timeless moment before collapsing against him. She held him tightly, quivering. Nick couldn't resist the convulsive pull deep inside of her, and he suddenly exploded, his body bucking.

It was at that precise moment that he realized he'd forgotten to use protection.

As soon as he caught his breath, he scooped her up and headed to the other room.

"What are you doing?"

"You said you wanted to shower with me. Now's your chance."

Much later, the lights were out and they were tucked in bed, her head on his shoulder. He thought she was asleep when she asked, "Have you ever been married?"

That didn't take much thought. "Nope." After a moment, he said, "My kind of work is tough on marriages. Just ask Ron."

After another long pause, she asked, "Have you ever been engaged?"

Now there was a question he wasn't certain he was ready to answer. He'd never discussed his personal life with anyone before. He also realized that not answering her would hurt Ashley, and he didn't want to do that.

She deserved his honesty.

He shifted, so that he could slide one of his arms behind his head. "Yeah, as a matter of fact, I was. Once upon a time, long, long ago."

"But you aren't now."

"That's right."

"Was it after you became part of the Secret Service?"

"The engagement was, yes, but Susan and I met in college. We'd dated back then before I graduated and went off to make a name for myself. She went on to law school while I was working overseas. We lost track of each other until I came back to the States and was assigned to a Washington post. We happened to run into each other one night at an embassy party. That's when I discovered that she had been hired by a Washington law firm. It was the old 'small world' thing, you know?"

"Sounds as though fate brought the two of you together again."

Nick discovered that this was going to be tougher to talk about than he'd thought. This had all happened more than five years ago and he'd been over it a long time. And yet...

He cleared his throat. "Yeah. I guess that's what we thought."

"So what happened?"

He pulled away from her and sat up on the side of the bed. Although she had never suggested that they might have a future together, Nick knew that Ashley wouldn't be making love with him if she didn't have some very strong feelings for him.

Maybe this discussion might convince her that he wasn't good marriage material. Hadn't Susan already figured that out?

With his back to her and without turning on a light, Nick said, "I asked her to marry me. She accepted. I gave her a ring. We set a date, notified our families—all the usual stuff you do." He got up and went over to the sink, found a glass and filled it with water. "But life has a nasty habit of getting in the way of our plans sometimes," he said, turning around and looking at her across the room.

The room was much darker than the one the night before. He couldn't see her face…and she couldn't see his.

She waited.

He wished to hell he hadn't started this. What difference did it make, anyway? He was no longer engaged. End of story.

She continued to wait.

Finally, he walked over to the windows and looked outside. He could see the mountains rising in the distance, dark shadows against a darker sky.

"Uh, we were both really busy," he finally said. "It was a campaign year and I was traveling quite a bit. She understood because her firm was working on a huge lawsuit, which was taking up all of her time. We stayed in touch by phone, continued to make our plans, talked about the future, a honeymoon and all those things that people do."

Everything was coming back much too clearly. He could remember how much he'd looked forward to their telephone conversations…how much he'd missed her.

In a gruff voice he said, "One night I called her and she was really upset. I tried to get her to tell me what was wrong. She kept saying we'd talk about it when I got back to Washington. Finally, I got angry and pointed out that it would be another six weeks and whatever it was that had upset her needed to be dealt with then, not later."

"Did she tell you?"

He turned away from the window and faced her. "Oh, yeah. She told me. She'd taken a home pregnancy test about an hour before I'd called. It was positive."

"Oh. And she was afraid you might be upset because of all the wedding plans?"

He stood very still. "You could say that, since there was no way in hell I could have gotten her pregnant."

"Oh."

Nick could picture himself in that other hotel room that night, stretched out across the bed, talking with his fiancée. He could still remember the print hanging over the bed, the exact color and design of the multicolored bedspread and the matching drapes. He could hear the low muttering of the television he'd forgotten to turn off.

He forced himself back into the present and deliberately sat down on his side of the bed. This close, he could see the pale oval that was Ashley's face.

"It seems that one night—and she swore it had happened only once—she and one of her co-workers had worked late as usual on their big case. One thing lead to another and…"

As far as Nick was concerned, that pretty much told the story.

Ashley waited, but when it became clear he didn't intend to say anything else, she said, "That must have been tough for you to hear."

"It wasn't one of my shining moments, I'll admit."

Now there was an understatement. If he hadn't been clear across the continent from her, he wasn't sure to this day what he might have done. In this case, his job had saved his sanity by keeping him away from Washington until he could adjust to the new turn of events.

Nick realized after a while that he was sitting there nude in the dark and that he was cold. He slid under the covers and Ashley immediately wrapped her arms around him and held him close.

"But everything turned out okay, as it happens," he finally said, feeling her warmth radiating along his side. "You

know the old saying—all's well that ends well. It ended well
enough."

"How?"

"She married her co-worker, they had a little girl, and
they are sublimely happy practicing law in the same office.
A match made in heaven."

"I'm sorry you had to go through that."

From the sound of her voice, his flippant tone hadn't fooled
her much.

"It sounds trite to say that I'm glad it happened *before* we
were married, but that happens to be the truth," he said.

"I'm sorry for prying into your past, Nick. I know talking
about it is painful."

"You have no reason to apologize. For some reason you
seem to think I'm still carrying a torch for Susan. I'm not. I
still care for her, but the man she chose to marry is as opposite
to me as he can be. If that's who makes her happy, then we
were saved from a disaster."

"I think she was crazy to mess up what the two of you
had."

"No. I had no right to think I was husband material. I've
been on my own for too many years. I prefer it that way."

"How old are you?"

"Thirty-two."

"That's pretty ancient, all right."

"I'm sure it is, to a twenty-one-year-old."

"I'll be twenty-two next month—February fourteenth."

"Really? So you were a Valentine baby."

"Yep. Mom said the nurse brought me to her on a red
satin pillow shaped like a heart. I still have it, as a matter of
fact."

"Which makes you a romantic, I bet."

"Sometimes. Perhaps."

"My loss of control last night ruined your first experience with lovemaking. That should have happened with your
husband. I can't tell you how sorry I am."

She leaned up on her elbow so that she could reach his

mouth for a kiss. Then she murmured, "Please don't go there. Neither of us deserves that. The timing may be wrong, but we both know that this is where we've been headed since we met. You've mentioned the sparks before. Why are you blaming yourself?"

He thought about that, and he thought about something else that he hadn't put together until right now. "Talking about Susan reminds me of something she said to me back then, something that didn't mean anything to me at the time. Now I realize that what she tried to explain happened between her and Jeff was what happened to you and me last night."

She kissed him again. "Spontaneous combustion." She leaned back. "Is it so wrong to want you as much as I do? We're headed into a dangerous situation. Neither of us is certain that we'll survive the outcome. Why can't we enjoy this time we have together? I'm not asking for your future—just your present."

Nick wrapped his arms around her and drew her against him.

"You're too generous for your own good, Ashley. You need to understand that nothing can come of a relationship between us."

"All right."

"I mean it."

"I know you do."

"I'm too old for you. I'm too old to change. You have your whole life ahead of you."

"I'm not arguing with you."

"I robbed your husband of that first time with you."

"It was my choice, Nick. Don't forget that. I want you so badly. If this is all there is, so be it."

He'd run out of arguments. He kissed her with a passion that seemed to grow greater the more he made love to her. He didn't want to think about what that could mean.

Chapter 15

El Paso, Texas
Saturday, January 2

Nick woke up abruptly. Once he became aware of where he was, he relaxed and looked over at Ashley, curled up beside him asleep. He glanced at his watch. It should be getting light soon and they needed to be on their way.

From looking at the maps he'd picked up, it was a thousand miles from El Paso to New Orleans. Traffic in west Texas would be next to nothing. Once they reached San Antonio, they would lose some time. Houston would slow them down even more. He still thought they could make it in eighteen hours or so.

He went in to shower and while standing under the invigorating spray recalled the dream that had awakened him. He'd dreamed about Susan last night for the first time in several years. After they had called off their engagement, he'd dreamed about her for months. In his dreams, he was getting his revenge for what she had done. Last night's dream had been different.

He'd dreamed that Susan was demanding to know why he had betrayed her with Ashley. He'd tried to explain. She hadn't understood. She'd kept telling him that he had betrayed her until he woke up.

What was he thinking of, anyway, sleeping with Ashley Sullivan? He'd taken a hell of a chance making love with her without protection. He'd also betrayed his position of trust to watch over her. Once the dust cleared, he'd probably lose his badge over his behavior this trip. Not only was he not reporting all the information he had to his superiors, he was taking advantage of a young woman's vulnerable state.

He had trouble looking himself in the eye when he shaved.

Ashley was equally quiet when she woke up. She disappeared into the bathroom with no more than a nod at him while he shaved. He heard the shower come on. By the time he searched through his clothes and dressed, she came out of the bathroom dressed, her hair pulled high on her head.

They loaded the car in silence. The sky had lightened but the sun hadn't appeared.

Nick closed the trunk and looked at her. "I thought we'd have breakfast before we leave town. There aren't all that many towns between here and San Antonio. Are you still willing to help with the driving?"

She nodded. "Whatever I can do to help. I just want to find my parents."

Over breakfast she asked, "How do you intend to look for my family once we get to New Orleans?"

"Sam gave me the name of the tanker they're supposedly on. If his information is correct, they should be anchored at the shipping docks."

"And if they aren't there?"

"We'll watch for them for a few days. If they don't show up, I intend to take you back to Washington."

"Are you going to be in trouble for coming down here?"

"It will depend on what happens once we get to New Orleans. If I have unnecessarily endangered you, then of course I'll be in trouble."

"Is that why you've been so quiet this morning?"

He pushed his plate away. "Ashley, even if I haven't endangered you physically, I've taken some unnecessary risks. We had no protection last night."

She met his gaze without blinking. "I'm aware of that."

"It was careless behavior on my part."

"There were two of us involved, remember? I never gave it a thought, either."

"Are you prepared to face the consequences?"

She smiled. "The consequences being…having your baby?" Her smile grew wider. "I can think of worse things."

"You mean, you'd go through with the pregnancy?"

"Absolutely. The timing might be a little awkward, but I can't think of anything more rewarding to me than to have your child."

He shook his head. "You don't know me well enough to say that. I'm not husband and father material. I've tried to explain that."

"Oh, I've heard those explanations, Agent Logan, and the truth is you're scared to death of the idea of marriage and fatherhood."

He bristled. "I'm not afraid. I'm—"

"'Scared to death' was the phrase I used and I'm sticking with it. It takes a brave man to commit to a relationship, to stay with it through whatever life throws your way. Don't worry. I don't intend to force you into something you aren't ready for."

He took a deep breath in an effort to gain control of his temper. "You think I'd just walk away and let you deal with this?"

She shrugged. "Why don't we wait and see what happens? We don't know anything at the moment. Weren't you the one who agreed we live in the present? Well, you're certainly jumping into the future with both feet." She glanced around them and said, "I'll meet you at the car. I'm going to the restroom."

Nick paid for their meal and waited in the lobby for her to appear. When she did, he didn't give her an opportunity to speak. "I'm going to do my job," he said in a low voice, then took her arm and escorted her out to the car.

"Oh, yes. I forgot about your dedication to duty." She took the keys from him and got into the car. He took the passenger seat.

They'd been on the road more than an hour when Nick said, "What did I do or say to cause you to be angry with me?"

She didn't answer right away. "Did I ever tell you about my first big crush?" she finally asked.

"You know you didn't."

"I was a late bloomer, I guess. I never understood what all the whispering and giggling was about among the girls my age. Maybe it was having a couple of younger brothers, but I never saw anything particularly mysterious about the opposite sex. However, during my senior year in high school, I started dating an older man." She glanced at him and grinned. "Three years older and already in college. I'd known who he was for some time and never thought he'd notice me. When he did, I was ecstatic." She shook her head in wonder. "Talk about a crush! I had all the symptoms."

He waited, but she didn't say any more. Finally he prompted, "So what happened?"

Her voice flattened. "What happened was, he got tired of trying to date me with a gaggle of Secret-Service men following us everywhere. He couldn't even kiss me good-night without an audience. He finally told me that he couldn't take the fishbowl routine. He wished me well, said he'd like to continue our friendship and went on his way."

"I'm sorry," was all he could think of to say.

"Well, I can't say my heart was actually broken, but it certainly carried a few dents after that."

"Did you remain friends?"

"Of course. We just went skiing together last week."

"Are you saying that you and..." He thought of the three men who were with them.

"Joe. It was Joe who helped me understand that even if a man was interested in me, he was definitely influenced by who my father was." She looked at him and said, "As are you. If I had been anyone else on this trip with you, you wouldn't be backing away from me so rapidly now. We would be enjoying getting to know each other, wondering if the relationship would develop into something other than a couple of nights in bed together. I might be wondering if I would ever meet your parents, while you might be wondering the same thing. You see, Joe was right. I live in a fishbowl. It's the only life I've ever known. I understand your wariness much better than you think. If it will soothe your conscience, I've enjoyed the few days we've been together, just the two of us. They have been a real novelty in my life. During these past few days I've been more frightened than I've ever been in my life. I've also experienced pleasure that I never knew existed. I've also had to face the fact that I may never see my family again." She looked over at him. "I'm willing to deal with everything that has happened to me, Nick. Everything. I accept the consequences of the choices I made. I suggest you do the same, rather than trying to take on all the blame."

Nick settled back into his seat and closed his eyes. He needed to rest in order to take over driving when Ashley grew tired. He also wanted to think about what she had said.

She wasn't holding him responsible for what had happened between them. She was right that he blamed himself, because he kept thinking of her as an innocent child. She was not a child. She was taking on a heavy burden by attempting to help him find her parents.

Nick realized how much respect he had for the woman who had struck him as a spoiled brat just a few days ago. He'd misread her aversion to the lack of privacy her life offered her to a childish refusal to cooperate with the rules and regulations set by government agencies.

This wasn't a life that she had chosen. It had been chosen

for her, and she was attempting to find a way to deal with it. She was a strong woman, much stronger than he had given her credit for.

She was also right about his behavior toward her. The fact was that he was falling in love with her. Hard. And it did scare him because he didn't like feeling vulnerable. She'd read him right.

He almost smiled. Was there anything more frightening to a man than a woman who understood him too well?

They reached San Antonio about four in the afternoon.

It was considerably warmer than Colorado had been. Each of them looked in their bags for something a little cooler to wear. Nick discarded his sweater and wore a short-sleeved pullover. Ashley wore a cotton turtleneck that she'd brought to wear beneath her sweaters.

After a quick meal they got on the road again, continuing east. Nick drove.

"How far are we from New Orleans?" she asked once they left San Antonio.

"According to the maps, its another eight to ten hours of hard driving."

"We'll make it tonight, then."

"Late, but yes, we can make it."

"Good," Ashley said.

Nick had the same sense of urgency. He was thankful that Ashley had taken the wheel earlier. Now he was fresh and eager to make time. They were in Houston a little before eight that night. He filled up with gas. Once he crossed the Louisiana border, Nick knew swamps and bayous would be the order of the day.

It was after two in the morning when they finally reached New Orleans. Ashley awoke when they stopped for gas and a city map. Once he located the shipping area, he drove to that part of town, while Ashley studied the streets as they passed.

"What do we do now?"

"Find a place to stay. I'm going to wait for daylight to see if I can spot the tanker I'm looking for."

Ashley could feel her adrenaline pumping. Now that they were here, she wanted to do something. But they'd been on the road for more than seventeen hours. They both needed rest before searching for her family.

Nick found a motel and checked them in. Neither of them paid much attention to the room or the beds. Instead, they each took a quick shower to get rid of the sticky feeling caused by the Louisiana humidity and were asleep within minutes of crawling into their beds.

His wrist alarm went off much too soon, but Nick was up and in the shower as soon as he heard the beeping sounds. Ashley continued to sleep. He hurried through his shower and got dressed, being as quiet as possible. Then he wrote her a note and slipped out the door.

Once outside, he went to the car and drove back to the docks. There was more activity there now, and he knew he could use that to hide his presence. He drove a few blocks away and parked the car, then returned on foot, hoping to blend in. He'd worn his jeans and a sweatshirt, which looked similar to the work clothes on the men he saw laboring in the area.

He spotted the tanker bearing the name Sam had mentioned and felt his first sense of relief in several days. It looked as though Sam had given him straight information, after all.

There was nothing about the tanker to draw the eye. It was one of several waiting to unload its liquid cargo.

He wondered if whoever had kidnapped the Sullivans had already taken them off the ship? He needed to get on board as soon as possible, but he didn't dare during daylight hours. There was too much activity going on around the docks.

He needed to find a location that would be inconspicuous where he could watch the area for the day.

Nick turned away, careful not to call attention to himself. He retraced his steps to the car, stopped for beignets and the strong chicory coffee served in the city and returned to the motel.

When he slipped back inside the room, he was relieved to find Ashley still sound asleep. He set his offerings on the table, then eased himself down on her side of the bed.

There were faint shadows beneath her eyes that hadn't been there a week ago. The past few days had definitely taken their toll. He leaned down and placed a light kiss on her forehead, then one on each eyelid. They fluttered open and she looked at him in surprise.

"You did it again," she murmured, sounding more asleep than awake. "You're already dressed." She reached up and pulled him down to her, giving him a leisurely kiss. He wanted nothing more than to strip off his clothes and crawl into bed with her.

He couldn't let himself do that.

"Uh-huh," he said, pulling away from her, ignoring his racing pulse. "And I've also been out and brought back breakfast."

She stretched, then pushed herself up on one elbow. He brushed her hair away from her face as an excuse to touch her. "Want some coffee?"

Her eyes opened a little more. "Sounds good. Is that what I smell?"

"Mmm-hmm. If you've never tried New Orleans-style coffee, you're in for a treat."

He waited while she showered and dressed, then set out their breakfast at the small table by the window.

As soon as she joined him, she asked, "Have you been to the docks?"

"Yes."

"Did you see the ship you're looking for?"

"It's there. I need to watch it today, see who's getting on and off. I'll wait until tonight to attempt to board her."

"I want to go with you."

"Not yet. I need to know more before we can make our move."

She was quiet for moment. "All right," she finally said.

He looked at her in patent disbelief. "You're agreeing with me?"

She nodded, then smiled. "I know. Uncharacteristic of me, isn't it?"

"Absolutely, but I appreciate it very much. I'm going to need you later on, once I've located them." He could only hope they were all alive and able to leave the tanker unaided.

That night Nick left the room dressed in black. He carried a woolen ski mask to cover his face once he was on the water. He left the car at the motel and proceeded to the docks on foot.

The weather was cooperating with a heavy threatening sky. Rain had been forecast and it looked as though the predictions were going to be correct. There was still work being done along the docks.

He continued past the area and followed the river, hoping against hope he would find a skiff that he could "borrow" without the owner missing it.

When the rainstorm hit, it hit with explosive force. Nick found cover and watched as people scurried home. While he waited, several small boats came ashore. He kept his fingers crossed that one would be left unwatched.

His wishes were granted. An older man pulled his boat out of the water, clumsily turned it over, camouflaged it with a tarpaulin, then ran through the rain down a side street and disappeared into a bar.

Nick had learned patience early in his career. He waited another half hour before venturing toward the boat. The rain now fell in a steady downpour. It was not a good night to be out on the water.

So much the better for him.

He slipped on the ski mask so that his face wouldn't reflect light.

Within minutes he had the skiff in the water and had

jumped inside. He had the oars ready and began a steady rhythm to get him away from the shoreline.

The current caught him, which he'd counted on, as it now moved him toward the tanker. He drifted along its river side until he reached the anchor chain. Then he grabbed the chain and quickly tied up the skiff.

He'd been on tankers before and knew that the crew's quarters were in the nose, the officers' quarters and mess in the stern. If the president and his family were on board, they'd be in the rear. With that in mind, he climbed hand over hand up the anchor chain until he reached the side of the ship.

He paused in the shadows, watching for any crew members who might be stirring. Again the weather was working in his favor. Now came the tricky part—to find out who was on board without being seen. He slipped over the side and crouched in the shadows. There was a porthole across the deck from him but since there was no light inside, it would do him no good to get closer. Instead, he decided to search for an entry to the upper decks.

He stayed in the shadows and slowly worked his way around the deck until he found a hatchway leading inside. He eased it open, slipped inside and found himself in a long companionway that was empty at the moment. He started along the length of it, checking each wardroom he passed. These were part of the living quarters.

Nick opened the first two and found them empty. The third had a sleeping crew member. In the next one he hit pay dirt.

The President of the United States sat on the side of the lower bunk. He had several days' growth of beard. His eyes were bloodshot. He had on wrinkled slacks and a pullover short-sleeved shirt that had gone through some hard use. Most significant from Nick's point of view was the ankle iron he wore attached to an eight- to ten-foot chain shackled to the wall.

When Nick stepped inside and closed the door, Sullivan barely glanced up from studying his hands.

Nick slipped off his mask and moved to the president.

When he knelt the president looked at him. His eyes widened slightly, then he shook his head in disgust. "I played right into your hands when I asked you to guard my daughter, didn't I, Logan?"

Nick took a deep breath. "I'm not part of the group who did this, sir."

Sullivan gave a snort of disbelief. "Of course you aren't. Then how did you know I was here?"

Nick looked around. "I heard it was a possibility and I wanted to check it out. How often do they check on you?"

"You don't know the routine?" he asked sarcastically.

"I just came on board. So far no one knows I'm here." He picked up the chain and hefted it in his hand. "If I can get this thing off you, we can get you out of here."

"I'm not going anywhere, Logan, so don't waste your efforts."

"Would it help if I brought Ashley on board to convince you I'm here to help you?"

"Ashley? You're holding her, too, aren't you?"

"No. She's safe, although our van was ambushed earlier this week and Ron Stevenson was injured. He's recuperating in a hospital in Colorado. Hopefully whoever planned this thinks Ashley's either hidden away in Colorado or hidden in Washington. I spoke to Jason Freeman night before last. He's attempting to deal with your kidnappers."

Sullivan shook his head. "There's no dealing with them."

"Where's the rest of your family?"

Sullivan stared up at him with anguished eyes. "I haven't seen them since I was taken. I just hope to hell they're alive."

"If they're on board, I'll find them. What can you tell me about the routine here? Have you been fed this evening?"

Sullivan stood and, picking up the chain so that it didn't drag, walked over to the porthole and looked out. "Where are we? I've been looking for landmarks, but nothing looks familiar."

"New Orleans. Do you know how long you've been here?"

"Since sometime last night. We'd docked when I woke up this morning." He stared out the porthole. "Looks like quite a storm."

"Yes. And the skiff I'm in is tied up to the anchor and filling up with water. I don't have much time."

"Neither do I."

Nick didn't like the sound of that or the president's attitude toward his present situation. "If you don't want my help, I'll get back to Ashley. Whatever happens, I intend to keep her safe."

He started toward the door and was reaching for it when Sullivan said, "Wait." Nick glanced over his shoulder. "You really aren't part of this bunch of terrorists?"

Nick swallowed his irritation. "I told you I'm not. I don't lie, Mr. President. Especially about something as important as this."

Sullivan looked around the room, then back at Nick. "They took my watch. I have no idea what time it is, but it's been several hours since they last brought me food. When they do, I generally hear them in the passageway."

Nick looked around the small area, then opened the hatchway to the cubbyhole that served as the head. "When we hear them, I'll hide in here. Or you can turn me over to them. It's your choice."

"You're a cool one, Logan, I'll give you that."

"Mr. President, I took an oath to protect you and your family with my life. That oath hasn't changed. I don't know who is behind all of this, but at the moment my first priority is to get you to a place of safety. It would make my job a hell of a lot easier if you would cooperate."

Sullivan shook his head and turned back to the bed. He sat down and said, "They've got my wife and sons, Logan. They know I won't go anywhere without them."

Chapter 16

"Can you take me through it, sir? Explain to me what happened?"

Sullivan stood, his chains rattling in his agitation. He paced to the porthole, then turned. "What is today?"

"Sunday, January the third."

"Five days. It's been five days since I've seen Juliana, Jamie or Matt."

"What I was told was that your ship and the security ship suddenly disappeared from the radar screen. By the time the Coast Guard got to the area, the security ship was missing. Ray Clarke and the crew were found bound and gagged on the yacht. There were two agents with you who are still unaccounted for."

Sullivan shook his head as though trying to clear it. He didn't look as if he'd slept much. He swallowed hard. "It was the damnedest thing I've ever experienced. Ray and I were in the lounge having a drink together. Juliana had gone on to bed, saying she wanted to read. The boys planned to play some board game they'd brought along. Everything was very relaxed. It felt good to get away from everything for a few days. I think that's what Ray and I were talking about as we sat there."

"All of that confirms what they found, sir. There was an open book lying beside the bed in the master bedroom. The board game was in progress in the boys' room. I would say that your family was called out of their rooms on a plausible pretext and put up no struggle."

"I can only pray that's so." He was quiet for several moments, as though gathering his thoughts.

"Ray and I were visiting when we heard a noise and looked around. There were several men standing behind us, carrying automatic weapons. They wore ski masks, like the one you have, and I didn't recognize anyone. I was stunned. How could this have happened? We have agents around us at all times to prevent anything like this from ever happening!"

"I know, sir. I'm very much afraid you had someone on board who was working with these people."

"You mean crew members?"

"And possibly an agent or two. Who was with you?"

"Steve Rippy and George Fremont."

"Did you ever see them after the kidnappers appeared?"

"No. Four men held us in their sights while the others grabbed Ray and me. They must have hit me because that's the last thing I remember until I came to with a raging headache, a lump on the back of my head and tied hand and foot in a bunk."

"This one?"

"No. Eventually I figured out that I was on the security ship. But I didn't see anyone until we were alongside the tanker and I was moved."

"Did you recognize anyone?"

Sullivan shook his head. "I never saw faces. They were all dressed in dark clothes, like you are, and wearing ski masks, like you are. No one spoke. No one would answer my questions. It's been that way from the beginning."

"Actually, that's a good sign. If they don't want you to recognize them, that means they intend to release you eventually."

"Perhaps."

"Did you see or hear your family?"

"No. I assumed I was the only one taken at first, until they showed me a polaroid of Juliana and the boys bound and gagged, lying on bunks. They told me they wouldn't hesitate to hurt them if I chose not to cooperate."

"Then it's possible they're on this ship, too."

"I don't know. If they took them off the yacht, they may still be holding them on the security ship somewhere else. That's all I've been able to think about since I regained consciousness. Where were the people who were supposed to be protecting me and my family?" He looked over at Nick. "You think it was an agent, don't you?"

"There's a strong possibility of that, sir. I'm sorrier than I can say." Nick turned away for a moment, fighting his frustration. How could he expect the president to trust him if another agent like him had already betrayed him? He turned back. "The vice president received a call from someone identifying himself as a member of a well-known terrorist group. They played a tape-recorded message from you. Did you make that tape?"

"Yes."

"Do you know what their demands are?"

"No. I was told to cooperate if I wanted to see my family. I cooperated." He looked at Nick. "Are Rippy and Fremont a part of this?"

"I don't know. There are several people in the ranks who've done some suspicious things during the past few days. The detail leader was the one who notified us to take Ashley to an airfield near where we were skiing in the middle of the night. We were ambushed there, so that puts Greg Chambers on my list of possible suspects."

"Chambers? My God, he's been with me for years."

"Then there's an agent that I've known for years, Sam Masters, who's currently working out of the Denver office. We've been in some tight spots together, and I could have sworn he could be trusted. He's the one who told me where to find you. The only way he could have known that was if he was working with this group."

"Or he wants them to believe he's part of them. But he directed you to me. That counts for something."

"True. So here we are. If he chooses, he can tell them to be watching for me and I'll end up chained like you are."

There were some muffled sounds in the passageway outside. Nick stepped into the head and pulled the door almost closed behind him. From his hiding spot he waited until the outer door swung open. The man who stepped into the room could have been his double in height and weight. His head was covered with a ski mask. There was no way to tell the color of his hair. No wonder Sullivan hadn't been surprised to see him when he'd walked in.

The masked man set a tray of food on the table and walked out. Sullivan remained at the porthole looking out the entire time and ignoring his captor.

Nick waited for several minutes after the man left before he came out. Sullivan had sat down and was eating, carefully and methodically, out of practicality rather than enjoyment.

"You're not going to leave here with me tonight, are you?" Nick asked.

"I can't. Not until I know that Juliana and the boys are safe."

Nick sighed. "All right. I'm hoping they're here. If they are I'll find them. Do you have any messages for Ashley?"

Sullivan's eyes gleamed with a hint of hope. "Yes. I wish I had something to write on...and with." Nick slipped his hand into his jacket pocket and pulled out a small notebook and pen. Sullivan took them and rapidly wrote something, then signed it and handed it back. He stood and held out his hand. "Thank you, Logan."

"I haven't done anything yet."

"On the contrary. You've stayed loyal. I'll not forget that."

Nick slipped on his mask, pleased that he could pass for one of the group holding the president. That might save his neck. He cracked open the door and checked the passageway. He silently left the room and continued his search. He carefully checked out each room along the companionway, then went down the ladder and checked the deck below.

He was on the lowest deck when he opened a hatch and recognized first Jamie, then Matt, and finally spotted Juliana Sullivan across the room.

He stepped inside and closed the door.

Their room was larger. It held three bunk beds, one for each occupant. Like the president, none of the three in the room would look at him. Jamie and Matt sat on one bunk playing cards. The chains around their ankles made sure they weren't going far.

Juliana Sullivan stood at the porthole looking out at the rain.

"Mrs. Sullivan?"

She turned and gave him a searing stare. "Oh? You *can* speak. Does that mean you're going to answer my questions?" She held her chin high and met his gaze without flinching. She reminded him so much of Ashley that he almost smiled.

Nick removed his mask with calm deliberation. In a soft voice, he said, "I'm here to get you out of here, Mrs. Sullivan. I've already spoken to the president. He's being held nearby. As soon as I can figure out how to get all four of you off here without someone seeing us, I'm going to do it."

Her eyes widened with his words. Both boys scrambled off the bed and began to speak at once.

He hushed them all. "Have you been fed tonight?"

The younger boy—Matt—answered. "Oh, yeah. Hours ago."

"Do you expect them back tonight?"

Juliana answered. "Not if they follow their usual routine. Why?"

"I've got to find a way to get you out of those chains before anyone discovers my presence here."

"You mean you aren't one of them?" Jamie asked suspiciously. "You're dressed just like them."

"That's because we all have commando clothing for night reconnaissance. Those behind this kidnapping appear to be trained military personnel. Under the circumstances, it's hard to tell the good guys from the bad guys."

"You're one of the good guys?" Matt asked warily.

"Yep, but you're going to have to take my word on that for now."

"Can you take me to my husband?" Juliana looked dignified despite the fact that she had on a pair of pajamas and a robe. She had done the best she could to pull her hair back from her face. Nick could see where Ashley had gotten her exquisite bone structure.

"I could if I had the tools to get those leg irons off you. Unfortunately, I didn't bring anything with me. But I'll be back."

Jamie looked at Matt and curled his lip. "Yeah, him and Arnold, right?"

Nick grinned. "I'll admit I wish I had Schwarzenegger's help about now. Maybe he could pull those chains apart with his bare hands."

Juliana moved toward him, obviously hampered by the heavy chains. He quickly stepped to her side. "Aren't you the agent who was supposed to be with Ashley?"

"Yes, ma'am."

"They took her, too, didn't they?"

"No, ma'am, they didn't. Ashley's safe, Mrs. Sullivan. She's here in New Orleans with me."

She sat down abruptly. "Thank God," she whispered. "I just wish I understood what all of this is about."

"The most important thing at the moment is to get you out of here. If you'll stay here and not let on that anything out of the ordinary has happened—in case someone shows up—I'm going to see what I can find to release you. I'll be back as soon as I can."

He stepped back out into the companionway, checked both directions and then retraced his steps to the room where the president was being held. He slipped inside and found the man lying on his bunk. Sullivan didn't move, just watched Nick carefully until he slipped off his mask. When he recognized him, Sullivan sat up.

"Any luck?" he asked gruffly.

Nick grinned. "They're safe and sound two decks below. The three of them share a larger room than this one and are comfortable enough. Being together no doubt helped the boys to remain calm. Mrs. Sullivan sends her love."

"Can you get us out of here?"

"Yes, but you're going to have to give me time. I need to find something to cut those chains off you and your family."

"You mean they've got them…" Words seemed to fail him.

"It makes sense. They know you can't go anywhere like this. It saves on manpower. The thing is, we don't want to make them suspicious."

"How soon can you get back?"

Nick checked his watch. "Give me at least two hours."

"Hell, I can give you all night. I thought you were talking about days."

"I don't want to take a chance on their moving you, either off the tanker or taking the tanker to another location. I want to get this done tonight."

"Good enough." Sullivan held out his hand. "Good luck."

"Thank you, sir. I'm going to need it."

Chapter 17

Ashley could not sleep. She had been pacing the floor for an hour or more. She'd exhausted all her reading material—a couple of magazines she'd bought at the airport and had stuck in her bag, since forgotten, and a novel that she'd been trying to get through since before the Christmas break.

Nick had been gone for hours. She looked at her watch again. It was almost ten o'clock. He'd left at dark, almost five hours ago.

The rain had let up to little more than sloppy drizzle. There wasn't much traffic on the side street she could see from the motel window. Nick had chosen to stay near the docks. This place had definitely seen better days. It certainly wasn't on any tourist maps.

She turned and looked at the room, the dingiest of all they had stayed in on this trip. A maid had shown up in the late afternoon to change the sheets on the beds and half-heartedly vacuum. At least she'd brought clean glasses and Nick had brought her some ice before he'd left. He'd also made a run earlier in the day for food she could eat there in the room. In her own way she felt as much of a prisoner as anyone, but she understood the necessity.

Why wasn't Nick back? She continued to pace until she heard a key in the door. Following his instructions, she darted into the bathroom and hid behind the door. She heard it open and close, then the wonderful sound of Nick's voice.

"Ashley?"

She burst out of the room and leaped into his arms, kissing him repeatedly all over his face.

He wrapped his arms around her and gave her an exuberant kiss in return. When she was able to get her breath, she asked, "Did you find any sign of them?"

His grin lit up the room. "Are you kidding? I've got a note from your dad, and your mom and brothers are eagerly awaiting our return."

"Oh, Nick. You did it. You found them!"

He nodded. "And I need your help to get them out of there."

"Tell me what to do."

"I finally found a store open where I could buy some bolt cutters. Each of them has on an ankle iron and chain."

She paled. "Oh, no."

"Actually it works in our favor since they aren't being closely monitored. Once I get them loose, I'm going to bring them ashore, which is where you come in. You'll be waiting to take them to the car. We'll hide it somewhere closer to the docks than here. Once we get them that far, we'll bring them back here and decide what to do next."

"Oh, Nick, you're wonderful!" She threw her arms around his neck again.

"Let's see if we can pull this off first."

The first sign that things weren't going to go as smoothly as he hoped was finding the skiff gone when he returned to the river's edge. It had taken him longer than he'd hoped to find the bolt cutters. The owner of the skiff must have finally come out of the bar and taken it home.

The one he finally found was larger. On the one hand, it

would hold all of them with no problem. On the other hand, he would have a heck of a time controlling it on his own. But that couldn't be helped.

He turned to Ashley. "You stay down. If we don't show up by daylight, I want you to take the car and go back to the motel. I may have to hide on board ship until it gets dark once again. At least you have enough food there, so you shouldn't have to go out."

"Please be careful."

"You can count on it."

Traversing the Mississippi River in the larger boat was every bit as difficult as he'd guessed. He almost hit the tanker before he managed to tie the tender to the stern anchor. His arms were aching from trying to control it through the swiftly moving water. He rested in the boat for a few minutes to get his breath, then he hauled himself up the chain once again. He was glad the ship rode low in the water, an indication they had not unloaded their cargo. It would be easier to get Mrs. Sullivan back down there.

He waited in the shadows as he had before, watching and listening for any sign of movement. When he was satisfied, Nick crossed the deck to the hatch and eased inside.

Everything was still.

He gained more confidence. Gripping the cutters, he moved silently through the companionway until he reached the room where the president was being held. He eased open the door and saw the president stretched out on the bed once more.

If he hadn't been watching Sullivan's eyes, he wouldn't have caught the glance he gave past Nick's shoulder. Because he saw it, he swung around with the cutters at the same time the man waiting for him behind the door leaped.

He caught him across the throat, crushing his windpipe. The man slumped lifeless to the floor. "Damn," Nick muttered.

He spun to Sullivan and began to work on the chain closest to the ankle iron. The chain was thick and it took precious minutes for Nick to get through it. As soon as he was free,

Sullivan went over and pulled off the mask of the man on the floor. It was Steve Rippy.

"That answers one question, anyway," the president muttered. "Now, where's my family?"

"What was he doing in here? Could there be others waiting for us?"

"I don't give a damn. I'm going after my family. Are you armed?"

Nick silently handed him one of his firearms. He also had the pistol he'd taken from Ron at the hospital.

Sullivan checked it with expert precision before he said, "Show me where they are."

They stepped into the companionway with Nick leading the way. They went down the ladders to the lower deck. Nick paused and nodded toward the door. He signaled that he'd go in first. Easing the door open, he leaped across the room and spun around, checking for intruders.

Sullivan was right behind him.

Juliana spoke from the shadows. "Jim? Is that you?"

Nick flicked on his small flashlight. The three were in their bunks. There was no one else in the room. The president grabbed his wife and hugged her to him without sound. Nick started working on the ankle chains that held the two boys from going more than six feet in any direction.

"Dad?" Matt said softly.

Sullivan released his wife and quickly moved to the twin bunks. He touched each son. "Are you all right?"

"Yeah," Jamie croaked. "Now that you're here. We're just fine."

Sullivan turned back to Nick. "What's the plan?"

"I've got a tender tied to the stern anchor. We'll get you loaded into it and back to shore. Ashley is waiting there to take you to the car. She'll drive you to the motel where we're staying so we can plan the next step."

"What about you?"

"I'll return the tender to where I got it and meet you back at the motel."

The hardest part was fighting the current to get back upriver. At least Nick had some help with the oars. He and Sullivan worked together, fighting for every inch. It was obvious the tide had turned since his first foray to the ship.

By the time they touched the shoreline, he and Sullivan were both breathing hard. They were still downstream from where he'd left Ashley, but it couldn't be helped. He hid the tender, then led them to where he'd left Ashley. He was almost upon her before he discovered her hiding place.

She ran to her parents and brothers, hugging each in turn. All of them were silent, touching, stroking, with tears running down their faces. Nick finally said, "Take them to the car, Ashley. I'll see you soon." Then he hurried back to return the boat that had made the rescue possible. He intended leaving money in the storage compartment for the unknown owner, who probably would never know where the money had come from or why.

Ashley drove them back to the motel. Each of them still wore the leg irons. She signaled for them to be quiet until they were inside the room. After she turned on the light and locked the door, she said, "I don't know how thin the walls are, or if the rooms on either side are occupied, but to be on the safe side, we need to speak softly." She was speaking to her brothers, who had immediately thrown themselves down on the bed.

Juliana was the first to speak. "You boys get in there and shower right away."

With the reluctance that showed they weren't all that scarred by their recent experience, the boys quietly bickered over who had to shower first.

Meanwhile Ashley saw that her parents had not moved since they had walked in. They stood with their arms around each other, looking at their surroundings. Ashley smiled. "I know. It's not much to look at, but Nick wanted someplace close to the docks."

"You and Nick are sharing this room?" Juliana finally asked.

"Yes, Mom." She gestured to the chairs. "Please sit down. Nick should be back before long. Then we can figure out what to do next." She looked at their ankles. "I wonder how he's going to get those things off you."

"Ashley?" her father asked. "How long have you and Nick been here?"

"We got in late last night. Why?"

"Why didn't you get separate rooms?"

"Because I didn't want to be alone."

"Ashley, I—" her father began.

Juliana interrupted him. "Jim, this is not the time or the place to have this conversation. I'm certain that you and Ashley can discuss this once we're back home safe and sound."

"Dad, you really don't need to worry about my virtue. We drove over a thousand miles without stopping for more than gas, food and an occasional rest area. We were both exhausted."

"Where did you stop the night before?"

"El Paso. And we each had our own bed." *Even though we didn't use the extra one,* she silently added. She had no intention of mentioning that to her father.

"You've never been afraid to stay by yourself alone before, dear," her mother said gently.

Her father said, "Nick mentioned that your van was ambushed and his partner injured. I suppose that would be enough to make anyone nervous."

Juliana gasped. "Oh, darling, I had no idea." She rushed to Ashley and held on to her. "I can't believe all that has happened. We've always been so protected. It seems strange being here as a family, and yet we're alone." She looked around at her husband. "We certainly haven't experienced this much privacy in the past twenty years."

Matt came out of the bathroom, drying his hair. "Guess I have to put the same clothes back on, right, Mom?"

"I'm afraid so. But for now you might as well get some rest." She nodded to one of the beds. "I'm so thankful that Agent

Logan was able to get us out of there." She shivered. "Jim, did you ever find out who was behind our abduction?"

"No, but you can count on the fact that I'll find out."

Several minutes later when Jamie came out of the shower, Sullivan turned to him. "You two are going to have to share one of those beds. Ashley and your mother will sleep on the other."

"Dad, you need your rest. When Nick gets back, he can rent another room for us and you can—"

"For us?" her father repeated ominously.

"Now, Jim!"

"Dad, I know that it will never matter to you how old I am, I will always be your little girl. But the truth is, I'm almost twenty-two years old. I'm an adult. I make my own decisions."

"Another topic to be discussed more fully at another time," Juliana said, her gaze going to the boys.

Sullivan walked over to the window and peered outside. "Shouldn't Nick be here by now?"

"He had to return the boat. He also wanted to watch the tanker to see if there was any sudden flurry of activity. He said this would be the most dangerous time—if they should find you gone before we can get you away from here."

Sullivan continued to peer through the window. "If they follow the routine we had coming over here, they won't miss us before morning."

"Jim," Juliana asked, "what are we going to do? Can we call for Air Force One to pick us up?"

"That was my first thought. Now I'm not so sure."

"What do you mean?"

"Honey, we were set up out there on that yacht. Something's going on that's being engineered from within. We know that at least one of the Secret-Service agents was working with the kidnappers. There could be more. Until we know who's behind this, we don't dare trust anyone."

"I know," Matt said indignantly. "I thought Steve Rippy was my friend. He told me and Jamie that you wanted to see us.

Then when we step out on the deck, two other guys suddenly grab us and they handcuff us and tie our ankles together."

"What about taping our mouths so we couldn't yell?" Jamie added.

"If it's any consolation, boys, Mr. Rippy has already paid for what he did to you." He turned to Juliana. "Was it Steve who came to you?"

"Yes. He told me that you and Ray asked him to come get me. I thought that was rather strange, but I put on my robe and came out of our cabin. I was following Steve when someone grabbed me from behind, placing cuffs on my wrists, as well as covering my head with something. I tried to fight, but then whoever it was lifted me and tied my feet. When they finally uncovered my head, I discovered the boys were with me in a small cabin. I didn't recognize where we were."

"The security ship. That's where they took me. What I haven't figured out is why."

They heard a noise at the door and all quieted. They watched the door swing open. When Nick stepped inside, there was a collective sigh of relief.

"It's a little crowded in here," Nick said.

Sullivan replied, "Ashley suggested you get another room, which I think would be an excellent idea. We'll let the family share this room while you and I can use the other one. It will give us a place to discuss all of this in greater detail."

Nick could see that Ashley was not pleased with her father's suggestion, but he agreed with him. He nodded. "I'll see what I can do."

It was after midnight. When he went to the front desk, he discovered a different clerk from the night before. Nick asked for a room without explaining that he'd checked in the night before. After paying cash, he was given a receipt and key and returned to the Sullivans.

The room was on the same floor, but halfway down the hall. Nick gathered his things and he and Sullivan went to the other room.

Once inside, Sullivan said, "If you'll excuse me, I need a

shower and would very much like to shave, if I can borrow your razor."

"Of course."

Nick went after ice and got some sodas out of the machine. By the time he returned, Sullivan was shaving. Like his sons, he'd put on his pants, but hadn't bothered with the shirt. Nick found a clean shirt in his bag and silently handed it to him.

"Thanks." After he'd finished shaving, Sullivan rubbed his jaw and said, "I feel much better now."

Nick set out glasses, filled them with ice and motioned for Sullivan to choose his drink. Once Sullivan sat down across from Nick, he said, "Tell me everything you know and we'll see if we can get to the bottom of this."

Nick nodded. "All of this started for me when I received a call the morning of December twenty-first informing me that I'd been assigned to the White House detail starting immediately, on the four-to-midnight shift."

Sullivan poured himself a drink and took a long swallow. He looked much better now than he had earlier in the evening. Of course the shave helped, but the lines of strain were much less evident, as well.

Nick continued, "Less than an hour later I received a call from Homeland Security requesting my presence at a meeting in Evelyn Cramer's office as soon as I could get there."

"I see," Sullivan said.

"When I arrived, there were four members of the department there. It was Ms. Cramer who told me that several weeks before, one of the Secret-Service agents on White House detail agents had come to her saying that he'd been offered a quarter of a million dollars if he would be willing to work with a group who, as he was told, wanted to right an injustice. After a long discussion it was agreed that he would accept the offer, but would report to Ms. Cramer with any information he might gather."

"Who was the agent?"

"Colin Crenshaw."

"Colin!" He sat up in his chair. "You mean—"

"He was on his way to meet his contact when he had his accident."

"Are you saying his death wasn't an accident?"

"There's no way to prove that now, so I understand. It was very unfortunate timing, all the same. Colin had told them he thought he had some answers for them. Unfortunately he was never able to tell them what he'd discovered."

"So where did you come in?"

"She figured Colin's contact was one of the agents already in the White House. She wanted to see if I could find out who it was."

"Then I shipped you to Colorado to play nursemaid to my daughter. Why didn't you protest?"

"I had already requested a transfer the day after I was assigned to Ashley. The same person who turned me down recommended me to you as most qualified to go with your daughter."

"Greg Chambers."

"That's correct, sir."

"Did Colin name him?"

"No. According to Ms. Cramer, Colin had mentioned that he didn't know who was passing on the information since he'd had no direct contact with whoever it was. She was hoping his latest message meant he'd been able to find out."

"She believes it's someone in the White House?"

"Yes, sir."

"My God, then it could be anyone! Who has a motive?"

"The terrorists are demanding the release of some of their people currently at Guantanamo. The group must have bribed some key people working near you is my best guess."

"Then the fact we escaped means they no longer have a lever to use. We're no longer in danger and can return to Washington with no one being the wiser about what has happened."

"Except we won't know who in the White House betrayed you."

"That's true. Unfortunately."

"We also know that if something happened to you, Jason Freeman would be our next president."

"Are you suggesting that Jason would have me killed in order to take my place?"

"History is full of incidences where that is exactly what happened."

"Then what can I do to prevent this from reoccurring?"

"We can smoke them out."

"How?"

"Right now no one in Washington knows you've escaped. If we keep it that way for a few days, we can watch to see what happens next. Will the terrorists admit they were unable to hold you? Somehow I doubt it. However, whoever is behind this in the White House will eventually learn that you've disappeared. At that point I think they'll panic and perhaps overplay their hand. When they do, Evelyn Cramer will have them."

"How do you explain my not returning from vacation to the general public?"

"The press secretary mentions you've returned and have the flu. This is the season. I think the whole thing can be cleared up in a matter of days."

"Do you have some ideas about what we can do to disappear, as you put it?"

"Yes, sir, I do."

Chapter 18

The next morning the president and Nick returned to the other room. Nick tapped on the door. After a long moment Juliana Sullivan answered. Nick recognized that the blouse and jeans she wore belonged to Ashley. She had obviously washed her hair and was now brushing it dry.

"Good morning," she said with a smile. "You're both up rather early, considering the fact that you probably sat up half the night talking. Come in."

Once inside the room Nick saw that the boys were still asleep. Ashley must be in the bathroom.

Juliana walked into her husband's arms and hugged him. Nick turned away to give them some sense of privacy. He walked over and sat on the end of the bed that she and Ashley must have shared the night before.

"Honey, Nick has a plan that I want him to explain to you," Sullivan said, leading his wife to the table and motioning for her to sit down.

Ashley stepped out of the bathroom, her hair wrapped in a

towel. "Oops. Didn't know you were here," she said. She was dressed except for shoes.

Her dad motioned for her to join them. "I want you to hear this, too, Ashley."

She rubbed her hair with the towel, then walked over and sat on the bed beside Nick while she pulled a comb through her hair. Nick didn't miss the look the Sullivans exchanged. He wanted to put his arm around her shoulders and say to them, "Yes. We are a couple. Deal with it." But of course he didn't.

By the time he and Ashley's father had talked through the necessary logistics of his plan last night, they'd been exhausted and had gone to bed. He knew that sooner or later he and James Sullivan would have a heart-to-heart talk about his intentions toward his daughter. Nick preferred later to sooner.

"So what's your plan?" Ashley asked.

"Okay. Here's what we have that I think can work for us. The American people believe that the Sullivans are on a yacht fishing in the Gulf. Later they'll hear that the president has the flu and has canceled his appearances. No one will be expecting to see you as a family on vacation in the Southwest."

"Are you saying that we shouldn't stay here in New Orleans?" Juliana asked.

"Yes. I'll rent a van for all of us." He looked at each one of them. No one said anything. "My suggestion is that we go shopping and get you some different kind of clothes—tourist wear, so to speak—that would not be something you usually wear. As Ashley has long ago discovered, clothes provide a simple disguise that works with the general public."

"But where would we go?" Juliana asked.

"I'm suggesting that we drive back to Colorado. It will take three to four days, which I think is long enough to bring this matter to a head back in Washington."

They looked at each other. "We could go home," Juliana suggested.

"Home?" Nick asked.

"To Boulder," Ashley explained. "We still have our home there."

"How many people know about it?" Nick asked.

Sullivan smiled. "I doubt that anyone remembers that we had a place in Boulder before I became governor and we moved to Denver. From there we moved to Washington. We very seldom have the opportunity to go back to Boulder, although we have a couple living there looking after everything." He took Juliana's hand. "I think it would work. Besides, if Nick's calculations are accurate, we would probably arrive in Denver in time to fly back to Washington."

Sullivan looked at Nick. "Is Freeman aware of where we are?"

"No. He won't know until he's beyond any suspicion of being a part of this."

"You'll never convince me he's behind this."

"That's been my take on the situation, as well. However, is it worth risking your family's safety to let him know where you are?"

"I suppose you're right."

"Do you remember Harvey Cameron?" he asked Sullivan.

Sullivan thought for a moment, silently repeating the name, then smiled. "Of course. Harvey worked with us years ago."

"Well, Harvey was the one who rented the car in his name. I'll follow you and take the car back to him—I've got his phone number—if you will allow him to once again be your security. Ashley and I will fly out of Denver and no one will know we've seen you."

"Are we going to return to Colorado wearing leg irons?" Juliana asked with a slight smile.

"Actually, with a little time, I think I'll be able to pick the locks on them. It takes patience and a steady hand. I'm a little rusty at it, but at one time I could pick a lock with no problem."

Sullivan shook his head. "I don't believe I want to know how you learned that particular skill, Logan."

"All part of my training as a government employee, sir."

"That's what I was afraid of."

Nick managed to remove the president and first lady from their bondage. Since the boys still slept, he suggested that he and Ashley go shopping for the family and bring back some breakfast for everyone.

Ashley wrote down everyone's sizes. They found a discount store and divided up the list. It was important that the clothes be warm enough for where they were going, as well as masking who was wearing them. By the time they left the store, Ashley was giggling.

"What's so funny?"

"Can you imagine what Dad's going to look like in this? He hates loud colors."

"Good."

"And these hats will make the boys look ridiculous."

"Even better."

"And Mother! She's going to think I've lost my mind."

"Let's get them some food, so we can get on the road. We have a lot of miles to cover. The faster we're out of New Orleans, the better."

"Did Dad talk to you about me?"

"In what respect?"

"He was upset when he found out we've been sharing a room."

"Really? He never discussed the matter with me. What did you say to him?"

"Not much. Mom didn't think we should discuss it at the moment."

"Good point."

After renting a van, they stopped at a fast-food place and stocked up. Ashley followed the van in the car back to the motel. Both of them had their hands full when they reached the door. Nick fumbled for the key, but was rescued when Jamie suddenly jerked the door open. "It's about time, you guys," he muttered, reaching for the bags advertising the national fast-food symbol. "I'm starved!"

"Me, too," Matt said, rushing to greet them.

"When does the maid service come?" Juliana asked. "It wouldn't do for all of us to be found here."

"She didn't show up yesterday until almost four o'clock. I think you have plenty of time."

Sullivan said, "Let's eat, change and get moving. We'll follow you since you know the way."

"We want to ride with Nick," the boys said almost in unison. "Us guys have to stick together."

Ashley rolled her eyes but didn't comment.

While they were eating, Nick removed the leg irons from Jamie and Matt. Because of the earlier practice, he was able to make it look much easier than it was. The boys were very impressed with his skills and wanted him to teach them how to do it.

Their mother had to remind them of the need to change into the new clothes so they could leave.

Within an hour they all looked like a rather tacky tourist family hitting the road, exactly the look Nick had planned. They would also have warm jackets and sweaters to wear once they reached the Rockies.

Nick kept a steady pace as they headed to Colorado. Their first overnight was spent in San Antonio, the second in El Paso. The family got into the spirit of the journey, stopping at various places to sightsee and buy souvenirs. At each stop Nick made the arrangements, this time getting connecting rooms. If this were a normal situation, there would be at least three more agents with them. However, the added men would have been more noticeable, particularly since Nick and Ashley pretended to be a couple whenever they stopped to eat. The group appeared to be a typical family on vacation. no one gave them a second look.

Once they reached Denver, Nick put in a call to Harvey and explained the situation. Harvey promptly agreed to take over guard duty of the president and with hours met them at the airport. Harvey turned in the rental car there and prepared to be their driver for the van.

When they were ready to leave, Nick stood back and watched as the family all hugged and kissed Ashley, gave her instructions, warnings and admonitions. Sullivan spoke to Nick in a low voice. "You take care of her, you hear?"

"That's my job, sir."

"So it is. Just make damn sure she gets back to Washington safely."

"Yes, sir, I will. Or die trying."

The older man nodded, satisfied. Then he herded the family to the van. Harvey shook Nick's hand and said, "Looks like you've had quite a time since I last saw you."

"Just part of the job."

As soon as they arrived at Washington National Airport, Nick and Ashley caught a cab to Georgetown, where Nick's apartment was located. Ashley made no effort to find out where they were going or why. Unlike Nick, she couldn't sleep on a plane. Now that they were back in Washington, she was experiencing a letdown after the incredible tension of the past several days.

They pulled up in front of an apartment building. Nick paid the driver, then assisted Ashley with her bags. They went into the lobby and he signaled the elevator. Ashley waited until they reached the hallway to his apartment to ask, "Do you live alone?"

He looked at her in surprise. "Yeah. Why?"

"Just wondering."

"You think I'd allow you to be recognized with me by someone else after all of this?"

"Guess I wasn't thinking."

He opened the door and motioned her inside.

The first thing she noticed was that the place was small. There was a living-dining area, a galleylike kitchen and a door she discovered led to the bedroom.

"Make yourself comfortable," Nick said absently, sorting through mail he'd picked up in the lobby. She wandered to the bookshelves and studied his collection. They read many of the same books. Good to know they had similar tastes, although she'd already discovered that about him. Then she looked at a couple of framed photographs—obviously family. A colored Christmas photograph of a smiling family. Cute kids. An older couple, the man looking a little uncomfortable in a suit and tie. An obvious studio picture.

No unaccompanied females in any of them. Ashley smiled to herself. So there wasn't another woman in the picture. Good to know.

When Nick followed her into the room, she was standing at the window looking out. She turned and smiled. "Lovely view."

"Right." He glanced through the window at the brick wall a few feet away. "I don't spend much time here."

"So what do we do now?" she asked.

"I thought we would stay here tonight—give us a chance to regroup. We'll go to the White House tomorrow. As far as anyone knows, we flew directly from Colorado."

She went into the small kitchen and opened the refrigerator, then closed it, laughing. "Do you have any idea how old that lone apple is in your refrigerator?"

"Why? Are you hungry?"

"I was until I saw that thing. It looks like the mummy of some ancient relic."

"Probably is. I think I have some frozen dinners in the freezer, maybe a pizza."

"Actually, if it's all right with you, I may just take a shower and go to bed. I'm more tired than anything."

He nodded toward the bedroom. "The bathroom's through there. Help yourself to whatever you find." He glanced at his watch. "I have some phone calls I need to make."

Maybe it was the Washington air, but Nick had reverted to his detached professional demeanor. Ashley knew she was tired and overreacting, but she felt as though the two nights they'd shared were in the far-distant past and that Nick had dismissed them from his mind.

Perhaps that was what she needed to do, as well.

Hours later Ashley roused slightly and discovered Nick quietly crawling into bed.

"What time is it?" she mumbled.

"I'm sorry. I didn't mean to disturb you. It's almost one."

She ached with the need to touch him, but she refused to be the one who initiated any intimacy between them. Nick seemed to have no reticence, however, and gathered her into his arms. He nuzzled her neck and kissed first her ear, then her cheek.

"I've missed you," he finally said on a sigh.

"I've been right here," she replied.

"I know. You are a temptation I don't need right now. I can't seem to resist you." He kissed her and she relaxed into his very thorough, leisurely possession.

He had promised himself not to make love to her again, not to take advantage of the unusual circumstances that had thrown them together with such intimacy, but the fact was that he loved her with an intensity that ripped him up inside, because he knew he couldn't have her.

She was here with him now, her warmth and tenderness completely undoing his firm resolve.

In the quiet of the night he made love to her, taking his time. He concentrated on bringing her as much enjoyment as he was capable of. Her sighs of pleasure were his reward.

When she finally fell asleep in his arms, Nick lay awake, holding her, staring into the dark.

Nick stirred early the next morning and eased away from Ashley. He slipped on a pair of jeans and paused, taking in the picture of her in his bed. He forced himself to turn away and retreat into the kitchen, where he made coffee and turned on the news.

He poured his first cup of coffee and sat down at the bar,

focusing on the television. It took him a moment to understand what he was seeing. A fire burned out of control on some docks somewhere. His uneasiness mounted as his certainty grew.

"The flames shot high overhead the New Orleans docks late in the night as firefighters fought to save nearby ships and other tankers carrying inflammable cargo. Officials are still uncertain what caused the explosion on board the tanker, nor do we know how many were on board."

"That's the ship my family was on," Ashley said, standing in the doorway to the bedroom.

"Yes."

"They could have still been on there."

"I know."

Ashley shivered and walked over to him. She'd found another one of his shirts to sleep in. She was still warm and rumpled from sleep. "It's early," he said when she leaned against his shoulder. "Why don't you try to get some more sleep?" He hugged her to him, enjoying her warmth against his bare chest.

"Do you think whoever was responsible for the explosion thinks my family was on there?"

"I don't know. We'll try to find out, though." He kissed her. "I need to shower and get ready. Are you prepared to face everyone today? You can't let on that you know your family is safe."

"They tried to kill my family."

"We can't be sure of that. The explosion could have been an accident."

She leaned back so that she could see his face. "Do you believe that?"

"Not really."

"Neither do I."

"The explosion could also have been to destroy any evidence that the Sullivans had ever been on board."

"If we'd been three days later, it could also have meant their death."

"Try not to think about it that way. They're safe."

Ashley dressed quickly and drank coffee while she waited on Nick. When he appeared he was in his working attire—dark suit with white shirt and a dark tie. Once again he was the agent—highly trained, single-minded, with a smile that could slay her at ten paces.

She followed him out into the hall, paused while he locked the door, then continued following him to the elevator. Once the elevator stopped, they exited into the underground parking garage. He walked over to a late-model sports car, hit the security button on his key chain, so that the lights blinked a greeting and the doors unlocked.

"Well behaved, isn't it?" she said, getting into the passenger seat.

He got in on the other side. "Who?"

"Your car. It did everything but wag its tail when we walked up."

His expression was more than a little puzzled. "Has anyone ever told you that you have an overactive imagination?"

She nodded with dignity. "A few times. I've ignored them."

"Uh-huh."

They didn't speak while they made their way into D.C. Ashley was content with the company. She was still feeling the relief of knowing that her parents were out of the hands of the kidnappers.

They pulled up at the gate to the White House.

Ken White saw Nick and recognized his passenger. "Good morning," he said, opening the gate for them. "How's the world treating you these days, Logan?" he asked.

Nick gave him a mock salute. "Can't complain." He drove through and parked near the entrance.

"Is this where we say goodbye?" she asked with commendable nonchalance.

"You wish," he muttered. "No, Ashley. I've got to report for duty and as far as I know I'm still assigned to you, so you'll be seeing me later this afternoon."

He helped her out, then grabbed her bag while she slung the knapsack over her shoulder.

After they were inside, Ashley gave him a little wave and headed toward the living quarters. He turned and went in the other direction, to the detail leader's office.

Greg Chambers was on the phone when Nick paused in the open doorway. Chambers said, "I'll get back with you," and hung up. He came around the desk with his hand out. "Man, am I glad to see you. I was beginning to think you'd turned up missing, too." He looked out into the hallway. "I hope this means that Ashley is safely back."

"Yes, sir. She arrived with me and has gone to the family quarters."

Chambers closed the door and motioned to a chair. "Sit down and tell me what's going on."

"I was hoping you would be able to do that for me. How is Ron?"

"We had him flown back after his doctor released him to us. He's at Bethesda Naval Hospital."

"That's good news. I hope to get over there to see him today." Nick glanced around the office, the first time he'd seen it, then looked at the man behind the desk. "What's the news on the president?"

Chambers's expression became grim. "We've received two more calls from the terrorist group. The first one came in on Sunday—giving us until tomorrow or they would begin to maim their prisoners."

"When did the second call come in?"

"This morning, giving more specific threats."

"What does the VP say he's going to do?"

"He pointed out to the cabinet members and presidential aides that if we ever give in to terrorists' threats, there will be no stopping them."

"Has there been any luck on locating them?"

"Not yet."

"Any more tapes played purported to be the president?"

"No." Chambers shook his head. "There's some talk that it may already be too late to save him."

"Has a reason been given to the public for his delay returning from vacation?"

"Illness. Once Ray Clarke was out of the hospital and was supposed to be back from vacation, we had him visit the White House. He's given an interview describing the uneventful nature of the vacation and mentions how unfortunate that his friend now has the flu. I know the VP will be pleased to have Ashley back home. Since most everyone believes she was also on board, it will make it seem she was the only family member who avoided the illness."

"Do you want me to resume my shift this afternoon, sir?"

Chambers smiled. "Oh, I think you deserve a couple of days off, don't you? Why don't you report back on Thursday?"

"I'd like that, sir. Thank you."

As soon as he left the White House, Nick went directly to Homeland Security. He'd already contacted Evelyn Cramer the night before and told her he would be in her office sometime that morning.

He was shown into her office as soon as he was announced.

Evelyn Cramer was a petite woman with a white halo of hair around her grandmotherly face. She looked nothing like a tenacious bulldog who could unearth secrets, then bury them even deeper.

She held out her hand and smiled. "I'm relieved to see you, Agent Logan. You said you had good news for me. I'm eager to hear it."

"The president and his family are safely out of the hands of the terrorists."

"Thank God!" she said. "That *is* good news. How did you manage to rescue them from the high seas while skiing in Colorado, if I may be so bold as to ask?"

"What makes you think I had anything to do with their rescue?"

She gave him a look that bored right through him. "Because your assignment was to get to the bottom of all this. If it meant rescuing our president, you would do it."

He shook his head. "I'm afraid you have entirely too much faith in my abilities, Mrs. Cramer."

"You're saying that you had nothing to do with it?"

"Not exactly. But if I hadn't gotten some information that led me to where they were holding him, I wouldn't have been able to—"

She leaned back in her chair and smiled. "I rest my case."

"Don't make me out as a hero on this one. It was just dumb luck that I managed to find them. As a matter of fact, they were being held in chains on the tanker that blew up in New Orleans last night."

"What? Did you set that off?"

"No, ma'am. I swear I had nothing to do with that explosion. I'm wondering about the reason for it, though."

"Where is the president now?"

"He and his family are at home in Boulder with local security coverage."

She nodded. "Who knows about this?"

"You're the only one in D.C. I've told. It's up to you how you want to handle the news."

"Why the security?"

"We weren't certain who could be trusted to protect them. Steve Rippy was one of the men who betrayed him."

"You're certain about that?"

"Very certain."

"Where is Rippy now?"

"Dead."

"I see."

They looked at each other without expression. After several minutes of silence, Evelyn said, "Well, we were able to do a bit of sleuthing, ourselves. We've picked up the members of the terrorist group who were making the phone calls. From them, we were able to pick up two other agents who were working with them."

Nick asked, "What about Sam Masters?"

She frowned. "That's right, you know Sam. He hasn't been detained. Should he be?"

"It was Sam who told me where I could find the Sullivans."

"Are you vouching for the man?"

"I suppose I am. I don't think he had any idea what he was getting into when he joined the group. He certainly didn't do it for the money. Maybe he was bored and looking for something to do with his spare time."

She made a note on the file in front of her. "Thank you for that piece of information. We also managed to find the security ship."

"And?"

"The crew and agents had been bound and left on board by the two agents we arrested. They were fortunate that everyone was still alive and as well as could be expected, given their circumstances."

"Where were they?"

"Off the coast of Mississippi, not far from Biloxi."

"So what do we do now?"

"I would say that we let those who knew about the kidnapping be advised that the president has been found and is safe, that those responsible for all of this mayhem have been arrested and are behind bars, and that peace reigns across our nation once again."

"You're saying that we can trust the men in the White House to do their job protecting the president."

"That's exactly what I'm saying…and the sooner the better."

"Then I'll leave all of this in your very capable hands."

She stood and shook hands with him. "I appreciate all you've done for us, more than I can possibly say. Take care of yourself now."

"Yes, ma'am, I intend to."

Chapter 19

Washington, D.C.
Wednesday, January 8

Ashley appreciated being home although the family quarters seemed dreadfully empty. She didn't want to speak to anyone about her recent experiences. Nick had stressed to her the need not to discuss anything with anyone, including the vice president.

She decided to stay in her room and rest. At least she had the fact that she would see him this afternoon to look forward to. She took a long leisurely soak in the tub, emptying her mind of all thought. She had another two weeks before she needed to return to school.

Would Nick be assigned to her there, as well? Somehow the thought of being followed around by Nick wasn't nearly as upsetting as it had been a couple of weeks ago. Her perception of him had made a definite shift in that time.

Later she took her time finding just the right clothes to

wear. Nick had seen her in jeans and ski clothes. Now she wanted him to see her looking as feminine as possible.

By the time four o'clock rolled around she was more than ready to speak to the agents outside her door. She opened the door. She did not recognize either man.

"Where is Agent Logan?" she asked.

"I don't know, ma'am."

"Oh." She closed the door and walked over to the phone. After looking up the number in the White House directory, she rang the detail leader's office. The phone was answered immediately.

"Chambers."

"Hello, this is Ashley. I was trying to locate Agent Logan."

"He's taken some days off, ma'am. Could someone else help you?"

"Oh. No, thank you." She hung up and stared at the phone in bewilderment.

Days off? How could that be? What had they done to him? She couldn't let this happen. That he might disappear had never crossed her mind. So here she'd been, working on being as alluring as possible, and he might have been captured and was being held somewhere.

Just like before there was no one she could trust. Only now she didn't have Nick with her, either. She had to find him.

When Nick walked into Ron's hospital room later that afternoon, he discovered that Ron already had visitors. Two little girls dressed in colorful dresses and shiny patent-leather shoes were sitting on the bed with him. A very attractive woman stood at the foot of the bed, watching the three of them with a smile on her face.

"Nick! Good to see you, man. Come on in and meet my family."

"You're looking a lot better than you did last time I saw

you," Nick said with a grin. He held out his hand to the woman. "Nick Logan."

"Janine Stevenson," she said, taking his hand in a firm clasp. "These are our daughters, Corinne and Sasha."

So this was Ron's former wife. Nick nodded to the girls who watched him with eyes just like their father's. "I can't stay long. I heard they finally released you from the Colorado hospital. I know you're glad to be back here."

"You got that right. I called Janine once I could make some sense after being so doped up. Explained to her what had happened. We've been on the phone daily ever since."

Janine smiled. "Ron's told me some really nice things about you, Mr. Logan."

"Nick."

"Nick. He said you saved his life. For that, you have our undying gratitude."

Nick could feel his ears burning. He shrugged. "Please don't give me any credit. Ron would have done the same thing in my place."

"Uh-huh. He told me not to waste my breath trying to thank you, but I had to try."

Nick looked over at Ron, who was grinning from ear to ear. "You put her up to this, didn't you?"

"Nope. Not me. I didn't think my worthless hide was worth saving, anyway."

"Please don't even joke about it, Ronnie," Janine said, coming around the bed. She leaned down and kissed him. "All I've been able to think about since you called was that the call could have been someone else informing me you'd been killed." She shuddered. "It doesn't bear thinking about."

Nick noticed that each of the girls had coloring books and were busy adding lots of color to the pages. "Budding artists, I see."

They giggled, but didn't say anything.

"So how are you and Ashley getting along these days?" Ron asked. "Still fighting?"

Nick grinned. "Naw. I gave up on that. She always wins, anyway."

"When did you get back?"

"Last night."

"Everything all right at work?"

"Yep, everything's fine. The president is back from his vacation, but he's a little under the weather. Guess he caught a flu bug. I've got a couple of days off. I'll probably use them by sleeping around the clock." He nodded toward Ron. "I'm going to miss working with you, so hurry up and heal, will you?"

"I'm doing my very best."

"Well, you take care of yourself," Nick said, backing toward the door. "Any idea when they're going to let you out of here?"

"The doctor mentioned the end of the week, provided I had someone to help me for a few days at home."

Janine said, "I told him that he would be coming home with us. He's going to have all the help he can handle for as long as he wants."

Nick looked at Ron and smiled. "I'm glad to hear it. Really glad. I'll keep in touch."

"You do that. I'd like to hear how Ashley finally managed to get you to see things her way."

Nick laughed. "Now that's a story that will take a little time in the telling."

By the time he left the hospital, Nick realized that he was going to be fighting the five-o'clock traffic getting back home. Not that it mattered. He had no plans for the night.

After parking in his usual spot, he took the elevator to the lobby. He wanted to speak to the manager of the apartments about a leak he'd discovered that morning in the bathroom sink. As soon as he stepped into the lobby he spotted an agent. What could have happened in the few hours since he left the White House? He walked over to him and said, "Are you waiting for me, Tim?"

The agent smiled. "In a manner of speaking. You have a visitor waiting for you upstairs."

Ashley.

He forgot about the water leak or speaking to the manager. Instead, he took the elevator to his floor. As soon as he entered the hallway, he saw her leaning against his door and talking to the other agent assigned to her.

"Sorry," he said, walking up to them and fishing in his pocket for his key. "I wasn't expecting company." He gave Ashley a quick glance before meeting the agent's gaze.

Agent Kelly nodded. "I'll wait downstairs. Give us a call when you're ready to return, Ms. Sullivan."

Nick opened the door and motioned for her to enter. As soon as he closed the door, he asked, "What are you doing here?"

"Wasting my time worrying about you, from the looks of things."

"Why would you worry about me?"

She sat down on the sofa and looked at him. "Now there's a good question. You told me you'd be working this afternoon. Instead, I'm told you have a few days off. How am I supposed to interpret that? I actually thought about the possibility that you'd been kidnapped and were being held somewhere."

"Ah, Ashley," he said, sitting down beside her and pulling her into his arms. "I'm sorry. I should have let you know."

"No kidding."

He kissed her. "I missed you today."

"I must be completely out of my mind, but I missed you, too. I was getting used to spending twenty-four hours a day with you. So I'm having withdrawal symptoms." She sat up. "I'm sure I'll get over it."

He got up and walked into the kitchen. "How long have you been here?"

"I don't know. A while."

"Are you hungry?" he asked, opening the refrigerator.

"I don't think your withered apple is going to be much nourishment for the two of us, do you?"

He turned and looked at her. "You're really ticked off at me, aren't you?"

She got up from the sofa and sauntered over to the kitchen counter, opposite him. "You could say that. Do you know how foolish I feel—now that I know you're all right—rushing over here trying to find out what horrible thing could have happened to you?"

He grinned. "What did you expect to find? A note on the door telling you I'd been abducted?"

Her mouth twitched into a reluctant smile. "Who knows what I was thinking. This whole thing has made me crazy."

"So what can I do to make it up to you for not having been captured by unknown terrorists?"

She propped her chin on her hand. "You could take me out to dinner," she said thoughtfully.

He eyed her warily. "Like a date?"

"Mmm-hmm."

"You know that our being seen out together will start tongues wagging, don't you?"

"Whose reputation are you concerned about? Yours or mine?" She straightened and looked him squarely in the eye.

"Well, it's not mine. It's just that everything you do is news. Once the media sees us out as a couple…" He let his words trail off.

"I'm not asking for a lifetime commitment here, you know. Just dinner."

Only then did it hit him how she was dressed. Gone was the tomboyish look. Instead, she wore a designer dress that flattered her figure. She'd done some kind of intricate thing with her hair. In short, the woman looked stunning.

He walked out of the kitchen and paused beside her. "I think dinner is the safest suggestion you could have made." He held out his hand and she took it.

They stopped at the lobby to inform the men protecting her where they were going before getting his car from the parking garage.

* * *

It was early enough that they were seated at a well-known restaurant without reservations. Nick had a hunch that the two agents seated at a nearby table were very curious about them.

He couldn't blame them in the least.

"What have you found out today?"

"The men responsible for the kidnapping have been arrested, as well as the agents who helped them."

Her eyes widened. "Really! How can you be so calm? This is wonderful news."

"I agree." He held up his glass in a toast. "The mystery is solved."

"What about that agent in Colorado?"

"Sam? I'm not sure. I reported his help in locating your family. Who knows if that will be enough to get him out of this mess."

"What happens to a rogue agent like the ones involved in this case?"

"None of them can be publicly charged with what they managed to pull off. The facts will never be released. However, I'm sure enough charges will be found to keep them in jail for a considerable length of time."

"What about my family?"

"It's my guess that Air Force One will bring them home today."

"That's wonderful news!"

"Now you and your family will have time for that discussion about sharing a room with me."

"I can handle them."

"Shall I be watching for a shotgun?"

She reached over and touched his hand. "Absolutely not. You've definitely gone beyond the call of duty on this one. Besides, I have all of these things to do to get ready for school. I'll probably be so busy in the next two weeks I won't have time to—"

"Ashley?"

"Yes?"

"You aren't going to make this easy for me, are you?"

She looked at him, confused. "Make what easy?"

"I've been working on how to make this noble gesture to get out of your life."

"Oh, is that what it is? Well, don't bother. I've been telling you all along—there's no commitment necessary."

"Except for the one I want to make."

She stared at him uncertainly. "Nick?" she whispered. "What are you saying?"

"That despite your bad temper, your stubbornness and this determination you have to always get your own way, I love you more than words can possibly express. If the truth were known, some of those traits are probably what made me fall in love with you in the first place."

"Nick, you have, without a doubt, the worst timing of anyone I've ever known."

He blinked at her. "Excuse me?"

"Why couldn't you have told me you loved me when we were in bed together?" she teased. "Or at least in the privacy of your apartment, so that I could respond in an appropriate manner. Now all I can do is…is…"

"Behave yourself in public like a well-brought-up young lady is expected to do."

"You did this on purpose?"

"I'm not going to make love to you again until we're married—that is, if you decide you want to get married, and if you decide that it's me you want to marry—so it's much less stressful on my nervous system not to spend time alone with you."

"You're doing it again. You've decided that you're going to make all the rules in our relationship."

He lifted his brows. "So we do have a relationship?"

"You'd better believe it, Agent Logan. It's a ripsnorting

one, too, let me tell you, so you might as well get used to the idea."

He leaned back in his chair and grinned. "I can hardly wait."

Chapter 20

"I really appreciate your coming by tonight to pick me up," Ron said to Nick once they were in Nick's car and headed to the White House.

"Glad to do it."

Ron settled back into the seat with a sigh. "It feels good to be out of the house, I've got to admit. I was getting a little stir-crazy."

Nick grinned. "Makes sense."

"You can imagine my shock when the Man himself called to see if I could come to this little get-together tonight. Do you have any idea what's going on?"

"Possibly. We'll see soon enough. I received a similar call. Today was my day off. When he mentioned that you were also invited, I thought we could ride together."

They drove along in silence for a few minutes before Ron asked, "You still assigned to Ashley?"

Nick cleared his throat. "Uh, no. I'm not."

Ron's grin flashed white in the shadowy interior of the car. "She finally got rid of you, did she?"

"Actually the prez suggested to Chambers that I be reassigned...to Mrs. Sullivan."

"Did he say why?"

"No, but I have a strong hunch it's because Ashley agreed to marry me. And her parents want to keep a close eye on me. I don't think they're too pleased with me at the moment."

Ron straightened and stared at Nick in disbelief. "Marry you? I must have been out of the loop longer than I thought. You care to fill in some of the blanks for me?"

"Actually, I'm in a state of shock, myself. I agree with the president. All of this happened too fast. We don't know each other that well. She has to finish school. In addition, I've got to deal with my career and what being engaged to the president's daughter is going to do to its stability." He pulled up at the gate of the White House, showed his card and was waved through. "So I've been staying away from her since we returned to Washington, except when I'm with her mother."

"Is the engagement official?"

"I haven't given her a ring, if that's what you mean. It certainly hasn't been announced. I think the prez is hoping that we'll both come to our senses."

"Do you agree?"

Nick thought about that question while he parked the car. He waited until they were almost to the door before he said, "I love Ashley enough to stay out of her life if it will make her happy. At the moment I'm just going to wait and see what happens."

"You're a brave soul, I'll give you that. Courting the daughter of the head of the free world takes guts."

They passed through security and were escorted to a large reception room where the president and first lady were greeting new arrivals.

Sullivan's face lit up when he saw Ron. He shook his hand firmly and said, "It's good to see you on your feet again, Agent

Stevenson. As you know, I had no idea when I asked you to go on the ski trip that we'd have this much excitement."

"It's good to be here tonight, sir. Thank you for inviting me."

When Ron stepped over to Mrs. Sullivan, the president turned to Nick. "You know, Logan, I've recently faced a very humbling realization," he said, holding out his hand to Nick.

"How's that, sir?" Nick asked, shaking hands.

"I have much better luck getting dignitaries from all over the world to heed my advice and counsel than I do my own family. It certainly keeps things in perspective for me."

"I'm afraid I'm not following you, sir."

Sullivan gave him a half smile. "My daughter is a very determined woman, Logan. I don't believe I'm going to be able to dissuade her from her chosen course. She's firmly resolved to marry you, come hell or high water."

Nick felt his pulse surge, his body reacting to what his mind was slower to grasp—he was being welcomed into the family. "I am very much in love with your daughter, sir," he said quietly. "I want her to be happy."

"We're in agreement there. I've had to come to accept that she's not going to change her mind where you're concerned." Sullivan glanced around the room. "I'm already getting a glare from her for holding up your progress. We'll talk some more later."

Nick quickly shook hands with the first lady, then joined Ron, who stood nearby. Ron was the first to speak. "I don't recognize too many of these people, do you?"

Nick recognized the vice president. Gregory Chambers was also in attendance. He was surprised to see Evelyn Cramer there, as well. Several cabinet members mingled with the guests. Then he spotted Ashley coming toward them, and Nick forgot everyone else in the room.

She looked beautiful tonight in a black dress that managed to be very classy and as sexy as hell. He fought to control his response to her. This was neither the time nor the place to wrap her in his arms and never let go of her.

Professionalism was called for at the moment.

"Ron!" she exclaimed, pausing in front of the two men. "It's wonderful to see you looking so well." She took his hand and squeezed it. "You're looking much better than the last time I saw you. How are your girls?"

"When I left them tonight they were giving their mom fits. She was trying to get them to bed and they wanted no part of that." He paused, and in a lower voice said, "Janine and I were remarried the day I was released from the hospital."

"Oh, Ron, that's great news. I couldn't be happier for all of you." She reached for Nick's hand. To anyone watching them, it would look as though she was greeting the men equally—unless they heard what she said. "Did you tell him our news?"

"Oh, yeah," Nick drawled. "He's still in shock."

Ron chuckled. "You have to admit the last time I saw you two, you couldn't be in the same room without snarling at each other."

She glanced at Nick, then made a face. He watched them without expression. "Uh-oh. He's doing his great-stone-face routine. Only now I know that's because he's having to work at hiding his emotions." She leaned a little closer to him and whispered, "Aren't you, love?"

"You enjoy tweaking the tiger's tail, don't you?" he replied in a low tone.

She laughed, then sobered enough to ask, "What was Dad saying to you just now?"

"Nothing that would interest you." He glanced around the room. "I don't recognize some of these people. Do you?"

"Well, you recognize Uncle Ray and his crew, don't you? There are some Coast Guard people here, as well. I think I know why they're here, but I'd be guessing at this point." She waved toward the buffet table. "Let's get something to eat and find a table. Dad will explain everything later, I'm sure."

They were filling plates when a familiar voice spoke behind

Nick. He glanced over his shoulder and saw Sam standing there. "Thought I recognized you," Sam was saying. "Good to see you, Nick." He nodded to Ron and Ashley.

"What are you doing here, Sam?" Nick asked.

"Beats me. I was summoned. I obeyed." He gave them a cocky grin.

Everyone was seated some time later when President James Sullivan stood and waited for the room to fall quiet before he began to speak.

"Look around the room, ladies and gentlemen, and note each and every face, for each of you are heroes in a silent war that was waged and won because of your loyalty and unstinting support. Because of the nature of the situation, there will never be any recognition for any of you other than this gathering tonight. Officially the kidnapping never happened. After tonight it will never be referred to again. Unofficially I want to thank each and every one of you for your loyalty and devotion to duty during this time. Many of you here in Washington worked around the clock to find the perpetrators. Know that your efforts will never be forgotten."

Ashley glanced around the room. Even her brothers were there, sipping on sparkling grape juice and looking oh, so grown-up in their new suits.

Her father continued, "I know there are many unanswered questions for most of you. We hope to be able to answer them in time if at all possible. With that in mind, I'm going to ask Evelyn Cramer of Homeland Security to come forward."

Ashley blinked in surprise. Who was this woman and what part did she play in all that had happened?

"Good evening, ladies and gentlemen. President Sullivan has asked that I share with you the confidential report on the investigation our office conducted with regard to the conspiracy that resulted in the kidnapping of the presidential family."

She quickly summed up what had been discovered and when. When she brought up Sam's name, Logan, seated next to Ashley, leaned forward. "I was notified by one of our agents, who was an unsuspecting member of the terrorist group, that he had received word of plans being made to cause a disruption in the government. His reasons for being part of the group had nothing to do with the conspiracy. However, since he was already in place, he offered to work with us on the matter. We had him transferred to the area where the core group had their headquarters. Despite his efforts, he was unable to prevent the kidnapping, but he did manage to discover where the family was being held. With that information, another agent was able to arrange their escape. We owe them both a great debt of gratitude and thanks for the many risks they incurred."

Once again the president took the floor. "Agent Sam Masters, a special citation is being placed in your personnel folder for the work you did in this matter, even though the reasons given for the citation are intentionally vague." He glanced over to where Nick and Ashley sat and smiled. "As for you, Agent Nicholas Logan, you are receiving the highest award any man can offer to another—my daughter Ashley's hand in marriage. I hope you will consider that sufficient reward."

There was a stunned silence before a great many people erupted in applause, laughter and congratulations.

Nick responded with a grin, "More than sufficient, sir!" which increased the laughter.

In the midst of the hubbub, Ray Clarke, who was seated at the president's table, spoke up. "You don't know how thankful I am to have you here at all, Jim," he said. "You know you've always been family to me. I'm sure I speak for everyone here when I say how devastated I was when the news broke about that tanker exploding and I thought you were still on board. I never want to experience anything like those few days of hell and grief again."

His words brought a hush to the group. Most of the people there wore puzzled expressions.

Jason Freeman, the vice president, finally broke the silence. Wearing a slight frown, he said, "I'm afraid you've lost me, Ray. What tanker are you talking about? What explosion?"

Ray smiled at the people around him. "I suppose Jim didn't tell you about that part of it. He told me about being chained away from the rest of the family, not knowing if they had been captured, not knowing where he was or where he was being taken. They barely escaped with their lives!"

There was a general murmur among the listeners.

Jason spoke up. "You were on a tanker?" he asked the president.

Ashley noticed that Greg Chambers set down his glass and stood. Ray had his back to Chambers and didn't see him.

President Sullivan stared down at the table for a long silent moment. When he looked up, moisture filled his eyes. His face looked drawn. "That's correct, Jason," he said to his vice president. "I was. Ray explained it exactly the way it happened. The only problem is—" he turned his gaze to his friend of many years "—I never told you that I was on a tanker, chained away from the rest of the family, not knowing if they were alive. I never told anyone. Only my family, Nick Logan and my captors know where I was—besides the person who arranged the abduction in the first place.

"I guess my question to you now is—why, Ray? What caused you to do this to me and my family?"

Greg Chambers and another agent stood directly behind Ray Clarke now. Chambers pulled Ray to his feet and slid handcuffs on his wrists before Ashley registered what was happening. In fact, every person in the room sat as though frozen in suspended animation while James Sullivan and Ray Clarke looked at each other across the table they had shared.

"They weren't supposed to hurt you," Ray finally said in a choked voice.

"That doesn't answer my question, Ray," Sullivan replied in a low voice.

"I had no choice, Jim. None whatsoever. They had information that would have ruined me. Don't you understand? They promised me that they would let you go regardless of the outcome of their negotiations. I believed them. I would never have wanted you harmed!"

"It was your money that turned the agents, wasn't it?"

"I had no choice," Ray repeated.

Sullivan looked at the man who had been so close to him for so many years. "We all have choices, Ray. Whatever they were holding over you might have ruined your business, but by cooperating with them, you've ruined your life and could have destroyed me and my family. I hope that God can forgive you. I'm not certain I can."

Greg Chambers nodded to the agent, who then escorted Ray Clarke out of the room. The closing of the door seemed to animate everyone once again.

Ashley turned to Nick. "Did you know about this?"

"We couldn't prove it, Ashley, which is why this little gathering was staged tonight." She went over to her father. Nick followed.

She looked at her father. "Oh, Dad, I'm so sorry. Did you have any idea it was him?"

He shook his head. "No, honey, I'm afraid I didn't. I knew there was a continuing investigation going on despite the arrests. Quite frankly I didn't want to know the name of the person working within our small circle who had betrayed me."

The vice president came forward, looking stunned. "I'm sorrier than I can express, Jim," he said. "I had no idea that Ray was involved. He was here every day, wanting information about you. Everyone understood his concern. He'd been injured when you were captured. It never occurred to any of us that he had a hand in this."

"Actually it occurred to Greg Chambers," Nick said. "He's taken all of this very personally. He lost too many agents in this deal, men he trusted who betrayed everything he stands for."

Ashley said, "At one time you thought he might be part of it."

"Yes. I could never quite get over the ambush at the airport."

Ron joined them. "Who was behind that, anyway?"

"As soon as the leak in the White House heard that we were taking Ashley back home, he notified the terrorists in Colorado."

Sam joined the group around the president. He turned to Ron and said, "I owe you an apology for not being able to prevent your being shot. By the time I heard about the planned ambush, it was too late to do anything." He looked over at Nick. "That's why I risked blowing my cover by going to the cabin with the information I'd picked up. There was a leak somewhere. Information was getting through too quickly and things were getting out of hand."

Ashley asked, "Did you know I was there?"

Sam smiled. "No. Nick had me convinced you and Ron had already flown out of Colorado." He looked over at Chambers. "You didn't tell me about Ron, so there was no reason not to believe Nick."

Chambers nodded. "Like you, I realized there was a leak somewhere and my agent had been shot. I wasn't taking any more chances."

Ashley placed her arm around her father's waist. "I'm so sorry, Dad. I know this must be devastating to you."

"I suppose that's what betrayal is, honey. Only someone close to us has our trust and can actually turn on us. It's hard to face the knowledge that someone you love can do this to you."

Later that evening Nick took Ashley away from the White House for a few hours. Her parents had gone into seclusion. Her brothers were still bewildered by the turn of events, and she was too restless to stay inside.

So they walked. Ashley knew that there was a car following them nearby, but she no longer cared. She was still caught up in what had happened earlier.

"I just can't believe it! I used to call him Uncle Ray when I was small. He's as close to being family as anyone we know."

"I'm just glad the arrest turned out as peacefully as it did. None of us was sure that he would actually admit to knowing about the tanker tonight. We could only hope."

"You honestly thought he was the one?"

"After the investigations, we could find nothing in the vice president's background or Greg Chambers's background to warrant their participation in this. Once we discovered some kickbacks in real-estate deals that Clarke had paid when he first got started, we had a hunch it was enough of a lever to have been used against him."

She stopped walking and looked up at him. "You've been in on this investigation all along?"

"Yes."

"And you never told me."

"It's what I do, Ashley. This is the life I lead. No matter how close I am to you, how much I love you, there will be parts in my life that I cannot talk about. Do you understand what that can mean in a relationship?"

She went up on tiptoe and kissed him. "Just who do you think you're talkin' to, Agent Logan? My entire life has been spent watching a marriage work quite well under similar circumstances. So if you're thinking about trying to weasel out of anything by using your job as an excuse—"

He gave her a quick kiss in return and immediately released her. "Behave yourself. There are people watching."

She laughed and swung her arms out, dancing in a circle around him. "Get used to it, fella. This is just the beginning!"

Nick grabbed her and, ignoring any spectators, kissed her until he had to finally come up for air. "I can't believe this is happening. It's too soon, it's too much, it's—"

"Nonsense. It's official now. I wouldn't be surprised if someone notifies the newspapers about the announcement tonight. It will make a good reason for the gathering without causing any media speculation."

"Spoken like the true daughter of a politician."

"I've been thinking—I see no reason to suffer through a long-drawn-out engagement. Why don't we get married on my birthday next month?"

"Next month? What about school? I don't want you dropping out."

"Oh, that's no problem. I'll transfer credits and stay here. That would please my folks just fine. We could have a small wedding with just our families. What do you think?"

Nick stood and watched her in the reflected lights around them. He knew he'd never be able to tell this woman no. He hoped she never discovered the hold she had over him. If that ever happened, his life would be hell.

He smiled at her look of expectancy. "If your family will agree to a Valentine's Day wedding, I'm all for it. I can't seem to concentrate on anything else these days except thinking about all the things I want to do to you when I get you alone."

She grabbed his hand and began to walk once again. "I may be able to think up a couple of good reasons to convince the family an early wedding would be just the thing!"

"Ashley, are you trying to say…?"

"Nope, but they don't have to know that, do they? By the time I get through with them, they'll be thanking you for wanting to marry me."

"Uh, Ashley, you aren't going to tell them what happened between us, I hope."

She gave him a very seductive smile. "Only if I don't get their blessings any other way!"

He had no doubt in his mind that she would do exactly that. She was determined to get him threatened with a shotgun yet.

Epilogue

Christmas in the White House. Ashley wandered through the rooms, looking at all the decorations. Now that she no longer lived there, she could better appreciate the history and the privilege of being a part of this magnificent old building.

This would be the first Christmas she would spend with her husband. His parents and both brothers and their families were also having Christmas at the White House this year.

Nick had gone to the airport to arrange for transportation to bring them here. She had teased him about making up for his missing Christmas with his family last year by having everyone gather in the nation's capital. He'd just smiled and made no comment.

Ten months of marriage had not made much of a dent in her husband's stoic facade, but she didn't care. She knew how to get past his guard and get him to unbend. Not that she took advantage of her knowledge. She would never do that. She smiled at the thought.

Jamie showed up at her elbow. He'd grown at least three inches taller during the past year. Now she had to look up at him. "It seems weird, having you sleeping here again," he said, draping his arm around her shoulders in a casual effort to show off how tall he was.

"Don't worry. It's only for tonight. Tomorrow we'll be back at the apartment."

"Do you miss living here?" he asked, his curiosity obvious.

"Not really. Although Nick and I are looking to buy a house. We're tired of the apartment. It's really too small for more than one person."

"Mom said to tell you Nick and his family are here. She wants you to come greet them."

"Jamie! Why didn't you tell me?" she asked, hurrying to the stairway.

"I just did," he replied, baffled by her irritation.

She found everyone gathered in the same room where she and Nick had been married last February in front of the same group of people. As soon as he saw her, Nick started toward her. Ignoring everyone, he kissed her as though they'd been parted for days rather than hours.

Matt said, "Blech," causing everyone to laugh.

Nick grinned. "Sorry. Must be this room. Every time I'm here I think I'm supposed to kiss the bride."

Hours later the group was gathered together before bedtime when President Sullivan said, "I wanted to share something with you since there are such few occasions when we're all together like this."

He had everyone's attention.

"As you know, this will be my last public office. I've enjoyed the work, but I believe I've earned the retirement."

There was a ripple of amusement among them.

"I just wanted to say that I'm encouraging Nick to consider going into politics. I think he'd make a good representative of the party. I'd like to see him move forward by running for the House of Representatives in the next election."

Everyone looked at Nick to see what his reaction was. It was Ashley who spoke. "Not so fast, Dad. At least let me get out of school first. Besides, we're already talking about starting our family. I'd like my children to have two parents rearing them."

Sullivan said, "Now wait a minute. I helped to rear you, young woman."

Ashley looked at her mother and winked. "Sure you did, Dad. Besides, I was looking forward to having some privacy once you leave office. I was promised there'd be no more agents trailing along behind me."

Mrs. Sullivan looked at Nick. "How do you feel about all this, Nick?"

He shared a love seat with Ashley and had his arm around her. "I think Ashley makes some good points. I'm not at all sure that I would want to work in the public sector of government. I'm comfortable with what I'm doing."

His dad spoke up. "Come on, son. Don't you want to be the president of the United States someday?"

Nick smiled before looking down at Ashley curled up beside him. "Actually, Dad, my ambition is to be married to the future president of the United States someday."

* * * * *

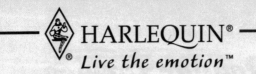

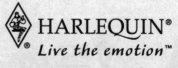